Twins of Time

To Anna
Best Wishes
Maria Boosey

by

Maria Boosey

Bloomington, IN   Milton Keynes, UK

authorHOUSE®

AuthorHouse™
1663 Liberty Drive, Suite 200
Bloomington, IN 47403
www.authorhouse.com
Phone: 1-800-839-8640

AuthorHouse™ UK Ltd.
500 Avebury Boulevard
Central Milton Keynes, MK9 2BE
www.authorhouse.co.uk
Phone: 08001974150

This book is a work of fiction. People, places, events, and situations are the product of the author's imagination. Any resemblance to actual persons, living or dead, or historical events, is purely coincidental.

First published by AuthorHouse 2/6/2007

ISBN: 978-1-4259-8809-8 (sc)

Printed in the United States of America
Bloomington, Indiana

This book is printed on acid-free paper.

DEDICATION

To Liana my Mother, my rock. Herbert my Father, sorely missed. My best friend and daughter Gina, her partner Dylan and my grandson Brookin, the sun in my life.

ACKNOWLEDGMENTS

With special thanks to Darin Jewell, for making my dream a reality.

My family, especially Gina and close friends, especially Christine Carter, for all their support and encouragement.

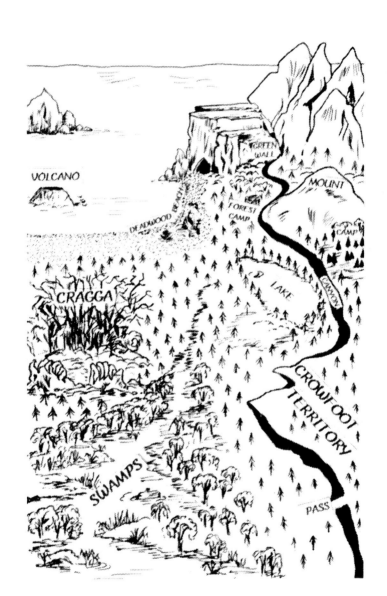

CHAPTER ONE

The Key

It was nearing the end of a damp and chilly March in the year of 1985. A blanket of early morning mist seeped into a sleepy Cornish village on the outskirts of Bodmin Moor.

There was one particular cottage where the windows had lit up at intervals, from dusk till dawn. The peculiar thing was that the light from one of the windows was signalling an SOS out to the moors. It was home to four generations of women (well at least it was at the start of this day).

Six-year-old Jill was lying in her bed. Her bright blue eyes stared wide-eyed into the half-light. She twiddled with her long blonde hair, listening to the sounds of doors opening and closing, the toilet flushing, but mostly the click, clicking of the light switch in her Great Nana Eleanor's room, which was next to hers. Then as the bulb popped she heard her mother whispering loudly. '*No* Nan! You *must* get back to bed!'

'They'll come soon. I *know* they will! *I must warn them!*' replied Eleanor, who was clearly distraught.

Jill's disgruntled father called out. 'Pamela! The baby's awake!'

Then Jill heard her nan get up. 'It's all right Pamela. You see to Simon, I'll see to Eleanor.'

Eventually there was silence. Jill turned onto her side and looking across to her younger brother Ritchie, who had slept through all the noise, drifted off to sleep. (Little did she realise that this day would be imprinted in her memory for the rest of her life.)

There had been a tense atmosphere in the cottage for some time. Whenever Jill asked what was wrong, the baby was given as an excuse. She was beginning to think they wished he'd never arrived. In fact, if it hadn't been for her Great Nana Eleanor, she felt sure her happy bubble was going to burst.

Eleanor, who was eighty-nine (but adamant she was ninety-eight), had a child like quality about her which Jill adored. They spent lots of time playing and laughing together.

It was a Saturday morning. Jill was first up. Jumping out of bed into her favourite pink fluffy slippers, she crept into her parents' room and peered over the edge of the moses basket. Simon was fast asleep. This wouldn't do, so she blew gently on his face. To her joy he smiled and began to stir. (Of course, he really had wind of a different nature and his discomfort had caused him to cry.)

'*Jill!* I've hardly slept a wink!' mumbled a very tired Pamela as she tossed back her quilt. Jill beamed as her mother dragged herself out of bed.

The cottage soon became active. Jill's nan and granddad were preparing breakfasts, Pamela was feeding the baby, Ritchie who was only three, was pulling out the contents of the kitchen cupboards.

'*No!*' scolded his father, peering out from behind his newspaper at Ritchie who had caked his mousy brown hair in jam.

Jill just seemed to get in everyone's way.

'Jill darling, take Great Nana her cup of tea.'

'OK, Nan.' She carefully climbed the stairs clutching the china cup and saucer. The cup wobbled. She watched the little tea waves all the time, so as not to spill a drop.

She knocked on the bedroom door and waited for a response, but none came. 'I've brought your cup of tea Great Nana!' There was still no reply, so she went in.

It was the smallest room in the cottage. Dark wooden beams crossed the white slanted ceiling and green floral wallpaper complimented the red sash curtains that adorned a little window.

Jill became a little concerned as the bed was made but there was no sign of Great Nana. Frowning, she carefully placed the saucer on the bedside table and looked around the room. Just then a shuffling noise came from inside the wardrobe. 'Great Nana, is that you?' she asked warily … BANG. The wardrobe door burst open and Eleanor leapt out. Screaming, Jill jumped onto the bed, and then fell about giggling. 'Ha ha, got you!' laughed Eleanor.

Eleanor sat next to her on the bed and then reached under the pillow for her camera, which was her prized possession. She aimed it at Jill, who quickly grinned and posed. '*Bigger* smile!' she ordered. Jill smiled *so* broadly her gums were showing. Click, FLASH. The photograph whirred out.

They sat waiting with bated breath as the picture began to develop. Jill began to laugh, as her ridiculous expression became clear. Eleanor stared sullenly at the snapshot. 'Don't you like it?' enquired Jill, looking worried.

Eleanor smiled. 'I shall keep it *here, always!*' she replied, as she tucked it inside her sweater and softly patted her heart.

'JILL, BREAKFAST!' called her nan from the bottom of the stairs.

'COMING NAN! - I'd better go Great Nana, don't let your tea go cold!' As Jill kissed Eleanor on the cheek, she could smell the strong scent of lily of the valley (Eleanor's favourite perfume), she then hurried downstairs.

Tucking into her boiled egg with toasted soldiers, Jill noticed a lack of conversation at the breakfast table, where normally the contents of the newspaper were read out loud and discussed.

Presently her father went into the front room where Pamela had laid Simon down to sleep and was sitting with her face cupped in her hands.

'Have you told Jill yet?'

'No John, I've been far too busy with the baby.'

'You're cutting it a bit *fine*. Do you want me to?'

'No - no, I'll do it now,' replied Pamela, sounding stressed.

Just then the phone rang. As Pamela answered it, Jill came into the room. 'Hello...? No, this is her daughter, just one second - MUM, IT'S FOR YOU! IT'S THE HOME!' Jill's nan hurried in and Pamela passed her the receiver.

'What home, Mummy?' queried Jill, looking rather puzzled.

'Oh, it's a *special* home darling. You know Great Nana hasn't been very well lately?'

'Hasn't she? Why, what's wrong with her?' asked Jill frowning.

'Well, it's not actually physical, you see when she wanders off without telling us it's *very* dangerous.'

'But she *loves* going for walks,' declared Jill.

'Yes but she *can't* go on her own.'

'Then *I* can go with her!' argued Jill, earnestly.

'But you're not always here darling and - well we've found this *beautiful* house with a *huge* garden, where she can walk around safely. There are *lots* of people to take care of her and we can visit *whenever* we like. It's not too far away and-' Jill stared at her mother horrified.

'YOU'RE SENDING HER AWAY? HOW *COULD* YOU!' she screamed and then ran upstairs.

Eleanor, who had been eavesdropping, closed her door as Jill approached. Jill paused at Eleanor's door and then continued to her room, threw herself onto her bed and sobbed uncontrollably.

'She'll come round,' said John, trying to console Pamela.

'Right, right, ... no that's fine; we'll see you then. Thank you, good-bye.'

'Is everything all right, Mum?' queried Pamela.

'Yes, but we'll have to get ready to leave, they need her in a bit earlier than planned.' Pamela's mother had a pained expression as she left the room.

Jill's nan and granddad worked, as did her father who was saving for a deposit on a house. Pamela was so busy with the children, she couldn't constantly watch Eleanor. Simon's arrival had made the situation even more difficult.

Eleanor's husband Whitlow had passed away two years earlier. In her grief Eleanor, showing signs of dementia, had begun to live in the past and would wander off causing concern.

Recently during a storm, she had sneaked out in the early morning hours. The milkman had alerted the family as he thought he'd seen her heading towards the moors, clutching a parcel. Eleanor was nowhere to be found.

Nearly the whole village had joined in the search for her. She was found later that evening, cold and wet on a cliff top at the ruins of Tintagel Castle. Her fingernails were clogged with soil and the mystery parcel was nowhere to be found. Apart from the danger she was in, she had almost caught pneumonia.

'Jill – Jill? Wake up darling. It's time to say good-bye to Great Nana.' Jill rubbed her eyes and holding tightly onto her mother's hand, accompanied her downstairs.

Ritchie was pushing his favourite toy truck on the lawn; John was lifting a suitcase into the boot. Eleanor was standing with nan and granddad by the car. Jill pulled away from her mother and stayed by the cottage door. Not wishing to upset her further, Pamela continued over to say her good-byes.

Eleanor looked across at Jill's sad face and smiled but Jill couldn't find one to return. She tried so hard to think of happy things to disguise her pain, but nothing worked.

Eleanor came over to her, removed her false teeth and crumpled her frail wrinkled face till it resembled a cabbage. Jill began to smirk. Replacing her teeth, she took hold of Jill's tiny hands in hers and squashed them so tightly her knuckles turned white. Jill could feel something hard and sharp being pushed into her palm. She looked closely into her Great Nana's face and deeper still into her eyes where there dwelled little tears that grew and grew. Time slowed and the tears pulled away from the corners. Snaking a path through a maze of wrinkles they wound their way down Eleanor's cheeks. More tears followed in their hollowed paths. Then with a little gulp, Eleanor let go of her hands and patted her chest where Jill's photo lay close to her heart. Nothing was said, but Jill had taken note; whatever it was her Great Nana had sneaked into her hand, it was for *her* eyes only, *their* secret.

As Jill watched them drive away her spirit slightly lifted. As soon as the car was out of sight she ran into the cottage ahead of her mother.

'Jill, are you all right?'

'Yes Mum, I'm fine. I think Simon's awake!' While her mother attended to Simon, she hurried up to her room, fist still clenched tight.

Sitting on her bed she slowly and carefully unfolded her hand. There, indented into her palm was a tiny silver key, with the prettiest ornate top she had ever seen. She looked long and hard at the little key but had no idea what it belonged to, if anything. Still that wasn't important, the fact that her Great Nana Eleanor had given it to her made it the most precious key in the world.

Upon hearing footsteps on the stairs she panicked and quickly pushed it through the mouth of her favourite china doll, which was the nearest thing to her.

*

The next day, Jill woke to hear voices coming from Eleanor's room. Climbing quickly out of bed she hurried down the hallway and listened at the door.

'Have you looked under the mattress Pamela?'

'Yes Mum, it *must* be here somewhere!' On hearing this Jill gasped … 'Oh Jill! I thought I heard something,' said her mother, opening the door. 'We're just - clearing the room ready for the nursery. Are you feeling OK darling, you look a little flushed?' Jill nodded, hurried back to her room, picked up the china doll, hugged it tightly and then hid it under her bed.

During the summer months that followed the family visited Eleanor quite often.

On one particular visit Jill spent a few minutes alone with her great nana and asked her about the key. But Eleanor appeared vague and didn't want to talk about it. In fact she had become increasingly distant with each visit.

*

The summer had passed and the cottage garden was ablaze with autumn's reds and golds.

On this particular day, Jill was in the garden gathering leaves into piles and then jumping into them. The next thing she knew her mother was whisking her inside.

'Jill, help granddad with your brothers! Are you sure you can cope Dad?'

'Yes, we'll be fine won't we Jill!' Jill nodded, although she didn't have a clue what was going on as her mum, dad and nan left hurriedly, speeding off in the car.

Later that evening, Jill found Ritchie fast asleep on his bed. She removed his slippers, covered him up and then went to find her granddad, who was rocking Simon off to sleep in the nursery.

'Get yourself off to bed Jill. *Mind* you don't wake Ritchie and don't forget to clean your teeth,' he whispered, warmly smiling.

Blowing him a kiss, she made her way to her room.

The next day everyone returned. Once again a silence and sadness fell about the household.

It was early in the morning a week later, when Jill was told she would be having the day off school. Her mother sat her down and carefully explained that Great Nana Eleanor was going to a special home in the sky. She was just taking in what her mother had said when the doorbell rang.

It was Pamela's sister Margaret, who'd travelled up from Devon where she lived. 'Auntie Margaret!' called an excited Jill running to greet her.

'Hello beautiful!' said Margaret fondly, as she lifted her up and swung her around.

Margaret had a loud, eccentric personality that masked a sadness that dwelled deep within her heart. For when she was only fifteen she'd fallen pregnant and would not reveal the father's identity. Unable to cope with the situation, she'd put the baby up for adoption. He was taken away at birth. Apart from her Granddad Whitlow, whom she was very close to, the family never spoke of it again.

Margaret's grandparents never got to see the baby, which caused Eleanor *great* distress. In fact the family believed it was the start of her mental deterioration.

Giving up her baby and feeling responsible for Eleanor's condition had seriously affected Margaret. She'd since married a divorcee called Bob.

Jill thought she was wonderful.

Shortly after Margaret arrived, John returned from the airport where he'd been to collect Pamela's brother, Edward, who had travelled from his home in Australia to attend the funeral.

The last memory Jill had of that day was sitting with her family in a long, shiny, black car. Carefully held in her hand was a lily of the valley. Gazing at the pure white little bells that stood out so boldly against the black clothes everyone was wearing, she became mesmerised and drifted off into a little world of her own.

Eventually the car passed slowly through the cemetery gates and soon came to a halt. It was a day of sunshine and showers. Eleanor was to be laid to rest alongside her beloved Whitlow.

Looking over to where the priest awaited them, Jill saw a beautiful vivid rainbow that seemed to fall at his feet.

As the entourage walked towards him and the rainbow's end moved away, Jill became distracted by what appeared to be little rainbow coloured balls of light that stayed and danced around on the grass by the graveside. Suddenly the balls of light sped off towards the rainbow. She looked up at all the sad faces, to see if anyone else had noticed them, but it seemed as though nobody had. Margaret tapped her on the shoulder and winked. Jill wasn't sure if she'd seen them or not.

Jill walked forward, dropped the delicate flower onto the coffin and whispered; 'Good-bye Great Nana and don't worry, your secret's *safe* with me.'

CHAPTER TWO

The Secret

The years had passed quickly. It was the first day of the summer holidays in 1990.

Jill was now aged eleven (going on sixteen). Ritchie, now eight, was tall and slim for his age. Simon had blonde hair and blue eyes like his sister and had just turned five.

Their father John had been promoted at work. However, the promotion entailed moving. A suitable house had been found at Southend-on-Sea, in Essex. Luckily the move coincided with the holidays, giving the family time to settle into their new surroundings.

The removal van was being loaded and the cottage was in turmoil. Jill was helping her mother, who was collecting some last minute bits and pieces from the loft.

'Oh my!' sighed Pamela.

'What *is* it?' called Jill from halfway up the ladder.

'It's just so stifling up here. There's no air! I may leave the rest till we come back up to visit. There's nothing we need urgently … OUCH!'

'Are you all right Mum?' she asked, sounding worried.

'Yes darling, I just kicked great nana's box.'

'What box?' asked Jill intrigued.

'Oh it's just some of her things we put up here when we decorated the nursery.'

'Can I see it?' said Jill eagerly.

'Well - OK, I'll pass it down … Careful now, it's heavy.'

Jill grasped the beautiful mahogany box that was the size of a large shoebox. Carefully placing it on the floor, she eagerly opened the lid.

'Not *now* Jill, there's still lots to be done!' whinged Pamela, making her way down.

'Oh, but *Mum*!' complained Jill.

Just then her nan joined them.

'How's it going Pam?'

'Fine Mum, it's too hot up there though.'

'Nan, look!' declared Jill excitably, pointing at the box.

'Oh, you've found my mother's keepsakes! Come with me and we'll go through them together.'

'But Mum, I just told her she can't!' said Pamela firmly.

'Nonsense Pamela, you're not off for a while yet. Besides, I can spend some precious time with Jill and I think we could all do with a nice cup of tea.' With that she picked up the box and made her way downstairs to the kitchen, with Jill hot on her heels.

As her nan proceeded to make the tea, Jill excitedly rummaged through the contents of the box.

'Oh Nan, these pearl necklaces, they're beautiful!' she exclaimed, lifting a bunch in the air.

'Aren't they just. Those pearls are very rare. Be careful now, they're very old and delicate.'

Jill carefully laid the necklaces down in rows and then delving back in pulled out some photographs. Her nan passed her some juice and biscuits then sat at the table with a cup of tea.

'What are these *strange* photos, Nan?'

'Let me see?' she said, taking them from her. '… Oh, the birthmarks!'

'*Birthmarks?* But whose are they?' she queried.

'Well, this one was on my brother David, God rest his soul. Now this one belonged to your Uncle Edward. I recall how your mother used to try and wash it off him at bath time. These two *you* should recognise.'

'Aren't they Ritchie and Simon's?'

'That's correct.'

'But why on earth did Great Nana want to photograph *those*?'

'I really don't know, she used to say, *some birthmarks stay and some go but a memory must live forever.*'

'Whatever did she mean Nan?'

'I'll never know, Jill. My mother was a very mysterious lady. I do know she hid them from your Great Granddad Whitlow. Still they're not worth hanging on to, we can throw those ones away.'

'Oh no, *please* may I keep them?'

'Why of course you can,' she replied, handing them back to her.

'Who's this Nan?' queried Jill, passing her a yellowish, brown photograph that was creased and cracked in places.

'… Ah - this is the - *only* photograph she had of her … family. She used to *keep* it in her - *notebook*, which – has - long since - vanished.' Her nan seemed strangely alarmed. Sipping at her tea she suddenly leapt from her chair. Coughing and spluttering she ran to the sink with her hand over her mouth.

'Nan! Are you OK?' said Jill sounding worried, as her nan grabbed hold of some tissue and wiped her face. 'I'll fetch Mum!' she blurted, leaping to her feet in a panic.

'No, it's all right Jill, I'm fine darling. It went down the wrong way that's all. Come and sit back down.'

Her nan then began anxiously rummaging in the box.

'Is something wrong Nan?' said Jill frowning.

'Oh no, I just thought – Oh – pay no mind to me Jill. Now where were we?' she huffed.

'The family photograph?' Jill noticed a glazed look on her nan's face as she continued.

'Oh yes. This is your Great Nana's Mother and Father, Edwina and Henry, with her twin baby brothers, Lance and Miles. I was about your age when my mother informed me that they had all been lost at sea in a terrible storm.'

'Oh, how awful!' cried Jill. 'Was she with them? Was she rescued?'

'I don't know, Jill. You see she showed me the photograph and said I was *never* to ask her about it again.' With that her nan placed everything back into the box, and pondered. She then removed a necklace and some of the photographs and closed the lid.

'I'll tell you what Jill, if you *promise* to keep and treasure this box with *all* its contents, I'd like *you* to have it.'

'*Really?* But of course I will, Nan! Thank you so much!' she said, with a beaming smile.

'Now let's put the box with your things. I'll tell your mother I've entrusted it to you.'

Soon it was time to leave. The removal van had set off ahead of them. Auntie Margaret had come up to join the rest of the family and friends who'd gathered to see them off. There were lots of hugs, kisses and tears.

As the car pulled away, Jill stared through the back window at everyone waving till they became tiny specks in the distance.

'It was nice of nan to give you great nana's box, wasn't it Jill.'

'Yes Mum.'

'Make sure you take *good* care of it.'

'I will, I promise,' she replied heartily, then sat back and shed a little tear.

*

The family soon settled into their new home. The house was Victorian with large rooms and tall ceilings. Jill's room was on the top floor with a stunning view of the sea.

On the seafront there were a multitude of amusement arcades, shops and cafes. The beach accommodated a pier and theme park, which is where Jill and her brothers spent most of their time.

One particular day, the children decided to walk to the end of the pier. Simon was carrying a polythene bag containing a goldfish that Jill had won for him at the theme park.

A gang of boys on roller skates began to taunt them after hearing their Cornish accents. One loud boisterous boy in particular appeared to head the gang who referred to him as Rocky. He had short-cropped brown hair, was quite stocky and wore grubby slashed jeans. Jill was becoming anxious as Rocky made fun of them for the amusement of his gang.

'That fish should be in the sea!' snarled Rocky, as he tried to grab it from Simon.

'Pick him up Ritchie!' cried Jill as she stepped in front of Simon. But Rocky swiped at the bag, knocking it from Simon's hand. As it fell to the ground three other boys ran across to them shouting, drawing everyone's attention to the gang, who quickly dispersed.

Simon was sobbing as Ritchie picked up the bag which had just enough water left in it to sustain the fish, which was unharmed.

'I think you should call him Lucky!' said Jill quietly, as she stroked Simon's hair and wiped the tears from his eyes.

(If only she knew just how lucky it was, because sometimes things happen for a reason.)

'Are you OK?' asked one of the boys.

'Yes, we're fine. Thank you for helping,' replied Jill, slightly taken aback by the boy as she stared at his penetrating green eyes.

'My name's Matt, this is Jack and Podge.'

'Hi, I'm Jill and these are my brothers, Ritchie and Simon.'

Jack crouched down to Simon. 'That's a great lookin' fish kid,' he said, smiling at Simon with the cheekiest dimples indenting on his handsome face.

'Rocky and 'is gang are bad news. Come on, we'll walk yeh back to the seafront,' said Matt, reassuringly.

Jill, who was instantly smitten with Matt, happily agreed.

She and her brothers ended up spending the rest of the day with the boys with whom they soon struck up a friendship, during which time she discovered they called themselves the Surf gang.

After spending more time together in the days that followed, Jill developed a crush on Matt but the feeling wasn't mutual. Podge, who was ten, struck up a quarrelsome friendship with Ritchie, whom the gang nicknamed Dapper because he was always immaculately dressed. Simon was not always allowed out because of his age, but they all made a fuss of him when he was.

It wasn't long before Jill discovered that Matt and Rocky hated each other. She also learned that all the Surfs had been in trouble with the authorities. She thought it wise to keep this information from her parents, knowing they would not approve of the company they were keeping.

One particular evening when Ritchie and Simon had stayed at home, Jill was out with the Surfs in the arcades on the seafront, when they bumped into Rocky and his gang.

Rocky approached Matt and they became engaged in an argument. Jill got upset and came to Matt's defence. Furious with her for embarrassing him, Matt shouted at her, to go home and stay away from him, permanently. She burst into tears and ran off. Jack turned to go after her but received such a glare from Matt; he stayed.

Jill was so upset she wanted to be alone and wandered quite a way along the coast before climbing under a small boat that was propped upside down on the sand.

Hours passed, her parents, beside themselves with worry, informed the police she was missing.

Eventually, an officer found her after hearing her sobs and escorted her home.

Her parents were furious and grounded her for a week. She felt the whole world was suddenly angry with her and didn't understand why, as she was the one that was hurting.

That night she cried herself to sleep and wished they'd never left Cornwall.

*

The next day, Jill woke to find she was cuddling the doll that contained the key. She lay for a while staring at the doll and then gently shook it to hear the key rattle inside as she recalled the day Eleanor gave it to her.

'Jill, are you awake?' called Pamela from the top of the stairs.

'Yes Mum.'

'I'm just taking the boys to the barbers. Get yourself together and then tidy the kitchen for me. I'll be a couple of hours.'

'OK,' she called back glumly.

Sitting up, Jill caught sight of her reflection in the dressing table mirror and stared at her matted, salty hair through red, puffy eyes. She got herself showered and dressed but having no appetite for breakfast, began her chores.

After tidying the kitchen she slumped at the table and pondered over the previous night. Feeling depressed she ran up to her room and threw herself on the bed, landing face to face with the china doll. 'Hum,' she murmured, and then attempted to shake the key out, but to no avail. Using a nail file she tried to lever it out. This didn't work either. Losing her patience she threw it on the floor, causing the head to crack open. 'OH NO!' she gasped.

Upon retrieving it she spied the key on the carpet but was more concerned about the damaged doll that was one of a collection her nan had bought for her. Panicking, she thought quickly and then remembered she kept some glue in her school bag, which was stored on top of the wardrobe behind her great nana's box.

Pulling over her dressing table chair, she climbed onto it and stretched up. But the bag was just out of reach. She went up onto tiptoe causing the chair to tilt and topple over. Screaming she fell, knocking the mahogany box off in the process. As it crashed to the floor the lid broke away. Jill landed beside it and stared in horror at the contents, which were strewn everywhere. With no thought to her own wellbeing she quickly gathered everything into a pile.

On picking up the lid, she noticed the panel of wood inside had broken away and there was something behind it. Carefully she pulled the panel clear and was amazed to discover a book of red leather, embossed with gilt flowers around the words: *Note Book*. On its side was a small silver lock. Jill's eyes widened as her mouth dropped open. 'Great Nana's missing notebook! The key!'

Quickly locating it, she placed it in the lock, held her breath and began to turn. Click. She carefully opened it to find, hand written inside its front cover, a calendar of short horizontal lines diagonally stroked through. The first date noted was the *27th of August 1901*. Underneath a sheet of ink stained blotting paper on the opposite page in the most beautiful handwriting was an inscription which read:

Should my notebook ever be discovered and all my innermost secrets revealed, then dear reader may the memory live forever.

Signed Eleanor Pearce 15th of August 1911.

'Memory live forever. Where have I heard that before? Ugh! 15th of August, but that's *today's* date!' Just then she heard the front door bang.

'SIMON! DON'T *SLAM* THE DOOR! HOW MANY TIMES MUST I TELL YOU!'

It was her mother. Quickly she hid everything under the bed.

'Jill, look at me!' called Simon as he ran up the stairs. Bursting into her room he spun in a circle, showing off his new hair cut.

'Wow, aren't you the dandy!'

'It's a tram-line!' he said, proudly.

'Come here and let me feel … I'm a tram!' she laughed, as she ran her fingers along the two parallel lines shaven close to his scalp, that travelled around the sides of his head and met at a point in the nape of his neck. Simon giggled.

'Ritchie has one too! See you later.' With that he hurried off.

'You OK Sis?' inquired Ritchie, popping his head round the door.

'I'm fine thanks Ritch. Like the hair cut, very *Dapper!*'

'Not bad aye,' he replied smugly, sweeping his hand across his head. 'Mum said to tell you lunch is nearly ready.'

'Is it? - Tell mum I'm not hungry.'

'OK - Oh, I forgot to mention the fresh cream cakes. *More* for me,' he replied smugly, as he left.

Jill, so excited at discovering the notebook, soon forgot all the events of the previous night. Even Matt was now at the back of her mind as her imagination, fuelled with adrenaline, began to run wild.

Retrieving the book, she made herself comfortable on the bed, but on hearing footsteps, quickly hid it under her pillow and lay down, at which point her mother entered the room.

'Why don't you want lunch? Are you sick Jill?'

'I'm *fine* Mum.'

'But your face is all red! I *bet* you caught a chill last night,' she said, placing her hand on Jill's brow. 'Oh dear, you are a little warm.'

Jill thought quickly, then replied, 'Actually, I - am - starting - to - feel - a - bit - *shivery*.'

'Right, get yourself into bed. I'll bring you up some supper later, now try and get some sleep.'

'*Thanks - Mum*,' she whimpered, with a weakness in her voice.

As soon as her mother left, Jill pulled out the notebook and began to read. Immediately she noticed something strange. The marked calendar began on the *26th of August 1901*, yet the first entry in the notebook was dated the *31st of July 1901*. Bearing this strange occurrence in mind she read on intently.

CHAPTER THREE

Eleanor's Notebook: The Storm

31st of July 1901.

How exciting, my first entry in my new notebook, which I bought especially for our holiday. I do so love writing on a new page and hope I can keep every one as neat as the first.

Mother is busy packing the twins' suitcases. She has been more flustered than I have ever seen her as Lance and Miles will turn one on the 31st of August and she has to arrange for their party at sea. Father has been away for such long periods with his work and did not want to miss the twins' birthday, which is why we are to join him on this trip. Lance is three minutes older, so he shall be first to blow out his candles. I can't wait for them to grow up so I can read them the events of this special occasion. We leave tomorrow at first light for Southampton and will sail around Cape Horn then up to Peru.

Uncle George arrived at 10 a.m. and has been in the study with Father for hours discussing business.

I wish Grace was coming with us. I shall miss my best friend immensely. Still, we shall have lots to discuss on my return. (As for Marcia Poole's jealous comments, I shall rise above them.)

I can hear Uncle George's penetrating voice. He must be leaving. I shall close this entry here.

1st of August.

With all the excitement I hardly slept last night. Uncle George has arrived to take us to the port in his shiny new automobile.

Lance and Miles are already dressed. They look so adorable in their suits. Lance's is navy blue, which compliments his blonde hair and fair complexion. Miles' suit is red, which flatters his dark eyes and curls.

Father gave Mother the most beautiful gold brooch to wear on the journey; a bouquet set with ruby and garnet flowers with emerald leaves. They bought for me the most fashionable coat and hat of the smoothest silk and such a pretty sky blue. Father says it matches my eyes and enhances my blonde locks. I have been so looking forward to wearing them. My new boots are going to take some time to lace up as they have so many eyelets so I had better start to get ready.

At last, a chance to write. We have boarded the liner Meridian Star, *which is preparing to set sail. I never imagined a ship could be so huge. I worry as to how such a heavy vessel will stay afloat. Mother, Father and the twins are next door. My cabin is quite small but I can view the sea through the porthole. However there's plenty of room up on deck where I shall go now to wave good-bye to Uncle George.*

What an eventful day. The sea air has tired us all. The weather has been fine and looks to stay that way. There are so many interesting passengers on board. Some are dressed in attire I have never seen before. The Captain made a welcoming speech at dinner and made everyone laugh with his humorous remarks.

2nd of August

Today Mother and Father taught me how to play Ping-Pong, which is the latest craze. It was such fun. I beat Father so many times. He insisted I must have played before.

Mother had to discuss the birthday cakes with the ship's cook so I joined Father on deck where he was talking to the Captain, who commented that I smelt like an English flower. (I was wearing my Lily of the Valley perfume today. How sweet of him to notice.)

3rd of August

Today was such a special day. Whilst playing with Lance on the deck, he suddenly let go of my hands and took his first steps. It was so funny when Miles tried immediately to copy him but fell on his bottom. We tried to coax him but he hasn't quite got his balance right yet. I am sure it won't be long.

Father missed the occasion. He said he was having a chat with one of the passengers from whom he purchased an oriental sword contained in a gemmed scabbard, for his collection. I think he was secretly practising Ping-Pong, ready for our next match.

4th of August

How quickly the time has passed. I thought the days would be drawn out with nothing but the ocean surrounding us.

Today I was sketching Father as he dozed on a deck chair when I heard a loud SPLASH. At first I thought someone had fallen overboard. Then the Captain yelled out from the bridge, pointing. 'LOOK! A MANTA RAY!' I ran over to the rails. Flapping its fins, it leapt out of the water. Its wings must have spanned at least eleven feet. It was as if it was flying and momentarily hovered looking into my eyes, as if it knew me. Then in a splash it disappeared from sight. (Oh, how I wish I could have frozen time and drawn this splendid creature.)

5th of August

Something disagreed with me at dinner today, so I am taking myself off to bed.

15th of August

I cannot believe ten days have passed. Mother said I had food poisoning. I have not left my cabin but plan to go up on deck today as the ship's doctor said the sea air might do me some good. Apparently, quite a few of the passengers were affected. It has come about that we all chose chicken from the menu. (I wish I had had the fish as Mother suggested.) I also missed Miles taking his first steps.

Here I am, relaxing on a chair on the main deck. Due to my sickness, I missed us passing Cape Horn. I so looked forward to seeing it. Father said that a haze had obscured most of the view and not to worry, as there is always the return journey.

Although it feels quite warm the ocean is choppy and a darker blue. The clouds are turning grey and appear to be thickening. The Captain has been over to inquire as to my well being and has assured me that the skies will brighten soon. I hope we're not in for bad weather (I don't think my stomach could take it). I feel weak so I shall take a little nap.

25th of August

It is only today that I feel I can put pen to paper following the terrifying ordeal I have endured. The last thing I recall was putting my notebook into my pocket and drifting off to sleep.

I was dreaming of Marcia Poole, who was being unusually nice to me. We climbed a horn shaped mountain and had just reached its peak when she pointed to a strange flower that was growing there.

As I bent down to investigate she lurched forward and pushed me off the edge. My brain sent shock waves to my stomach as I fell rapidly.

Before landing in my dream I woke with a start and opened my eyes to an even worse nightmare. The sky was black as night and lightening forked all around. The ship was tilting. I spied Lance, who was screaming hysterically.

It all happened so quickly. My chair began to slide towards him. Sweeping him into my arms I caught sight of Mother with Miles, clinging to a doorway as a ferocious wind threatened to separate them. The chair became entangled in some rope and came to a sudden halt. Mother screamed at me to keep hold of Lance. In all the commotion I tried to catch sight of Father but he was nowhere to be seen. I thought; This couldn't be real, this can't be happening, I must still be dreaming.

Everything stilled momentarily. I could see the grey clouds were shifting in a circle. It was then I realised we were in the eye of a hurricane. I looked across to see Mother making her way towards us, carrying Miles. 'NO MOTHER! GO BACK, TAKE HOLD OF SOMETHING QUICKLY!' *I shrieked. Then Father appeared. Somewhat dazed he was stumbling towards Mother, clutching the sword.*

Suddenly gigantic waves began to crash over the ship, which twisted and turned as it lifted up onto its stern. There were people and debris flying everywhere. I held on tightly to Lance whose arms were wrapped around my neck, but lost sight of Father, Mother and Miles.

All of a sudden there was no deck beneath us, we were flipped out of the chair and were airborne. I can't even begin to explain the horrendous fear that consumed my whole being. I squeezed Lance tighter and tighter so afraid of crushing his ribs, but so desperate not to lose him. Then in the darkness I spied some rainbow lights zooming towards us. It was at that point some debris must have hit me on the head and I blacked out.

When I eventually opened my eyes I expected to see the sky above from the ship's deck, but all I saw was darkness amidst which a dim light in the distance slightly lit my surroundings. I was lying on a bed of moss in what seemed to be some kind of cave. I began to wiggle my fingers and toes to see if they were still attached. Lifting my head I looked around for Lance but there was no sign of him. Beside me were some clay bowls containing a strange liquid that looked and smelt like the bottom of a pond.

I cried out for Lance. My words echoed loudly, pounding in my ears, which caused a searing pain in my head. I put my hand to my brow that felt like it was bound with some kind of bindweed and moss, which probably explained the tiny spider sitting on my nose.

A boy approached carrying a lighted torch. He knelt beside me and smiled, putting me at ease. I didn't recognise him from the ship and he was dressed in attire of foliage. His hair appeared to be black and his skin glowed pure white in the torchlight, that glistened in his dark eyes. He was very handsome and seemed to be about my age. 'LANCE!' I screamed. Pulling back from me he ran off.

Soon, people carrying torches and similarly dressed like the boy, surrounded me, lighting up the cave. Then the little silhouette of a figure I knew so well toddled in. 'Lance, Oh Lance!' I cried as he came towards me. I can't express the relief I felt. He appeared to be totally unscathed. I hugged him tightly and burst into tears. They pushed some torches into grooves on the walls and left us alone. I had no idea of day or night or where we were.

A few days must have past during which time the boy, whose name I discovered to be Whitlow, came back and forth with food and water. He redressed my wound daily, applying the smelly liquid and also attached beautiful rose coloured flowers to the binding to disguise the lingering odour. (How I wished at that time I had my perfume.)

Lance had made friends with children his age. The women caring for him frequently brought him in to see me. They all seemed rather pleasant and friendly.

Every night before Lance slept he would keep repeating, Mama, Dada and Miles. I had described my family to Whitlow, who assured me he was searching for them but as time dragged on I was becoming more and more anxious.

In the far corner of the cave was a divide, which served as our bathroom. Whenever I stood to go there my head hurt and I would come over faint.

This particular day I was starting to feel somewhat better and decided to explore. I entered a colossal chamber where lit torches cast ghostly shadows amongst shades of greys, blues and rusty red rocks. There were nooks, crannies and tunnels everywhere. Most amazing of all were two stairwells that had been chiselled into the walls. They led to a tiny opening at the top from where a shaft of sunlight shone like a star a galaxy away. People were climbing up one side and down the other, just like an army of ants foraging in and out of a giant hill.

I spied Lance playing in a clearing and was making my way towards him, when I heard my name resounding. Looking up I caught sight of Whitlow, who was anxiously making his way down. Pushing past someone, he lost his footing. My heart was in my mouth as he fell, landing on a ledge below, dropping a leafy bundle that he was clutching.

On seeing he was safe I ran over to where it lay. There was my notebook, which I had presumed lost. A little rough round the edges but otherwise undamaged. The key was still in the lock and my fountain pen tucked safely inside the binding.

By the time Whitlow joined me I had read my first entries and was staring at a family photograph I kept inside. He lifted my chin in his hand. The tears streamed down my face as I bombarded him with questions. Where were we? How did we get here? I told him I had to find out if my family had survived. He nodded reassuringly yet there was uneasiness in his eyes. Removing my dressing, he inspected the wound saying, 'You have to meet Woodruff!'

It came about that Woodruff was their leader.

Lighting a torch Whitlow led me into a tunnel, which was guarded by two people at its entrance. We seemed to have walked such a long way. Eventually the tunnel widened. Soon after we came to an opening of a cavern, where torches were burning brightly from within. Whitlow stopped and signalled for me to enter alone. Cautiously, I went in.

I immediately spied an old man sitting with his back to me on a fine leather chair at a polished wooden desk. The whole of the cavern's walls were lined with felled tree trunks that reached from the floor to the ceiling. Some of which had shelves carved into them containing all manner of books and artefacts. Others appeared to have cone type handles that suggested they opened. (It was like a museum.)

The chair swivelled. 'Eleanor, I believe?' he said turning to face me, with an air of authority, beckoning for me to be seated on a chair opposite.

'Yes, I am she,' I replied, looking into his lined round face on which his eyebrows climbed to his head of wispy white hair. He was wearing a red toga and sandals, liken to Roman times.

'I am glad to see you are up and about. Whitlow has kept me informed of your progress,' he remarked. He then went on to explain that I was in a volcano which had lain dormant for centuries beneath the sea apart from its summit. He and his people were known as Lavaights.

On the nearby shore was the Island of Echoco. In the lowland resided Newteleons, huge lizards that occupied the swamps. They were a secretive breed, that were masters of disguise, whose moods could change as quickly as their appearance and quite capable of devouring a human. Only the Lavaights were tolerated to annually clear the excess mosses from the bogs that contained medicinal properties. This arrangement benefited them both. Occasionally a soul was lost to the swamps or maybe the Newteleons. However they were not in a position to argue.

There was also the Crowfoot tribe that dwelled on a mountainous range across a canyon on the far side of the island. Their magic was strong when executed on their own kind. One of them, known as Arvensis, aptly named after a highly poisonous plant, was suspected of murdering the tribal chief, Hellebore. For his punishment Myosurus, the Chief Elder turned him into a crow. She banished him to live with the island's crows that inhabit a forest near the beach. Arvensis rules over these birds and resides in the shipwrecks on the shore.

'Best you don't venture there!' he advised. Staring at me with an inquisitive expression, Woodruff said, 'There have never before been survivors from the hurricanes. The Orbs chose to rescue Lance and yourself, for whatever reason I know not. Maybe they know something I don't!' I looked a bit puzzled by what I was hearing and he could tell by my expression that I did not have a clue about who or what the Orbs were.

Standing up, he walked over to one of the trunk doors. Upon opening it, a blinding rainbow of light shone out. He whistled. Then a little transparent rainbow coloured sphere the size of a tennis ball appeared, hovering at the door's entrance. I was totally shocked to see a little face peering out, a face, just a face of a baby boy with rainbow coloured hair. He pushed his nose into the bubbled wall, which shimmered.

Woodruff then picked up a book from his desk, opened it, and closing his eyes pointed randomly on a page. Looking up he announced, 'I hereby name you: Eyebright and assign you to Lance!' With that the boy nodded and retreated. Then a little girl Orb came forward. He repeated the routine and said, 'I hereby name you Orchis, sister of Eyebright and also assign you to Lance.' She smiled in my direction before retreating. He closed the door. 'They will always serve him!' he stated, snapping the book shut.

He informed me that as leader of his people and the Orbs, it was his duty to register all births and deaths. He was also responsible for naming all the newborn.

Opening a large ledger and whilst writing, he explained to me that on Earth there lived minute people called Kindreds that are unknown to humans. When a Kindred is born so too on Echoco is an Orb, known as the Kindreds' spirit. When an Orb dies the Kindred loses his spirit, and eventually dies too. They were very perceptive of each other. At this point he glanced up and as his eyes disappeared under his brow he said, 'The Orbs I have assigned

Lance are orphans. Maybe that's why they helped in your rescue!' He closed the ledger.

(It was at this point that I was beginning to think I had gone a little mad. Everything seemed real and yet my mind was refusing to take it all on board.)

I enquired if any ships passed the island, to which he frowned. 'Ships don't pass through. They just sometimes get caught up in a storm!' he replied abruptly. This left me even more confused. 'Go now!' he continued. 'Whitlow will accompany you onto the mainland tomorrow. Stay with him at all times. I cannot predict the reception you will receive, but under no circumstances enter the woods of Cragga. I wish you luck in your search but warn you to expect the worst!'

On hearing those words I felt sick in the pit of my stomach. As I turned to leave he commented, 'Oh and Eleanor, for your notebook records, you were unconscious for five days and today is the 25th of August.'

As Whitlow led me back to the main chamber I asked him why Cragga was out of bounds. He explained that no one ever ventured there. It was a cursed wood fringed with craggy rocks depicting clawed hands, where neither the sun shone nor rain fell. It survived by sucking the lifeblood and soul from any living creature that entered its domain. He then went on to explain that once a tree from the centre had been uprooted and deposited on the beach during a storm. They spliced the trunk to make firewood, but on finding the knots and rings in the grain resembling pained faces, they decided to bury it where it lay. I would certainly heed Woodruff's warning.

So, here I am in my own little cave. Tomorrow I will venture out with Whitlow. Lance is fast asleep. He has made so many friends, one in particular a little boy called Teasel who suffers from a nervous twitch. I know he will be looked after while I am gone and will adore the little Orbs. Hopefully he won't meet them till I return, as I can't wait to see his reaction. It is only six days till his birthday; I don't know how I shall cope if Miles is not here.

I have put today's date in as correct and have marked a diary inside the front cover to help me keep track of time and shall continue to write notes when I feel the need. We leave at first light, although I fear that where my head shall lead, my heart will not want to follow.

*

It was at this point Pamela came in to check on Jill, who was so engrossed in her reading she didn't hear her mother enter her room.

'Oh, you're awake! How are you feeling?' Jill just stared dumbstruck at her mother with her mouth gaping open. 'Jill, what's the matter?' Quickly, pulling herself together, she tucked the notebook unnoticed under her quilt.

'Sorry Mum, I must have drifted off and have only just woken up!' she blurted.

'I just want to take your temperature then you can get back to sleep.'

'M-u-m?' murmured Jill with the thermometer under her tongue.

'Wait a moment Jill!' said Pamela, as she studied her watch.

Jill's mind became boggled. The first thing she'd noticed was the change in her great nana's handwriting following the storm. Then she recalled the time her nan commented on the terrible tragedy at sea. She began to surmise that her great nana had survived the disaster and had been rescued. Maybe she was concussed or dreamt the whole thing up in an effort to cope with her loss. The Orbs however were playing on her mind. She recalled the funeral, and then dismissed such a ludicrous idea.

Pamela removed the thermometer. 'Hum, it's a little up but not serious enough to call the doctor in. Are you feeling hungry yet?'

'Not really.'

'All right, I'll look in on you later. Now what was it you wanted to ask me?'

'Oh, I was dreaming of Great Nana. We were visiting her in the home. I just couldn't remember what sort it was. Was it an - *asylum?*'

'Oh no Jill, it was a care home. She wasn't *mad!* Now don't worry yourself. Your Great Nana *knew* and *loved* you well. Now try and get some rest.'

As Pamela left the room, Jill quickly located the page she had stopped at and continued reading.

CHAPTER FOUR

Eleanor's Notebook: Echoco Island

We have camped for the night. Whitlow speared some fish and built such a cosy fire on which he cooked me a lovely supper. He's sleeping now as a mystical full moon dominates the clear night sky.

We emerged from the volcano to be greeted by a hazy mist. How wonderful the sea air smelt. We made our way down steps carved into the summit, to a wooden jetty, which secured thirty or more small boats. We boarded one and were soon on the island's shores. Whitlow said it would be best to scour Deadwood beach first, as Arvensis was not an early riser.

Making our way along the coast, I surmised Deadwood beach lay ahead as remains of ships appeared, ghosting in the swirling mist. Quietly, we searched as much of the area as possible but found no signs of life or Arvensis.

As we headed inland towards the forest, some Orbs flew swiftly overhead. Whitlow informed me that they were searching for several others that had disappeared during the hurricane from which Lance and I were rescued. Apparently they were quite capable of withstanding its force. Woodruff had noticed their absence, as he calls Orb register every night before they retire in their tree trunk quarters within his cavern. (I do hope they find them.)

How dark and dense the forest appeared. The crows, immediately aware of our presence, began to craah and flap around in the treetops. I couldn't believe the size of these birds that appeared almost on par with an eagle. I found them quite unnerving.

We combed the area for hours, walking through so many cobwebs and briars, my clothes are tattered and I am covered in scratches. (I hope tomorrow is a better day.)

My heart lies heavy after yet another fruitless day. The only lift to my spirits is this tranquil lake by which we've camped. Whitlow is restless. We have hardly spoken two words to each other this evening, as he knows I am beginning to realise my worst fears. I don't think we'll sleep much tonight. I must write, as I shall loose my mind if I don't distract from my thoughts.

This morning we came to the outskirts of Cragga. It was just as Whitlow described. The sun was high in the sky and yet Cragga was black as night. My bones chilled as a cold eerie wind blew from within its darkness in which I am certain I heard voices moaning and crying.

Whilst making our way around its perimeter I asked Whitlow how Arvensis had murdered Hellebore. He said the evil brave wanted to take over the tribe. On a particular day, Calyx, Hellebore's son, had strayed out of Crowfoot territory. A search party became divided on Cragga's outskirts; Cragga was taboo to the tribe.

Rumour has it, Arvensis, on spying Hellebore alone, maimed a fox ahead of him and sent it running, screaming, liken to a child, into Cragga. Hellebore ran to Arvensis, who was panicking and pointing, shouting, 'CALYX. IT'S CALYX!' They drew their hunting knives and ran together, but as they passed the craggy rocks, Arvensis faked a fall and pretended to break his ankle. Hellebore didn't hesitate in running in alone. Presently his painful cries filled the air.

The tribe's best hunter, Lingua, who doted on his Chief, had found Calyx. Leaving him safely with some braves, Lingua swiftly ran to where Arvensis stood. Lingua's wails were heard echoing across the island as he fell to his knees, clawing himself and the ground in frustration knowing he could not help Hellebore.

Eventually, Hellebore's cries ceased and as anticipated, he never returned. Lingua saw the fox's bloody trail and suspected trickery afoot. Myosurus, Hellebore's Mother, had no firm evidence of Lingua's theory; hence, Arvensis was turned into a crow and not killed for his suspected crime.

Hellebore's soul still dwells, protected, in the talisman that hung about his neck and his cries on that day, each year, echo across the canyon. Myosurus wails back to him. His soul cannot be laid to rest till his talisman is buried on sacred ground. But it is irretrievable. (This was not the best story to hear as the day began.)

The air became humid as we approached the swamps, the Newteleons' domain. Whitlow signalled for me to be quiet. Sitting me on a slimy fallen tree trunk, he scooped up some moss from the water's edge, at which point I saw a huge eye seemingly part of the trunk, open and close. I wanted to scream but bit my tongue. Whitlow thought my tense reaction was due to the soggy moss that stung as he applied it to my scratches. I pointed anxiously but he just took hold of my hand and led me off. Glancing back I saw the trunk slide into the swamp and disappear.

As we neared the end of this boggy land we came upon this crystal clear lake, surrounded by pine trees and active with shoals of fish darting everywhere. I have found a place I love on this island. If only I could now find the ones I love.

Well, here we are again, back at the lake before the return journey tomorrow. It took the best part of the day getting to the ridge, the only access across the canyon to Crowfoot territory. We travelled through forests and glades that skirted the mountains. It soon dawned on me; this vast area would take weeks to cover.

Walking in front of Whitlow I moved an overhanging branch, when suddenly a brave dropped out of the tree, landing in front of me. He was tall and muscular. He wore a hostile expression on his painted face. A bow and arrows were strapped to his bare back and he held his hunting knife firmly in his hand.

Slowly, he leaned forward and smelt my hair. (I recall he smelt like a campfire.) Staring into my eyes his face softened. Backing off he turned his attention to Whitlow, who addressed him as Lingua whilst humbly explaining our presence.

Lingua firmly informed us that there were no survivors on their territory. If there were he would have been the first to know. Then he told us to leave (which of course we did).

My heart lies heavy and my head feels numb. I still can't accept the inevitable. Lance's birthday is now only three days away. I shall try and be cheerful for his sake.

Where do I begin, so much has occurred? We arrived back at Deadwood beach before dusk. I could not give up hope and insisted we searched closer to the ships. Whitlow voiced his concerns, but in desperation I was past caring about the silly, scary crow.

Still we found nothing. That is when I broke down. Sobbing, I just put my hands to my face and dropped to the sand, whereupon something stung my knee. Flinching, I stood up and stared, dumbstruck at my Mother's brooch!

Just then, we heard a faint voice in the distance. Listening intently, we heard it again. 'Dada?' It was coming from a large wreck of a nearby galleon that was embedded in the sand. 'Miles!' I screamed. Whitlow called for me to wait, as I raced ahead of him.

I burst through a cabin door and could not believe my eyes! There was Miles sitting on the floor, playing with a live crab. 'Miles, Miles!' I cried. He looked up at me and smiled. Then I saw Arvensis. (No one had told me he was still human sized.) I froze, staring into his black eyes.

Whitlow rushed in and stood behind me, spear poised. Arvensis cawed loudly, spread out his huge wings and wrapped them around Miles, who began to giggle. Whitlow drew back his spear.

'Don't be foolish boy!' scorned Arvensis. To my amazement, he lifted Miles with the tips of his wings and held him forward, his tone softened as he spoke. 'I rescued him days ago and have been caring for him since!'

I grabbed hold of Miles and hugged him, crying. Whitlow still held his spear vigilantly.

At that moment, Woodruff, who had been alerted by a lookout, burst in with some of his men, all armed. Arvensis addressed Woodruff.

'You see, the child is unharmed. Caring for him has filled my heart with love.'

Woodruff seemed bemused but said nothing. As we turned to leave I overheard him telling Whitlow that he wondered why this carrion crow had not devoured the child.

We walked out onto the slanted deck to the most incredible sight. There on the sand stood a pure white, winged horse, with long sweeping mane and tail. Two twisting V shaped horns protruded from the animal's forelock. It was magnificent.

Astride its back was an old woman brave and behind her Lingua, who slid off and stood beside her. There was a mystical charisma about her. She was dressed in the brightest orange attire and many charms hung around her neck. Everyone bowed so I copied.

'Myosurus!' said Woodruff. Acknowledging him she beckoned for us all to rise and then signalled for me to come closer. I looked at Whitlow, who nodding reassuringly took Miles from me.

Placing her tiny hand on my head she closed her eyes and muttered words I did not understand. On opening them she gave me such a warm smile.

'Where is the other child?' she asked, addressing Woodruff. I thought this a bit strange as I was unaware she knew of our presence.

'Lance is in the volcano,' he replied and then proceeded to inform her of the strange occurrence with Arvensis whom she promptly summoned.

Arvensis came out. He appeared humble as he crouched before her. Ordering him to stand she stared straight through him. She then beckoned to her steed who walked backwards lowering his forelock and unexpectedly leapt forward, thrusting his horns towards Arvensis. I gasped and ran to Whitlow, who whispered to me, 'Hush she is testing him.' Arvensis submissively cowered away.

Myosurus spoke out. 'For your heroic deed of rescuing and caring for this child I shall reward you.' Arvensis lifted his head proudly. Myosurus beckoned to Lingua who reluctantly removed some parchment and a quill pen from a purse, tied around his waist. Taking them from him she struck the pen's nib into her finger, dipped it into her blood and began to write.

Then she announced, 'Let it be witnessed by all present. This contract, scribed of my blood and therefore indestructible, entitles Arvensis to eternal life, but he is to remain a crow!' (I noticed Arvensis's tail feathers twitch at this remark.) 'Should he default its terms, which state continued good behaviour, it can be served on him by the executor, hence causing him to die a terrible death! I name as the executor; Eleanor. Should there come a time she cannot fulfil this role, the onus shall fall to the twin brother of this child, the one known as Lance.' Arvensis bowed his head in acknowledgement.

Lingua took the parchment from her and as he handed it to me he squeezed my hand whispering; 'You must *keep it safe!' I sensed his concern. Lingua then leapt up behind Myosurus, following which the animal twisted around, spread its huge wings and flew away, spraying us with sand in its wake.*

I asked Whitlow about the animal. He told me it came to Echoco during a storm many years ago. Myosurus had named him Aquila, after a flower with a horn shaped spur and leaves that resemble an eagle's talons. He became sacred to them.

It was becoming clear to me that all the inhabitants of Echoco were named after plants. (How enchanting.)

I thanked Arvensis, who waved a wing at Miles. As we walked away, Miles began to cry and pull away from me. Arvensis asked if Miles could visit sometimes. I consented at which Woodruff huffed. Whitlow raised his eyebrows and we both smirked as with arms folded behind his back, Woodruff walked ahead muttering; 'It is a puzzle, can't put the pieces together yet but I know one exists. Got to be a reason!' Maybe because I had never seen the bad side of Arvensis, I was less concerned. Besides, I was so overjoyed at having Miles safe in my arms nothing else mattered.

When we returned to the volcano, Lance was thrilled to see Miles who seemed sullen when Lance hugged him. Then again he had been through quite an ordeal, as we all had.

I have just settled Lance and Miles down to sleep. They had such an exciting birthday. Everyone was so helpful.

The main chamber was decorated with seashells and seaweed hung on vines of which the children had great fun popping the pods. There was ample to eat and drink (well, that was before the food fight evolved). We even had music as the Lavaights blew through conch shells and played on drums that were normally sounded to warn of bad weather when the sea splashed over the summit.

The highlight of the day was the twins' presents from Woodruff, who had also assigned two orphaned Orbs to Miles, called Brier and Dodder. Dodder had the cutest plump face. Miles didn't seem too impressed and kept asking for Arvensis. Woodruff had made it quite clear that he was not welcome.

Lance was ecstatic upon receiving Eyebright and Orchis. I fear he has already forgotten Mother and Father. I wonder if Uncle George is missing us yet. I am sure he will send out a search party. Perhaps, contrary to what Woodruff said, we will be found.

We have just returned from the lake. Whitlow escorted me and then went fishing to give me some time alone. I decided to bury Mother's brooch, in an attempt to lay my parents to rest. I found the perfect spot beneath a tree that I marked with a little cross made of twigs. Overcome with emotion I poured my heart out and cried the tears that had so not wanted to leave my eyes.

As I sat reminiscing, my attention was drawn to little bubbles popping on the surface beside a boulder. It was at this point Whitlow appeared laden with fish. As we walked away I heard a splash and looked back to discover the boulder had disappeared. (How strange.)

I hope I can now begin to come to terms with my loss and start to rebuild my life and my spirit.

I do not know where this year has gone. It has been so long since I last put pen to paper that my ink had dried. Whitlow extracted some from a squid. He has been so helpful with the boys, who grow so quickly. Miles is turning into a little rascal, always up to mischief and a bit boisterous with Brier and Dodder. He rebuffs Lance most of the time and plagues me till I let him visit Arvensis, whom Woodruff blames for his attitude. I think he overreacts. Lance tends to spend more time with Teasel and the other boys. As long as they are happy I have no concerns.

Today is my fifteenth birthday and although I kept it low-key, Whitlow surprised me with not one but a cluster of beautiful pearl and shell necklaces. I know the waters around the volcano are shark infested and was so angry with him for risking his life, diving amongst the corals. Then he handed me a tiny present, wrapped in leaves. I could not believe my eyes. It was my perfume bottle, still half-full. I don't think he realised it had belonged to me. Leaning forward I kissed him on the cheek, to which his face turned crimson. It was then that I realised I was falling in love with him.

- CHAPTER FIVE -

Eleanor's Notebook: The Return

My heart is filled with great sadness and sorrow as I try to pen the recent events, which began, ironically, on the fifteenth of August 1902. (The first anniversary of my parents' death.)

I had risen early and taken myself off to the lake with my notebook, in case I felt inspired. After spending a few hours with my thoughts, I felt too depressed to write and made my way back.

I happened upon Lance, Teasel and some of the other boys in the forest, where they were building a camp. I was quite impressed at its size and structure. They had obviously worked hard, and I was looking forward to seeing the end result.

When I reached the beach I met with Miles, where Arvensis was helping him find shells for his collection that he stored in a cannon on the galleon. I recall smiling at Arvensis and thinking how strange when he stared at me momentarily, with a look that unearthed me. (I assumed he was aware of my low spirits.)

Whitlow had been anxiously awaiting my return, sitting on the summit where I joined him. He commented on how beautiful I looked. I was wearing all the necklaces he had given me.

Presently, Lance and his friends came past giggling amongst themselves. I knew that the affection Whitlow and I shared for each other was becoming apparent to all.

Whitlow suddenly became very nervous and on edge. He said he needed to talk with me. Perspiration began to form on his brow as he rubbed his hands together and began.

It was not long before I realised that he was professing his love for me. Taking hold of my hands he asked if I would one day become his wife. I looked up into his eyes, then straight past him, at which point the sky darkened. He turned his head to where my gaze was fixed. 'HURRICANE!' he yelled.

As hailstones began to pelt us, he picked up my notebook and secured it in an oilskin pouch tied around his waist, then told me to get inside. I screamed at him that Miles was still on the island.

As the sea raged the drums began to beat. We looked inland but a cloud so thick and black like one I had never seen obscured our view and was coming straight towards us. We were momentarily mesmerised by this strange phenomenon. It was not until it was upon us that we saw hundreds of crows, locked closely together and led by Arvensis.

Whitlow grabbed hold of me as we were swept into a choppy mass of black feathers and carried out to the path of the hurricane, where we were dropped helplessly into the sea.

Gigantic waves tossed us about. As our lungs filled with water, everything suddenly stilled. There was a strange serenity, it was almost as if we were flying as we sank. We gazed at each other in the murky depths, and then everything went black.

I woke to feel gentle waves lapping at my face. I tried to open my eyes that were glued with salty residue. On doing so I focused on an eye that was staring straight back at me. My whole body tingled as it dawned on me I was laying on the back of a manta ray. 'It is you, I know it!' I whispered, convinced it was the same magnificent fish I had seen from the Meridian Star a year previous.

I turned my head to where Whitlow was lying lifeless beside me. Quietly I called his name, again and again. Eventually he murmured and my heart soared with relief. I told him that we were safe but not to move suddenly as he might fall off.

We lay for two days on our slippery float that breezed through the water. As we neared unconsciousness it curled up its wing like fins and slapped us. We stirred with a start to hear voices shouting. 'AHOY THERE!' It was a ship, a trading vessel. They lowered a small boat to us. I kissed the manta ray and said thank you, to which it rippled its body.

As we clambered aboard the vessel, it leapt majestically into the air, flapping its fins as if waving goodbye, before disappearing into the depths. (I knew in my heart we would never meet again.)

The crew were very kind to us. I could not believe my ears when they said they were on route to England.

Presently the captain came to see us. Whitlow had already told me I was not to mention Echoco, so I told him we had both been shipwrecked from the Meridian Star a year ago. He looked at me as if I was mad, and then asked our names so he could radio a message ahead. I asked if he could get word to my Uncle George. He said he would try.

We docked at Southampton, where a crowd had gathered. As we disembarked, lots of photographers began taking our pictures. The crowd seemed to be mocking us. It was most bizarre. Then I spied Uncle George. He appeared somewhat older than I remembered. I presumed he had aged with worry.

My heart lifted as I ran towards him, calling his name. But instead of the warm, welcoming hug I anticipated, he pushed me away, with anger in his eyes and shouted angrily, 'IMPOSTOR!' I could not believe what I was hearing. I begged him to acknowledge me but he yelled furiously. 'MY FAMILY WERE LOST AT SEA *TEN* YEARS AGO! THERE WERE *NO* SURVIVORS FROM THE MERIDIAN STAR. WE SEARCHED FOR *MONTHS!* HOW *DARE* YOU TURN UP HERE AFTER STAGING YOUR SO-CALLED RESCUE, IMPERSONATING *MY* NIECE IN

AN ATTEMPT TO CLAIM HER ESTATE. SHE WOULD HAVE BEEN *TWENTY-FOUR* NOW, NOT A CHILD LIKE YOURSELF! I'VE A GOOD MIND TO HAVE YOU ARRESTED FOR FRAUD!' *With that he stormed off. I was absolutely speechless.*

Just then I spied a young woman in the crowd, holding onto a perambulator. As our eyes met she turned her head. 'GRACE!' *I yelled but she quickly walked away, disappearing from sight. I turned to Whitlow in desperation.* 'I'm so *sorry Eleanor. I knew our island was not of your time, I was just unaware of the delay period. Echoco exists in a time warp!' I could not take everything in. His words became faint amongst the noisy, jostling crowd and flashing cameras as I passed out.*

We were detained for some time by the authorities. It was hopeless to pursue my story as we would have been arrested or admitted to a mental institution. Eventually we were issued papers and released. Whitlow, having no surname, asked if he could take mine, to which I agreed. To top it all I discovered Marcia Poole had married my cousin Gregory, the son of Uncle George and was living a life of luxury on my inheritance.

I still cannot believe it is 1911; so much has changed. Luckily Whitlow had some pearls that provided some income to get us started. I told him to sell my necklaces, but he would not hear of it. He is determined to contact the Kindreds so we can return to Echoco. He knows of two Leaders, brothers called Ulex and Furse. Woodruff told him that on occasions they conducted meetings at the ruins of Tintagel castle in Cornwall. We've taken menial jobs and have rented a room in a squalid abode nearby.

March 1915.

Where has the time gone? Every Sunday for the last four years, Whitlow has taken himself off to the castle ruins, where at night using a flashlight he signals an SOS, which is one of the Kindreds means of communication. I anxiously wait, anticipating a smile in his eyes when he returns, but to no avail.

43

I have cried myself to sleep so many nights at the thought of never seeing Lance and Miles again. I fear for their safety, and wonder if anyone was aware that Arvensis had tried to kill us.

AUGUST 1918.

Whitlow and I were married last week. It was a cheap and low-key affair, with just a few friends from work who were our witnesses.

It was on our wedding night that he sat me down and explained that the first five boys born of his blood would bear birthmarks, each one a piece of a jigsaw. Joined together they would reveal the co-ordinates of a star constellation that could be seen annually above the Pacific Ocean in August. The central star marked the entry point to Echoco, which is only *accessible through a hurricane. Which explained why normally there were never any survivors. Apparently, when the eye of a hurricane is in alignment with this star a second twister forms in the eye and the vortex suction is channelled downwards through the second eye into the time warp.*

He asked me where I had put the contract. I told him it was safe. I knew he'd given up hope as the Sunday trips had ceased. He added that most birthmarks fade and with them so must the islands whereabouts. Then he swore me to secrecy.

I feel as though I've lived through so much in such a short space of time and I know, as does Whitlow, the birthmark map could take up to a century to evolve and there was nothing *we could do.*

31st of August 1925

Fourteen years have past. I am now twenty-nine. (How strange that I should really have been thirty-eight.)

Today is the twins' birthday. If they are alive and well they shall be three today, as they have been for the last three years of our time and will be for the next seven.

44

We have done quite well for ourselves and purchased an adorable cottage near Bodmin Moor. Whitlow has become a Professor of Oceanography, in which he feels closer to home as he studies the ocean and its phenomena. He has recently had a book published on the subject and signed the first edition for Woodruff. 'You never know,' he sighed, as he lay down his pen.

I have been busy with our two children, Susan and David, who was indeed born with a birthmark. For my own sanity I shall secretly keep an account of this and any future birthmarks, as they are the only doorway to my brothers. Not a day goes by when I do not think of them and the cruel hand fate dealt me. Why? I'll never know. I cling to the hope that one day I will return to Echoco. It is the only way I can go forward.

I shall keep this notebook safe, so that its contents shall only be known to me, but should you find yourself reading it; believe me, fate is dealing you a hand.

*

Jill stared at the last words, unable to move a muscle. Absolutely captivated by what she had read she turned the last page under which she found an envelope. Inside she discovered newspaper clippings. The first was dated August 17th 1901. The headline read: *Meridian Star disappears in hurricane in the Pacific Ocean.* The Pearce family were mentioned in the article, as it appeared Eleanor's father, was of some importance in the shipping business. The second was dated September 15th 1901 and headed: *Search for survivors of Meridian Star called off. All passengers and crew believed dead.* The third was dated August 16th 1911, headlined: *Girl bearing striking resemblance to Eleanor Pearce attempts to claim inheritance.* It featured a photograph of Eleanor and Whitlow on the dock at Southampton. Then went on to tell the story.

Jill surmised her great nana had acquired the previous clippings, which gave her the idea to attempt the fraud. Deciding her nan and mother knew, she assumed they'd desperately tried to find her notebook when she died to avoid bringing shame on the family.

What she couldn't understand was why her great nana had written this ridiculous story. She concluded that she gave her the key in the hope she may find the notebook as a child and therefore believe her story and not think badly of her.

Daylight was leaving Jill's room. Turning on her bedside lamp, she lay back on the pillow and thought for a moment. She recalled how her great nana had always insisted she was ninety-eight not eighty-nine and recollected the conversation she had with her nan. That's where she'd heard it before; *some birthmarks go and some stay but a memory must live forever!* Then there were the rare pearl necklaces and the photographs of four birthmarks, which her great nana must have studied often, as they were not concealed in her notebook. On the other hand, what if it was all true! Could *her great uncles be* alive *somewhere in a* time warp *and only now be* nine years old?

Just then there was a knock on her door. 'Jill! Are you awake?' It was her father.

'Yes Dad.'

He entered the room. 'I heard you weren't feeling very well?' he said, looking worried.

'I'm fine now I've had a rest.'

'Been reading! Anything good?' he asked noticing the book under her hand.

'Oh, just girlie stuff, not quite your cup of tea,' she replied, sliding it under the bed.

Her father closed the curtains. 'I've had a word with your mother; we've decided to un-ground you. If you feel up to it, get yourself out in the sea air tomorrow. It may do you some good.'

As he spoke Jill had the strangest thought. *That's exactly what the ship's doctor had supposedly said to Great Nana on this very date.*

Just then her mother came in. 'How's the patient? - See John, she *still* doesn't look right.'

'I'm *fine* Mum, honest,' she insisted, raising her eyebrows.

'I'll leave you two to argue,' said her father. He kissed Jill on her forehead and then left the room.

Pamela began to tidy her quilt. 'Stop fussing Mum!'

'I'm not fussing darling, I've been worried about you. You've been, well, I don't know - distant!'

'Mum?' she slurred.

'Yes sweetheart?'

'I've been wondering - do you think you'll have anymore children?'

'What a strange question Jill. I very much doubt it!'

'Oh, do you think Uncle Edward will?'

'You never know, he so longed for a son but after five girls I'm not sure he's meant to have one.'

'What about Auntie Margaret? Surely she'd want a child of her own!'

'After the baby I-'

'Baby? What baby?' she queried, frowning.

'Oh, it was a long time ago!'

'*What* Mum, surely you can tell me?'

'Well - I suppose,' said her mother, amidst a huge sigh. 'You see your Auntie Margaret fell pregnant at a very young age. She felt she couldn't cope, so he was given up for adoption at birth.'

'He!' declared Jill, with eyes agog.

'Yes, a boy. She didn't even name him, and has regretted her actions ever since. None of us got to see him. Jill? Jill? Why are you staring so?'

'Sorry Mum,' she replied, quickly shaking her head. 'I was just thinking how *awful* it must have been for her. So he was born before Simon and Ritchie?'

'Yes, but don't you worry your pretty little head about it. You do seem to be asking a lot of questions about the family today. Is there a reason?'

'No, not particularly. I've just been thinking of nan and grandad and that got me thinking of other things.'

'Yes, your nan did make a fuss of you whenever you were poorly. I'll tell you what, I'll phone her tomorrow and if it's OK we'll all go up and stay during the half term holidays. We could call on Auntie Margaret on the way home.'

'That would be great!' she replied enthusiastically.

'Right, I'll see you in the morning,' she said, then kissed Jill goodnight and went downstairs.

Jill went over the family tree in her mind. *Nan's brother David was the first boy born and then Mum's brother, Uncle Edward. Thirdly the mystery baby, followed by Simon and Ritchie. I don't know why I'm bothering, for even if the baby had been born bearing a birthmark, it would probably have gone by now and besides there's not much chance of tracing him.*

She decided to dismiss the whole affair and get some sleep.

Drifting off she began to dream and could hear her Great Nana's infectious laugh. Then she heard her calling her name, over and over. As she did, Jill found herself spinning and falling.

Landing on a beach she spied her Great Nana behind the shell of a boat, where she was huddled in a ball, sobbing.

'Don't cry, Great Nana, I *still* love you!' she assured her as she approached.

Eleanor gazed up at her and cried out, '*HELP* THEM JILL! *HELP* THEM, FOR I CANNOT!' Just then a loud 'CRAAAAAH,' filled the air. Jill's heart skipped a beat as she looked up to see a huge crow swooping towards them.

Waking with a start, Jill froze momentarily in the darkness. As she reached over to turn on the bedside lamp she could smell her great nana's perfume that she vividly remembered from her childhood. Then as she turned back, to her horror she spied the notebook lying on top of her quilt, open on the last page. She quickly looked around the room, but there was no one there.

Picking up the notebook, she noticed the thread bare remains of a pink ribbon on the inside back cover. She pulled at it, which caused the card to lift, revealing a secret sleeve. She was absolutely flabbergasted to find inside what appeared to be the contract, written in what looked like dried blood and worded just as her Great Nana had described in her story.

Jill gasped, then carefully closed the book and hugging it to her chest said, 'I'll try Great Nana. I'll try. I don't know how but if there *is* a way I'll find it!'

- CHAPTER SIX -

Back on Echoco

Not much had changed on Echoco, apart from the growing crow population whose large communal roosts were constantly increasing, so much so that many of them now resided on the wrecked ships on Deadwood beach.

Lance and Miles had grown apart. Miles had become a wild child after spending most of his adolescence with Arvensis, who'd taught him to fight and scavenge. On occasions he even cawed like a crow. Although Lance had often tried to get close to his brother he was often rebuffed.

The Lavaights had their daily chores. Miles, who was spiteful towards his orbs Dodder and Brier, assigned them his tasks. If they dared to inform Woodruff, he threatened to kill them. Brier having a quiet nature just kept his head down and got on with it. Dodder was always slower at completing his jobs, quite often making errors for which Miles would constantly pick on him, making Dodder nervous and jittery.

Miles had no interest in the Lavaight boys and particularly disliked Teasel, who was small for his age, with a mop of wavy chestnut hair that was so thick it made his head look too big for his body. Lance presumed Miles was jealous of their close friendship and continued to hope he could win back his brother's affection.

Lance, Teasel and some of the other boys spent hours on end in their forest camp. Their favourite pastime was playing conkers, which they'd learned about during their reading classes with Woodruff.

When the brown shiny nuts were ripe to fall in their spiky green jackets they would don clamshells to protect their heads, shake the branches and vie with each other for the champion nuts. They etched their initials onto the milky circles and hid them from each other in tree hollows.

Arvensis, having rid himself of the contract so cleverly masked by the storm, had continued to stay on his best behaviour, therefore diverting any suspicions of his involvement with the disappearance of Eleanor and Whitlow.

Following the tragedy, Woodruff had searched Eleanor's cave for the contract but found nothing. He concluded that she must have had it on her person and presumed everyone thought she'd given it to him for safekeeping, including Arvensis, or he would have returned to his old ways. (But Arvensis was biding his time, grooming Miles to assist him in an evil plot to take over the island.)

*

August was renowned for its abundance of hurricanes. On this particular evening, as the tail end of one left Echoco's shores, Dodder swiftly flew into Woodruff's cavern.

'You're late - *again!*' snapped Woodruff, as he reopened the register.

Dodder turning deep shades of red, hurried into the tree trunk doorway. Woodruff slammed the door shut behind him and left the cavern, but Dodder hadn't quite managed to get clear and his bubble became trapped. Glowing shades of indigo and blue, he struggled to pull himself free. This was not working so he began to push. The door suddenly burst open, catapulting him across the cavern and then ricocheted shut. Woodruff was nowhere in sight but Dodder could hear his voice as he approached. Quickly he hid himself in the shelving beneath an admiral's hat.

Woodruff entered the cavern. Hovering behind him were two Orbs, of which one had a package strapped to it. Perched on the other was a Kindred, an elderly little gentleman, only four inches tall.

Dismounting onto Woodruff's desk, the Kindred removed his soggy wet hooded cape to reveal a glittering regal attire of white and gold that flattered his silver hair and moustache.

'Here Ulex, let me take that for you, I'll hang it up to dry. Make yourself comfortable while I put your Orbs to bed … what should I do with this package?' asked Woodruff, releasing the Orb.

'Oh, on your desk will do nicely, thank you Woodruff. It was a bit rough that hurricane!'

'Yes, they seem to get stronger every year! If I'd known you were coming I'd have laid on some food.'

'Well, I sent word on ahead!'

'Did you? How strange, there hasn't been any Orbs come through for some time now!' said Woodruff, looking bemused.

He closed the door of the guest tree, inside which the tired little Orbs quickly snuggled down to sleep.

'Which is *one* of the reasons I am here!' said Ulex. They looked at each other perplexed. 'But first let us attend the package. It's for you!'

'For me Ulex? You shouldn't have!' he smiled, as he picked it up.

'Well, actually I didn't. It was recently discovered by a Kindred, buried in the ruins of Tintagel Castle, sealed with wax and addressed to yourself!'

'How mysterious,' said Woodruff as he carefully broke the seal. '*A book on oceanography*. My word! This is marvellous!' he declared, as he inspected its cover. 'I don't have *anything* in my collection on-' suddenly he silenced and the smile that had lit his face turned swiftly to a frown.

There on the back cover was a photograph of Whitlow. '*A Study of the Oceanic World by Professor Whitlow Pearce!*' quoted Woodruff. His hands began to tremble. Slowly he looked up. 'He *survived?*' he queried, totally shocked.

'What! You *didn't* know?' declared Ulex, somewhat amazed.

'And Eleanor?'

'Yes! Whitlow aged in Earth time and passed away as did his beloved wife Eleanor. We couldn't risk making contact with them.'

'I understand,' replied Woodruff, nodding his head.

Hands trembling, he opening the front cover to discover an inscription that read:

To my dear mentor, Woodruff.
Should this copy reach you, I just want you to know Echoco's whereabouts are safe, as is the contract.
Look to Arvensis!
Take care, Your friend,

Whitlow

Woodruff turned grey. 'I *knew* it!' he whispered under his breath.

'We were getting worried about you as no-one had heard from the island for so long, so I insisted I came myself to investigate! Mind you, I very nearly didn't get through at all! Pass through a hurricane and get hit by a bird!'

'Bird! What *kind* of bird?' asked Woodruff, with grave concern.

'Crow! Stupid thing was acting crazy, had to zap it with a grain!'

The Kindreds were known for mining powerful golden grains no bigger than a pinhead that were used with great care as they targeted the thoughts and subconscious of the holder.

Woodruff paused. Frowning, he turned to Ulex. 'But - *hundreds* of Orbs have been back to your time!'

'Then it appears we have a *mutual* problem!' replied Ulex.

'Wait I'll get my log!' said Woodruff, hurrying to a shelf.

Seating himself at his desk he began to search for the entry when Eleanor first came to Echoco.

'Here, look, these seven were the first to disappear. I was concerned for their well being but after extensive searches. I presumed they'd gone through to Earth time. The names that follow are their relatives. The list goes on...'

'Let me see!' said Ulex, who proceeded to walk up and down the pages muttering. 'Hum, I know many of these Orbs but can honestly say I've *no* recollection of seeing *any* of them logged in the visitors' book for years!'

'You mean - *none* of them?'

Ulex slowly shook his head sideways.

On hearing the news, Dodder began to tremble.

'*Arvensis!* It is as I suspected!' declared Woodruff.

'Tell me Woodruff! What goes on here?'

Dodder managed to contain himself as Woodruff explained about the contract, then concluded; 'He *must* have been killing all Orbs that came to and fro, which explains why there has been no news between us. He knows the contract is indestructible but probably thinks it lost to the oceans and now sees himself as invincible.'

'This is monstrous! What are we to do?'

'Whatever happens Arvensis must not learn what has evolved here tonight! If you can track down the contract we may be safe, but if he finds out it will immediately endanger the life of Lance!'

'The hurricane is still on your shores. I shall return and convey this news to the Kindred council. They'll know what to do. It explains why so many Kindreds have been losing their spirit over the years and dying!'

'I fear it is *not safe* for you to return, Ulex, for I suspect, whatever Arvensis is cunningly planning, will occur soon. We must be on our guard as he will now be aware that you made it through!'

'Fear not Woodruff, we *will* make it back and get help to you as soon as possible.'

'Thank you my good friend. Do you have more grains with you?'

'I have one. The rest were caught in the wind when I opened the bag. It will suffice.'

'Good. When you are gone I shall send word to Myosurus. She should be informed of what has come to light.'

'Can she help you, Woodruff?'

'I fear not as the tribe only attack those that threaten them directly.'

Woodruff woke the sleepy Orbs and escorted Ulex out. As soon as they left, the admiral's hat hovered clumsily in the air. Dodder got free of it and managing to open the tree room door with his teeth, quickly disappeared inside.

Sadly Ulex and his Orbs were not to make it back and the Orb messenger sent to Myosurus did not make it either. But Woodruff was right! Arvensis *was* planning to put his plan into action.

*

Dawn broke, the storm had calmed and everyone went about his or her daily chores. Woodruff had summoned Miles and Lance to his quarters.

When Lance arrived, Woodruff was unrolling a cloth on his desk.

'You sent for me, Woodruff?'

'Yes boy, come in … Where is Miles?'

'He left early this morning.'

'I see!' he remarked as he removed a short sword from the cloth.

'That's a fine sword!' declared Lance.

'Yes Lance. It's a cutlass. I used it for many a task when I was about your age. I would like you to have it.'

'Me?' he said, raising his brow in anticipation.

'Yes! But first you must earn it.'

'How?' he asked eagerly.

'I need some renovation work done to the stairwells. If your work is good, it shall be your reward. Do you want the task?'

'Oh yes please!'

'It may take a few days and means you won't have any spare time to go on the island!'

'I don't mind, honestly!'

'Good! Now off you go, you'll find all the tools you need at the stairwell with Orchis and Eyebright who will instruct you.'

'Thank you Woodruff.' Lance turned to leave.

'Oh and Lance, best you report back to me, let's say just before dusk, to inform me of your progress, and if you see Miles,' he added looking up from under his eyelids. 'Tell him I'd like a word.'

'I will,' he replied, and then hurried off.

Orchis and Eyebright were chatting with Dodder and Brier at the damaged stairwell as Lance approached.

'Hi guys, are you two off to see Miles?' inquired Lance, cheerfully. Brier nodded. 'Can you tell him Woodruff would like a word.' Dodder turned green as they sped off. 'Is Dodder alright?' queried Lance.

'He said he hadn't slept,' replied Orchis.

'Poor little fellow, he hasn't been himself for some time. Anyway - let's get started,' said Lance, as he rummaged through the tools.

Orchis, who had a soft spot for Dodder, sensed something was seriously ailing him.

Miles was having breakfast with Arvensis when Dodder and Brier arrived. Brier sheepishly spoke up. 'Lance said - to tell you - Woodruff wants to see you.'

'SHUT UP YOU INSOLENT BALL OF AIR. LANCE DOESN'T TELL ME TO DO ANYTHING! NOW GET OUT!' bellowed Miles, at which they instantly left.

'Spoken like a true leader,' praised Arvensis. 'Finish your fish and we'll take a stroll.'

'I've had enough thanks.'

'Good, come on then, we'll head to the cove, there's something I'd like to show you in the cave there.'

On reaching the cove Arvensis stopped momentarily and stared out to sea. 'It's a beautiful island, don't you think Miles?'

'Yes, I suppose.'

'I presume you've heard the rumours of *why* I was turned into a crow?'

'I don't take *any* notice of them, Arvensis.'

'Well, they're all false! Besides I want you to know the *truth*. It's important to me as *you* are!' said Arvensis abruptly, and then continued as they walked towards the cave. 'The truth be known, *I* was the tribe's *finest* hunter and Lingua was jealous of my favour with the chief. It was *he* who concocted the ridiculous story that led to my condemnation. The contract just added insult to injury. As *just* reward, I should have been *returned* to my former self.'

'Absolutely!' declared Miles.

Just then they entered the cave. It was a wondrous place with stalactites hanging down and great glistening pillars of stalagmites reaching up into the vast roof.

'Why have you brought me here?' asked Miles, looking totally bemused.

'Come, I will show you.'

Arvensis led him deep within and then pointed to a crevice in the wall.

'Put your hand in and withdraw what is *rightfully* yours!' he declared.

Miles delved deep inside, then grasping hold of a solid object, withdrew a sword with a handle of mother of pearl. 'Wow!' he exclaimed, holding it high and twisting it. 'What do you *mean,* it's *rightfully* mine?'

'It belonged to your father!' he said, with shifty eyes.

A chill ran down Mile's spine. 'My *father?* ... But-'

'It's time you knew the *truth* of what happened the day I rescued you!' Miles slumped to the ground confused. 'You see Miles; I heard your cries that day and flew into the storm. I arrived to find your parents huddled around you. There were several Orbs supporting them in the spiralling winds. Then I caught sight of your sister and Lance. She was knocked unconscious by this sword. As the lightning lit the sky I saw Lance grab hold of it, the scabbard blew away and he plunged the blade into the Orbs that were trying to save you and your parents. The Orbs burst and disappeared in the wind along with your parents. I knocked it from his hand, grabbed hold of you and flew you to safety. Shortly after, I came upon it on the beach and hid it here for safekeeping. I discovered it had belonged to your father as your sister had described it to me once in conversation.'

Miles lowered his head. His eyes shifted from side to side as he pondered silently. Frowning, he looked up at Arvensis.

'But - we were - *babies!*'

'Yes, and *very* astute for your age.'

Miles stared dumbstruck at the sword. Arvensis deserved an Oscar for his performance (if only of the fish variety), for it was *he* that had caught the sword in the wind and struck the Orbs, rescuing Miles for his own future plans. The only truth he told was the conversation he had had with Eleanor.

Miles stood up; his gaze still fixed on the sword. Bitter tears streamed down his face as he raised the glinting blade in his left hand, then cut it into his right, cawing loudly. His pain was overtaken by an exultation of power. As the blood trickled down the steel he yelled out. 'FOR THE PARENTS YOU DENIED ME, THE NEXT STRIKE IS FOR *YOU* LANCE!' His threatening words bounced off the walls.

Arvensis put a wing on his shoulders. 'Hush now boy, you will *have* your day but a good leader bides his time.' Then

Arvensis looked him straight in the eyes and said, 'You *must* promise me you will do *exactly* as I bid!'

'I promise!'

'Good, we must work quickly for we begin tonight. We shall take over this island bit by bit. I will need you to talk to Lance, but you must not let him see your anger. Do you think you can do that?'

'I - I'll try.'

'*Try* isn't good enough!' barked Arvensis.

'Yes, yes I can!'

'Good, come then, we have much to discuss.'

With that they made their way back to the galleon.

*

And so it began. It was nearing dusk when Miles returned to the volcano. Teasel and the other boys were in their forest camp. The Orbs had all returned to Woodruff's cavern except for Orchis and Eyebright, who were making their way there.

As Miles descended he caught sight of Lance, below. A red mist cloaked his vision and his palms began to sweat. He stopped for a few seconds to contain himself.

'MILES! WHAT'S WRONG? ARE YOU UNWELL?' shouted Lance. His words echoed around the walls, alerting Orchis and Eyebright. Becoming suspicious they concealed themselves nearby.

'NO, NO I'M FINE!' he called back.

Lance ran up to him.

'I thought you were going to fall!'

'It's nice of you to be concerned.'

'I've *always* been concerned about you!'

'Yes, I know Lance and I'm sorry for the distance I keep from you.'

'You do - I mean you are?' flummoxed Lance.

'Yes. In fact that's the reason for my dizziness. I have been busy all day preparing a feast fit for a king! Are you hungry?'

'Hungry? I'm starving!'

'Good then let's take this opportunity to put everything in the past and start afresh as *true* brothers!'

Lance couldn't believe his ears. 'You *mean* it?' he said, excitedly.

'I wouldn't have said it if I didn't. We could even spend the night in your forest camp!'

'That's a great idea! What about Teasel and the others?'

'Oh, the more the merrier.'

'I have to report to Woodruff. I'll let him know,' suggested Lance.

'Wait! I'll tell you what, you go ahead and inform the others before they make their way back and I'll meet you all at the camp. Besides Woodruff wishes to see me, I'm sure he'll approve.'

Lance's instincts told him to report himself but he was so ecstatic at the change in his brother, he didn't want to jeopardize the situation and agreed.

The night sky was devouring the last glimpse of daylight as Lance took hold of a lighted torch and hurried out. Miles made his way to the tunnel entrance where the guards stood. He chatted with them momentarily and after giving them some fruit to eat, proceeded to Woodruff's cavern. Orchis and Eyebright followed him at a discreet distance.

Miles entered the cavern to discover Woodruff crawling on his hands and knees with his back to him.

'Is that you Lance?'

'Yes,' mumbled Miles.

'I won't be a second, dropped a pen nib. It never ceases to amaze me how every time an item falls to the ground, it always disappears from sight. It hides, always hides! ... Ah, found it!'

Just as Woodruff knelt up, Orchis and Eyebright hovered in and were horrified to see Miles grasp a lump of carved wood from Woodruff's desk and bludgeon him on the back of the head. As he collapsed to the floor they quickly hid under the desk.

Miles covered him with a cloth and then went across to the Orbs' tree room, opened the door and yelled, 'QUICK! EVERYONE OUT. WOODRUFF LIES INJURED ON THE ISLAND AND A HURRICANE BLOWS IN. HE *NEEDS* YOUR HELP!'

While his back was to them, Eyebright and Orchis quickly grabbed the cutlass Woodruff had promised Lance and made a speedy exit. As they whizzed through the tunnel they caught sight of the guards who'd been poisoned, slumped at its entrance.

All the Orbs streamed out of the doorway. Dodder was last, quivering as he flew past Miles.

Lance had just reached the outskirts of the forest when he spotted Teasel with five of the other boys running towards him.

'Lance! Did Woodruff send you? We know we're late!' panted Teasel.

'No, wait! I've got some great news!' The boys suddenly froze in their tracks, staring towards the volcano. 'What is it? What's-' Lance silenced.

There, in the night sky, lit by a full moon was a rainbow, arcing out of the summit and across the island.

'A rainbow?' quizzed Lance.

'That's no rainbow,' said Teasel. 'That's the Orbs!'

As they gawped dumbstruck at the awesome sight, Miles appeared on the summit. Silhouetted by the moon he raised his arms and yelled from the depths of his lungs. 'RUN LANCE, RUN AND HIDE, FOR *WHEN* I FIND YOU, I WILL NO LONGER *HAVE* A BROTHER!'

Lance was mortified. They watched Miles descend and release all the boats from their holding but for one, in which he rowed back to shore. He dragged it onto the beach and then proceeded to smash a hole in its base.

Just then they heard the deafening CRAAAAAH, of a thousand crows that filled the sky. Many settled on the summit, others began to attack the Orbs, scattering them everywhere as they dispersed into the night.

The boys were in total shock. Suddenly Orchis and Eyebright appeared, grasping the cutlass between them. They gave it to Lance and told him what had occurred.

'Woodruff! Is he?' asked Lance in despair.

'We don't know,' replied Eyebright.

'Quickly, we must hide!' declared Lance.

'But where? The camp won't be safe!' said Teasel.

'The swamps, we'll hide in the swamps!'

'Are you *mad* Lance! I think I'd rather take my chances with the crows than the Newteleons. What about Crowfoot territory?' suggested Teasel as he began to nervously twitch.

'It's too far, we don't have time!' argued Lance.

The boys had no choice and headed off quickly through the forest towards the swamps.

CHAPTER SEVEN

An Unwitting Traitor

The nightly calls of the crickets and toads filled the air as the boys came upon the swamps. The torch Lance was carrying was burning down.

'It's so *creepy!*' remarked Teasel as they waded into the bogs.

'Just *stay* close together and keep your voices down. These creatures are nocturnal,' whispered Eyebright.

They soon found themselves waist deep in crud that floated on the surface.

'My father told me *huge* snakes live in these waters!' commented one of the boys, his voice quaking.

'Look, over there!' said Lance in a loud whisper.

As the torchlight flickered out, they spied a tree-logged area around one gigantic tree at least six foot in diameter, looming out of the darkness. Luckily Orchis and Eyebright glowed just enough for them to keep sight of it.

'Shush!'

'What is it, Eyebright? I don't hear anything? Not even the crickets!' puzzled Lance.

'*That's* the problem. Follow us, quickly!'

One boy fell and grabbed another's leg, who screamed, 'HELP! HELP! I'M BEING EATEN!'

Fear consumed them as panicking and shouting they splashed through the water following the Orbs.

Frantically they clambered safely onto the floating logs.

'Well, if they *didn't* know we were here, they *certainly* do now!' panted Teasel.

Just as he spoke they heard a loud splash in the distance. Holding their breath they listened intently but after a while when nothing materialized, they began to relax.

Every now and then the harrowing cries of the Orbs could be heard in the distance.

'We'll have to take turns at keeping watch,' said Lance.

Orchis and Eyebright positioned themselves in the branches above.

The boys were initially too frightened to sleep but as the night wore on, cold, wet and tired they turned to their own thoughts and gradually drifted off, apart from Lance and Teasel who kept watch.

Leaning back on the trunk Lance reflected on the day's events and blamed himself for trusting Miles instead of following his instincts. He couldn't believe how cold and callous his brother had become.

'I hope Woodruff is alive, Teasel. If only there were some way of finding out.'

'There's not much chance of t*hat*. Even if we made it to the shore we'd have to swim through sharks before getting past those carnivores at the summit.'

'What do you think will happen to them?'

'I don't know Lance, but they only have enough food and water for a week or so, *after that?*'

'They'll starve! There must be *something* we can do!'

'There's only one thing that will stop Arvensis and that's the *contract* but its whereabouts would only be known to Woodruff!'

They both fell silent as the true horrors that lay ahead began to dawn on them. As rays of moonlight filtered through the dense trees they began to doze.

In the early morning hours, there was movement in the swamp but the sleepy Orbs hadn't noticed as something large skimmed the surface towards them, gathering moss and crud in its path. Suddenly a Newteleon slowly rose out of the water.

Alerted, Eyebright and Orchis dropped, bouncing on Lance and Teasel's heads, who opened their eyes with a start to spy this great monster, glowing tinges of copper and green in the moonlight with swamp matter falling from its body.

Panting heavily it stared at them through small beady eyes and then a high spiky fanned crest lifted, skirting around its head. As its long spiky tail rose out of the water it drew back its front, clawed limbs. With their gaze firmly fixed, Lance and Teasel cautiously rose to their feet. The great beast let out a piercing squeal. 'AAAAARRRGH!' they yelled, running on the spot. The log rolled, consequently rolling all the others on which the boys, now awake were diving, terrified, this way and that.

As the Newteleon leapt forward, Teasel fell into the swamp. The beast swiftly pinned Lance to the trunk and flicked its tongue into his face, tasting its prey. Petrified, Lance squeezed his eyelids shut. Quick as a flash its jaws SNAPPED and embedded, not into Lance but a great limb of flesh that slithered over his face from above his head.

It was another Newteleon that screamed with a pained cry, 'NO! RANUNCULUS, NO!' Quickly evolving from the bark, it kicked its back limbs straight through the trunk that caved in behind Lance, who fell into the cavity and landed below.

He heard an awful din as the Newteleons began to fight, during which time the other boys managed to clamber in and join him.

Suddenly, there was silence.

Lance pulled himself up and peered warily over the opening. Ranunculus had gone leaving the Newteleon that saved him, floating limp and injured, surrounded by a yellow fluid that oozed from its wounds.

Orchis zoomed over to Lance. 'Quickly, you must help Peony to her feet,' she said anxiously.

'Peony?'

'Yes I know her. Her mother will have been alerted and will rain *more* blows on her for helping you!'

Lance and Teasel pulled themselves out and waded over to where she lay.

Peony's sleek torso was mainly dark blue. Her lower body was striped with red, green and orange.

Dawn was breaking and a mist formed around them as they struggled to raise her.

'Come on Peony, you *must* get up!' pleaded Lance. Slowly she opened her piercing yellow slit eyes and blinked.

'Lance, Teasel, quickly, get back in the tree!' called Eyebright panicking. But Lance felt torn and didn't want to leave her.

'Come *on* Lance!' pleaded Teasel as he splashed through the water. But it was too late. As Teasel clambered back in a huge black Newteleon, covered in orange and yellow blotches, moved swiftly towards Lance and Peony.

Peony dragged herself halfway up, to face her mother, who stopped by her and then sniffed towards Lance, who froze, petrified.

'FOOLISH CHILD, WILL YOU NEVER LEARN!' she shrieked, *swiping* Peony back down.

'But Scelaratus!' uttered Peony breathlessly. 'I knew of his sister. Trouble lies ahead!'

'MORE THAN YOU CAN IMAGINE!' she barked back at her, raising her claws to strike another blow at which Lance snapped too and drew his cutlass.

In a flash, Scelaratus swung her head towards him. The boys gasped. '*YOU, BOY!* I admire your courage, *foolish* as it may be but do not *think* of interfering. *This is our way!* My daughter has broken our rules and talks in riddles but you are *lucky* I have eaten tonight and anger has quelled Ranunculus's appetite!' she scorned, turning her attention to the tree, where the boys' heads quickly disappeared from sight.

Lance withdrew his weapon.

'I have no favour with the crows. You may therefore all hide in the tree till the sun begins to set, after that - we'll *know* where to find you! NOW GO FROM MY SIGHT BEFORE I SAMPLE YOUR FLESH!'

Lance looked at Peony who lethargically winked at him, then quickly joined the others in the hollow as Scelaratus dragged her away.

Orchis and Eyebright hastily covered the boys with leaves.

'Lance, we're going to find out what we can. We'll bring some food when we return.'

'It's *too* dangerous, Eyebright!'

'Don't worry, Orbs can fly and manoeuvre faster than a crow!'

'Not when there's *thousands* of them.'

'We'll have to take that chance. We'll switch to white light, then if we return in daylight there's less chance of them seeing us.'

'Very well,' sighed Lance. 'But take care!'

'We will.' With that they sped off.

Teasel began to jerk in spasms.

'Don't fret, we'll be all right!' Lance assured him.

'It's not that. I'm being eaten alive!' he winged.

Soon they all began scratching, as ants and other insects scurried all over them.

'After encountering the Newteleons, it's a luxury!' commented Lance. The boys' spirits lifted momentarily and they began to quietly chuckle.

*

Before the sun rose in the sky, Orchis and Eyebright carefully scouted the forest but found no signs of the Orbs.

67

Cautiously they made their way to the outskirts from where they could view Deadwood beach.

It looked as if it had been engulfed by an oil slick whereupon thousands of crows masked the sand. Arvensis and Miles stood tall above them on the galleon, surrounded by mature fighter crows. Arvensis was shouting.

'Can you make out what he's saying?' whispered Orchis.

'No! And we can't risk getting any closer.'

Just then they heard a noise. 'Psst, Eyebright! Over here!' They immediately recognised Brier's voice and flew elated to a tree hollow from which he emerged.

'Brier! Thank goodness you're safe! Where are the others?' asked Eyebright anxiously.

'They've disbanded all over the island. The word is they're congregating at the hideaway in the green wall. We're just waiting for our chance to join them, we dare not risk *one* crow following us!'

'We? Is Dodder with you?' asked Orchis apprehensively.

'Yes, there's just us two. He's too nervous to come out.'

The green wall was part of a cliff that edged the forest, so called because of the watery residue from the trees and shrubbery that camouflaged its surface. At its base was an inlet, concealed by thick bracken that led to a caved area, which was as yet only known to the Orbs.

'Have we lost many?' inquired Eyebright.

'Enough! What of the boys?'

'They're safe for now in the swamps.'

'The *swamps?*'

'It's a long story.' They heard Dodder gulp. Suddenly Orchis let out a shrill scream as a flock of crows swooped towards them. Swiftly they dispersed into the forest.

Whilst most of the crows gave chase, a few of them settled on the tree in which Dodder remained, trembling. They became aware of his presence and sat quietly in wait.

After a while Dodder became anxious and began to roll around, mumbling. 'Where are they? Must have been caught … S-S-Stay put, yes … What to do? What to do? - Woodruff would know - he knows *everything* - Ulex will return soon … A-Arvensis *mustn't* find out - Whitlow - the c-c-contract. Yes, - we'll all be saved!' The crows listened intently. Two of them stood guard whilst the others returned to the beach to reluctantly inform Arvensis.

When they arrived they saw Arvensis enraged, reprimanding a young crow for playing with the Orbs. Unearthed by his wrath they lost their courage, halted mid flight and flapped down amongst the others.

It wasn't long before the rumour began to spread and by and by all the crows began cawing uneasily.

As this sea of black feathers tossed and turned, Arvensis became suspicious. With a loud, hoarse 'CRAAAH!' he demanded silence. 'WOULD ONE OF YOU CARE TO STEP FORWARD AND INFORM ME OF *WHAT* LIES AMISS HERE?' he bellowed. Petrified, they remained silent. The fighter crows became agitated and began to scan the mass.

Arvensis summoned forward all those that had just returned. They flew up to him and submissively lowered their heads. 'I will *handsomely* reward any one of you that has the *courage* to speak up by allowing him to join my best ranks!' he said enticingly.

After a short pause, one of them raised his head and spoke out, following which Arvensis immediately struck him dead.

'LET THAT BE A WARNING TO YOU ALL! NOW BRING THE ORB TO ME, ALIVE!' he roared.

They scuttled off and soon returned. One of them, carefully holding Dodder's bubble in his beak, set him down.

'YOU!' snapped Miles at poor Dodder, who wibbled and wobbled uncontrollably.

'Leave this to me,' sneered Arvensis. 'I believe you have some information for me and, as you *rightfully* belong to Miles, it is in your best interest to relay it!' Dodder opened his mouth but the words would not come out. 'Don't be frightened little Orb, this is your opportunity to win back your master's favour,' he coaxed. His tone suddenly changed, 'THEN AGAIN YOU HAVE EXACTLY THREE SECONDS BEFORE I *BURST* YOUR BUBBLE!' Arvensis lifted his beak to which Dodder began to blurt out the conversation that had taken place between Woodruff and Ulex.

Arvensis was mortified. He began to pace back and forth, then looked to Miles. 'We *have* to retrieve it! I shall not rest until it is safely in my custody!'

Miles noticed Arvensis becoming more agitated and nervous. He'd never seen this weakness in Arvensis and could almost smell the fear that dwelled within him.

'What are we to do?' asked Miles. Just then the skies began to darken as thunder rumbled and lightning flashed in the distance.

'Hurricane! You see the spirits *smile* on me! I have a plan but in case it should fail we must dispose of Lance!' Miles began to smirk.

Unexpectedly, Dodder spoke up, as if in his helplessness he found some strength only to make matters worse by blurting out,

'There's not much chance of *that*. The Newteleons will have devoured him by now!'

Arvensis perked up. 'The swamps, they're hiding in the swamps! Thank you for that information, I'm sure your friends will be really proud of you.' Dodder slumped; as it slowly dawned on him he had unwittingly betrayed his friends.

Arvensis ordered Dodder to his cabin. Then he sent hundreds of crows to seek out as many Orbs as they could and bring them back alive.

'What are your plans Arvensis?' asked Miles.

'The Orbs in Earth time will hopefully have enough information on Whitlow and Eleanor for the contracts whereabouts to be traced. I need to send some Orbs to find out without arousing suspicion. They'll also ensure safe passage for two of my finest birds, who'll oversee the mission.'

'But how are you going to get them to comply?'

'Blackmail! We'll send Dodder and one other. That should suffice. Because Earth time moves faster than ours does, if the contract is located quickly they can return in the same hurricane. When they leave we'll kill the hostages, after which you can take an army of crows and seek out Lance. Do what you will with the others! Come, I'll get your sword!'

Before long the crows returned with their captives. Eyebright, Orchis and Brier were amongst them. They were herded into a holding below the sunken deck of the galleon.

Miles suggested that Brier should accompany Dodder. Brier was immediately brought to the cabin to join Dodder. Arvensis assured them, that once the contract was safely in his possession he would release the Orbs. They knew he was probably lying but had no choice but to comply.

The storm came to the island's borders and they were sent on their quest.

'Well, I suspect you are all a little - peckish!' quipped Arvensis addressing his flock.

'Ha, ha. Very funny,' sniggered Miles.

'WHO WOULD LIKE A TASTY LITTLE MORSEL THEN?' he yelled. The crows anxiously began to caw as Miles began to open the hatch.

'What are we to do, Eyebright? There's too many to out-fly!' cried Orchis.

Eyebright had an idea. He quickly called to all the Orbs to listen before they were ushered out.

'Ah, lunch has arrived. Which one of you would like to go first?' scoffed Arvensis. He was slightly taken aback when Eyebright flew forward.

'Me, please!'

'My my, a hero. You insolent fool!' he barked and then swiftly kicked him into the mass.

Eyebright flew straight up above their heads followed by all the Orbs who quickly surrounded him, prompting every crow to take to the wing.

The Orbs squeezed together, tighter and tighter till all their bubbles merged into one.

The crows raced towards the giant sphere, full of tiny faces that began to glow. Within seconds a brilliant, dazzling rainbow of light radiated in the dark sky, blinding their predators. As the crows fell about, crashing into each other, the Orbs disbanded with a pop, pop, popping and scattered to the four winds.

Arvensis and Miles uncovered their faces. 'YOU'LL PAY FOR THAT! YOU'RE DOOMED, ALL DOOOOOMED!' bellowed Arvensis. 'Go Miles, and seek out Lance! I shall await the return of the contract.' Miles nodded and eagerly headed off.

*

Back at Southend-on-Sea in Essex, it was September. The children had just finished their first week at their new schools in which they'd settled comfortably.

Jill was back on friendly terms with Matt and was making her way home from the seafront, where she'd spent the afternoon with the gang whilst her mother had taken her brothers shopping.

Jill was already counting the weeks to half term when they were off to Cornwall and then on to her Auntie Margaret's, where she was hoping to discreetly find out more about the mystery baby.

She arrived home and peeped into the lounge where her father was dozing on the sofa, with the television on. Upon hearing a report on the abundance of hurricanes currently in the Pacific Ocean, she paused in the doorway, listening. Immediately her thoughts turned to Eleanor.

After fetching a glass of water from the kitchen, she continued up the stairs. Suddenly she heard a noise coming from inside her room. Hesitating she hovered on the stairwell. *Was anyone else home?* she thought. Then remembering she'd left her window open, she presumed the wind had knocked something off the sill. However, she cautiously opened the bedroom door and peeped in.

Horrified, she dropped the glass that smashed. Simultaneously the telephone began to ring, her mother arrived home with her brothers and her father stirred abruptly from his sleep.

Her room was trashed. Then she heard her mother on the phone. 'WHAT? You're joking! But how? ... Oh Mum it's *awful,* how could anyone be so heartless! ... *Please* don't cry. Do you want me to come up? ... I'm coming anyway, ... No Mum, I insist!'

Jill's head became a blur. She heard her mother frantically shouting the news to her father. It soon became apparent that her great nan and granddad's graves had been desecrated.

Just then she spotted Eleanor's box, amongst the items littering the floor. Its contents, including the notebook, which she'd since hidden back in the lid, were strewn everywhere.

On spying the book she quickly ran over and knelt down to discover the secret sleeve open. 'Oh no! It's gone!' she cried. At which point her mother burst into her room and screamed. 'WHAT ON EARTH?'

'It wasn't me Mum, honest! I - I *just* came in!' she cried.

Pamela looked straight at the notebook in her hands and began to frown. Snatching it from her, she turned white, then ashen grey all in the space of a second. 'WHERE DID YOU FIND THIS? HAVE YOU READ IT?' she barked.

'NO MUM! I literally *just* found it with the box! It *must* have fallen out of the lid!' Jill had never seen her mother so distressed and felt she had to lie, although her blushing cheeks had guilty written all over them.

'JOHN! *JOHN!*' yelled Pamela.

Her father came rushing in. 'Jill! Your room! What happened?'

'It was like it when I came in Dad, I *swear!*' she declared, almost in tears.

'I can't deal with this John, I can't! Take care of it, I'm going to mother's!' cried Pamela. She then stormed out of the room taking the notebook with her.

Jill's father stood scratching his head. 'Burglars? … Best you start clearing up, Jill, while I check the rest of the house. Let me know if there's anything missing.'

Jill frantically searched for the contract, but to no avail. She came across the photographs of the birthmarks and clutching them to her chest sat on her bed numbed, as it dawned on her the *only* thing missing was the contract and she could hardly tell *that* to her father.

CHAPTER EIGHT

Spirits at Work

The contract retrieved, Dodder, Brier and the crows made the return journey to Echoco through the same hurricane, just as Arvensis had predicted.

Anticipating their return, Eyebright, Orchis and a group of Orbs rescued Dodder and Brier from the custody of the crows that were otherwise engaged in protecting the contract.

Meanwhile, Miles was approaching the swamps where the boys were becoming anxious. There'd been no sign of Eyebright or Orchis and it was getting late.

'It *must* be nearing sunset!' remarked Teasel, nervously staring up at the clouds.

'Maybe it would be best if we left now!' suggested Lance, in an undertone. They unanimously agreed and clambering out, heading off as quietly as possible.

'Where are we going?' asked one of the boys.

Lance looked blankly at Teasel. 'I hadn't given it a thought!' he said.

'Let's just get out of this place, then maybe we can think straight!' commented Teasel.

The waters became shallower as they neared the boggy edge of the swamp. All of a sudden they heard a commotion of loud splashes amidst crows cawing in distress, coming from the direction of their tree haven.

'Look's like we left just in time!' said Teasel, as they quickened their pace.

'Do you think they were scouts?' asked Lance, as they began to run on solid ground.

'Possibly. Quick, through those trees over there!' panted Teasel.

They burst through the shrubbery to be confronted by Miles, encircled by hundreds of crows in the surrounding trees.

'*Going* somewhere,' he snarled, pointing his sword towards Lance.

The boys froze in their tracks. Lance couldn't believe the madness he saw in his brother's eyes.

'THIS SWORD BELONGED TO OUR FATHER, BUT THEN AGAIN YOU'RE *AWARE* OF THAT FACT AS YOU USED IT TO *KILL* THE ORBS THAT TRIED TO SAVE OUR PARENTS AND ME! NOW ITS BLADE SEEKS A *NEW* SCABBARD!' he ranted.

'RUN!' yelled Teasel. The boys darted off in different directions, batting at the crows with their hands.

As Miles lunged forward Lance dived to the floor rolling out of the sword's path, scrambled to his feet and fled. Miles CRAAHED loudly at the crows, giving them orders to round up the boys and then pursued Lance.

Rapidly gaining on him Miles suddenly let out a distressing yell. A tree had fallen in his path. Lance stopped and looked back, concerned. While he watched his brother frantically clamber over the trunk, he heard a familiar voice in the trees whisper, *'Run Lance, run!'* which he did. But dusk had set in, his vision became blurred and his head disorientated. It was only when he felt rock beneath his feet that he realised he was running into Cragga!

Miles stopped on its outskirts and yelled, 'GO ON THEN, *DIE* IN CRAGGA! YOU'RE NOT *WORTHY* OF THIS SWORD'S BLADE!'

Swiftly like a fugitive Lance disappeared into the dark wood, believing that by running non-stop he'd come out the other side unharmed. Adrenaline surged through his weak tired body. His heart pounded in his ears as he accelerated, but his legs outran him. Tripping he fell over his own feet.

Lying face down sprawled on the ground the earth beneath him sank and the cursed soil slowly began to swallow him, sapping his remaining strength.

Helpless, scared and confused he laid thinking, trying to make sense of the things Miles had said. Unable to deal with his emotions, using his last ounce of energy he dragged himself out of his imprint and crawled into an old tree that was so hollow it had split completely in two (just like Lance and Miles). Exhausted he curled up and awaiting his doom fell into a deep sleep.

An eerie grey smog stretching as far as the eye could see began weaving its way through Cragga. Rearing its ugly head up and down it skulked round and round in search of the split tree between which Lance was sheltering. Then spying him in a crumpled heap, slowly stretched towards his face seeking confirmation. Suddenly its thunderhead arched. Wrapping its phantom body around the tree it thickened and blackened, spiralling upwards onto the tip of its tail. Swirling rapidly it formed a gigantic twister.

The tree creaked and groaned. Its roots spanning the length of Cragga trembled and quaked beneath the ground. Voices of tormented souls wailed and moaned as the jig-sawed halves of the trunk began to realign and slowly come together to consume Lance. The suction became so strong the roots cracked and snapped heaving a volcanic mount around the trunk's base as it began to dislodge.

Suddenly in the total blackness of Cragga's sky a tiny shooting star steered a path into the vortex. As the sides merged tightly together, the star extinguished dropping a flower into the eye of the twister that slipped through the last slit of space as the tree clamped shut. Then, as if the twister had swallowed some foul poison it weakened. Its tail broke away and folding up within itself formed a murky thundercloud above that flashed and rumbled in defeat.

Inside the musty damp trunk the little flower swayed gracefully down and gently settled on Lance's face. Glowing with an aura, it evolved into a dainty hand that tenderly stroked his brow. Stirring, he squinted at the hand to which the apparition of a beautiful young girl formed. Straining his eyes he tried to focus on the glowing figure before him.

The strong aroma of lily of the valley triggered something in his memory. *'Eleanor?'* he whispered. A smile lit the face of the girl.

'Oh Lance, my poor, *poor* baby,' she replied softly.

'Is it *really* you Eleanor?' he gasped in disbelief.

'Yes! Lance.'

'Are you – dead?'

'Well, my remains are buried at a cemetery near Bodmin Moor, but my spirit lives on.'

'Am I – *dead?*'

'Oh no! my little brother, but you *will* be if you stay here much longer!'

'But what should I do Eleanor, Miles is-?'

'Hush, hush, you don't have to explain I am fully aware of your plight. I don't have much time and I can't foretell the future but I do know you are the *only* person who can save them all. You *must* survive Cragga and retrieve the contract that Arvensis now has! If all else fails seek out your Great Niece Margaret on Earth, she will know you. Trust her and-' suddenly Eleanor tilted her head listening. 'There's no time to explain Lance, we must leave now!' she stressed urgently.

'But how do I escape?'

'Look to the soil for a talisman. It embodies the tormented soul of Hellebore, chief of the Crowfoot tribe. *Hurry!*'

As Lance frantically searched the earth beneath him they heard the harrowing cry of something unearthly that began ripping and clawing at the tree's trunk.

'Is this it?' he asked frantically, lifting a charm caked in mud.

'Yes! That's it! Quickly, tie it around your neck and join forces with our spirits.' Lance did as she instructed. 'Now, take hold of my hands.' As he did the beast screamed alarmingly prompting all the surrounding trees to lasso the trunk with their roots that entwined and tightened as the trunk shuddered in resistance to their will. The talisman glowed and for one split second the trunk *cracked* open, and in that second they purged up and out, as the tree snapped shut behind them. Following which the whole of Cragga roared and howled so loudly that it was heard across the entire island.

Miles and his army of crows, who'd captured all the boys stopped in their tracks. Never before had they heard an outcry of this kind. 'Hurry, get a move on!' ordered Miles.

When they reached the beach, the storm had passed and the moon lit the night sky. The boys stared in shock at the mass of crows loudly craahing and croaking. Miles waved his sword and the flapping birds clearing a path, pecked at the boy's feet and legs as they passed.

They ascended the rickety gangplank to where Arvensis stood waiting. 'Lance?' he inquired.

'Cragga!' blurted Miles. Teasel gasped.

'I *thought* as much!' nodded Arvensis smugly. 'What are we to do with this lot?'

'I have some work for them … for a little while,' replied Miles, raising his eyebrows.

'Very well! Listen to me you miserable bunch. You will do as Miles commands and if you value your tongues, you'll keep your mouths shut!' he threatened, leering at them. 'Crows! Usher them below decks. Come Miles, time to rest, we have busy days ahead.'

The boys stumbled through the murky hold where a green slime hemmed the walls just below the ramshackle bunks. There was already two inches of water in their dank rat-infested quarters as the tide came in. The hatch above their heads fell shut leaving them in darkness, but for little shafts of moonlight that shone through cracks. Deflated, they quietly crawled onto the bunks. Not a word was spoken, for there was nothing to say.

Slightly dazed, Lance found himself alone on the outskirts of Cragga. He could hear frantic drumming coming from Crowfoot territory and decided to make his way to the lake, which was the only place left to go.

On arriving he sat by the water's edge where unbeknown to him Eleanor had buried their mother's brooch. He spied the little cross, made of twigs. Picking it up he lay down and whilst curiously pondering, drifted off to sleep.

*

Morning broke. Lance was rudely awakened by something batting into him. Jumping up with a start and dropping the cross, he spied a great white cloud lying close to the ground, nearby. This strange spectacle unearthed him but before he had time to think a great chunk broke away and knocked him over.

Realising it was made of solid matter and so intrigued by this wondrous cloud that attacked him with chunks of itself, he grabbed a lump and threw it back. To which another flew straight back at him and a playful fight began.

Presently the bizarre cloud had completely engulfed him and, unbeknown to Lance, was airborne and heading across the canyon.

Catching him off guard, it catapulted him down to the ground. Lance was laughing as he landed, then stared up in awe as the cloud evolved into the full-bodied shape of a powerful buffalo with fluffy ruff and long white beard.

'Stunning, isn't he,' came a voice from behind him. Gasping, Lance swung round and gawped at Myosurus. Quickly looking about, he soon realised the cloud had brought him to a mount in Crowfoot territory that towered above their camp in the valley below.

Myosurus stared mesmerised at the talisman around his neck; a shiver ran from her toes to her head. Her tired eyes welled with tears of joy as she reached out for it. Lance removed the talisman and carefully laid it in her palm. Squeezing hold she closed her eyes tightly then turned raising her arms in the air calling out, 'HELLEBORE IS HOME!' Her words echoed across the mountains followed by jubilant cries from the camp below. Tying it around her neck, she turned back to Lance. 'For *this* you are to be *handsomely* rewarded. We know what has occurred on the island but cannot intervene. It is not yet *our* battle.'

Just then Lingua and some of the tribe's Elders appeared over the crest. Lingua was carrying two chairs. Sculptured on the backrest of one were animals, comprising of a buffalo head at its centre, a tiger's head on the right point and a wolf's head on the left.

'Come, sit with me Lance,' signalled Myosurus. The Elders sat crossed legged on the ground forming a wide circle around them. Lance walked towards the plain chair, 'No, here,' she said, pointing to the other.

'Surely not?' said Lance humbly.

'Don't argue. Sit!' she commanded. Lingua stood by her side.

Lance watched in amazement as the buffalo cloud descended forming a screen around the top of the mount. A silence fell and the Elders began to chant.

Presently Myosurus spoke. 'This autumn equinox marks my one-hundredth birthday, which shall be celebrated throughout this season. Just as the fall marks the decline of all that has matured, so too must I prepare for *my* journey. Lance has brought to us the most precious gift. Now when the time comes, my spirit can rest peacefully with our ancestors.' The expression on her aged face lightened. Rising she reached forwards as if beckoning for something then crossed her frail arms and proclaimed, *'To mark my Centenary and the return of Hellebore; I Myosurus of the Crowfoot tribe hereby assign to Lance; Three Great Whites.'* She then addressed Lance. 'Already you are acquainted with the buffalo. He is called Cumulus.'

Suddenly through the clouded mist leapt a great white tiger with piercing blue eyes, whose muscles rippled through its pristine striped coat as it landed in the circle. Bounding towards Lance it sat by his right side bared its sharp teeth and roared flicking its tongue on his knee as its jaws closed. Lance's whole body stiffened with a mixture of fear and excitement. Never before had he encountered such a large, majestic beast.

'He is called Cracked Ice,' she said, then looked expectantly to the mist.

No sooner had her gaze focused than the head of a great wolf with staring red eyes emerged. The stunning creature with a shimmering coat of long white hair, dropped on all fours and then pointed its nose towards Lance, sniffing his scent. Rising, with ears forward it paced over with tail swinging and sat by his left side. Raising its head to the sky it howled a chilling wail sending shivers of exaltation through Lance.

'He is known as Blizzard.' As Myosurus spoke, the mist of Cumulus lifted around them and reformed the great white buffalo cloud in the sky. 'These three are my reward to you, Lance. They will honour and protect you as best they can and will *sense* if you need them. Heed them well for they are very learned and unique, but *not* indestructible.'

'I – I don't know how to thank you for such an honorary gift, Myosurus.'

'By happily accepting them and by joining us in tonight's celebrations.'

'Forgive me but I fear I cannot while my friends are in danger! My sister's spirit told me that Arvensis *has* the contract!'

'Unless you rest and build your strength you will be of no help to anyone! The boys are captives but they all live. You will have need of *great* courage in the coming days. The contract *must* be retrieved and Arvensis *destroyed,* I am unable to change what has been written in blood. He thinks you are dead, that *may* be to your advantage but it won't be long before he discovers you *live*. Now come, you look as though you need feeding.'

They descended to the camp below where there was much activity as the tribe prepared a huge feast. Lance sat beside Myosurus and was joined by Cracked Ice and Blizzard who lay at his feet.

'I wish to introduce you to my grandson, son of Hellebore,' said Myosurus. 'CALYX!' she called. 'It is his twelfth birthday today which makes this a double celebration.'

'You called, Grandmother?' His shiny blue-black hair was tied back and his dark skin was decorated with red and white symbols that bore a striking resemblance to the markings of the woodpecker perched on his shoulder.

'Yes Calyx. This is Lance, he is our guest, and I wish you to attend him while he is here.'

'Very well Grandmother.'

'I'm sure he would like to hear your drumming skills,' she suggested.

'Oh yes please! Has the bird a name?'

'Hop,' replied Calyx smiling, then went off to prepare.

Myosurus explained that Calyx had found the baby bird injured, after it had fallen from its tree hole. He'd hand reared him and had since trained him to play the drums, which she wasn't sure was such a good idea as his beak quite often pierced the skins. But Calyx was the tribe's rainmaker and they made a good team.

Greater Spotted Woodpeckers cleverly warned of rain with their drumming. They inhabited Crowfoot territory and were highly respected by the tribe who called them little warriors.

Their war paint plumage of red and white showed at its best when they danced, hopping with wings spread, swaying their heads with ruffled crowns. The tribe often mimicked this dance as a ritual of gratitude following the forewarned storms.

Hop took his place on the biggest tom-tom with Calyx, after which the drumming and dancing commenced. The festivities went on well into the night. Amidst all the celebrations Lance momentarily forgot his worries.

Eventually, Myosurus retired and Calyx showed Lance to a teepee where Cracked Ice and Blizzard lay protectively at its entrance.

*

The next morning before anyone arose, Myosurus set off into the mountains to sacred ground, which was at the pinnacle of a particular mountain. Once there, she buried the talisman along with Hellebore's headdress, hunting knife and drinking cup. As his soul was laid to rest she was relieved to hear his voice in the wind, chanting a happy song.

As she sat meditating Aquila swooped down and landed behind her pawing the ground with his hooves. She acknowledged him by bowing her head. Following which he moved forward, wrapped his wings around her and lifted her spirit from her body. Beating its great wings they flew together, soaring into the future.

With her eyes focused on the points of Aquilas' twisting horns, she became enlightened of disturbing events unfolding. Then she saw the face of a boy, a chosen one who had yet to come to Echoco. She knew matters would get much worse before they got better, as in life no path is straight.

*

Back at the galleon, the boys were weary, hungry and listless. Miles had pushed them to their limit after deciding he wanted their forest camp for his own and had spent the morning working them to a frazzle preparing it. He asked Arvensis if he could have the cannon containing his shell collection to make it feel more like home. Arvensis consented and the task fell upon the boys, under the watchful eyes of Miles and the crows.

Removing it from the galleon was hard enough but didn't compare to the journey that lay ahead. With ropes secured about it they struggled in the soft sand that became impossible. They had to get planks of wood to lie under its wheels. The whole procedure took the best part of the day. Then on manoeuvring it through the forest, it kept getting stuck in the mud.

Nearing the camp, absolutely exhausted they came to an incline, which was to prove the most testing. Miles told Teasel to get behind and push! Their little faces glowed red as they strained and groaned to a standstill halfway up.

'We won't make it!' cried Teasel.

'Don't be stupid, you're almost there. Put your backs into it!' commanded Miles. The boys pulled with all their might. Their knuckles turned white and the veins protruded on their necks.

'I – I CAN'T HOLD ON!' screamed one of them as the rope began to burn and slice through his hands.

'KEEP HOLD!' barked Miles.

Just then the rope that was old began to fray. With a swift twang it snapped and whipped out of the boy's hands unleashing the cannon that shot rapidly back down the incline.

'TEASEL!' screamed one of them. Everyone stared in horror at his small lifeless body lying on the ground. Panicking they rushed down to him. One of them laid his head on Teasel's chest.

'Is he alive?' asked one of them anxiously.

'Is he breathing?' said another.

'Shush, let me listen! … I fear his heart has – *stopped!*'
came the reply.

'IF YOU'VE *QUITE* FINISHED!' yelled Miles.

'What about Teasel?' called one of them.

'Leave him there, the crows can scavenge his remains!'
The boys glared up at him, anger consuming them. Miles,
realising he'd overstepped the mark, instructed the crows to
escort them back.

'*We'll* be next,' commented one of them choking on his
tears.

As dusk set in the crows returned in search of Teasel's body
that had disappeared from sight. They searched the whole area
but it was nowhere to be found.

A group perched on the cannon became spooked as the
lonely wail of a wolf filled the air. Blizzard with red eyes
glinting in the half-light began bending his ghostlike body
through the trees nearby. This rare beast that they believed had
deprived them of a meal frightened off the crows.

Blizzard presently disappeared from sight, soon after
which, in the dark shadows of the trees, hundreds of little lights
began to glow. Zooming out they hovered around a boulder
close to the cannon that softened, heaving as if it were alive. It
was Peony whose disguise had masked Teasel, slithering off she
disappeared into the forest. The Orbs surrounded him, lifted
his limp body and hurriedly flew him away.

CHAPTER NINE

The Quest

Early the following morning Lance was preparing to leave. Myosurus came over to bid him farewell. 'Here Lance, take these, they will keep you warm as the nights turn cold,' she said, handing him a white woollen fleece jacket and a pair of moccasin boots.

'Thank you Myosurus.'

Blizzard and Cracked Ice came bounding over and they set off.

'Be strong!' she called after them. Calyx began drumming, to which a circle of braves, chanted as they danced.

Lance knew his priority was to retrieve the contract. He assumed it was hidden on the galleon and had to somehow get on board to search for it.

As they approached the canyon pass the drumming could still be faintly heard in the distance. By the time they'd crossed, the air began hovering around freezing. 'Strange?' No sooner had Lance spoken than a snowflake landed on his nose. He looked up at the sky that suddenly filled with snow and then great white flakes fell all about them. *Good magic, Myosurus!* he thought, smiling to himself. For Myosurus knew they would stand out like sore thumbs in the forest. Lance donned his jacket and boots. Shortly after which, a whiteout lay the snow deep on the ground.

Passing the lake they continued to the forest. They were in the thickest part when Cracked Ice and Blizzard who were playfully rolling in the snow, stopped abruptly. Blizzard's ears pricked forward. Snarling, he bared his fangs. Lance quickly climbed a tree to see what lay ahead. It was Arvensis, Miles and the boys with an army of crows.

On spotting a scout flying towards them, he quickly signalled to Cracked Ice and Blizzard to hide under the snow. Swiftly jumping down he pinned himself against the trunk. On approaching, the crow curiously flew down to investigate little puffs of smoke, (which was in fact Lance's warm breath hitting the cold air).

The crow caught sight of Lance but just as he opened his bill to sound the alarm, Cracked Ice leapt up and swiped him to the ground with his powerful claws, killing him outright. 'Well done, boy!' whispered Lance, patting him on the head. They shook the snow from their coats, covering Lance in the process. Blizzard began anxiously pacing back and forth panting, beckoning Lance to follow him as the entourage approached. Quickening their pace, they proceeded to the green wall.

They arrived to find the frontage of dense trees covered in snow. Blizzard howled softly, then led them behind a thick bush that concealed the entrance. They made their way down a narrow passage where lights twinkled ahead. On entering the cave some Orbs dashed past them carrying leaves, as they hastened to cover their tracks.

'Lance! You're alive!'

'Teasel! Oh thank goodness you're safe!' Blizzard rubbed affectionately against Teasel's leg.

'I was hit by a cannon and left for *dead*. Peony and the Orbs saved me!'

'Peony?'

'Yes!' Blizzard nudged him. 'Oh and not forgetting this wonderful animal!'

'He's called Blizzard and this is Cracked Ice,' said Lance, proudly.

Orchis came whizzing over.

'Orchis! Is Eyebright with you?'

'No Lance, he went out alone this morning. I'm beginning to worry about him.'

'I'm sure he'll be back soon. Are *all* the Orbs here?'

'Yes,' she replied.

'I don't know how long we'll be safe here, they're bound to be combing the island,' said Teasel.

'They are! I just caught sight of them with the boys, at least the weather will slow them down. Cracked Ice will guard the entrance. It will take a good crow to get past him.' Just as Lance spoke, a crow unexpectedly flew straight in above their heads. The Orbs squealed, but as Cracked Ice leapt at the crow, it suddenly dropped to the ground of its own accord.

Lance bent down to inspect it.

'Is it dead?' inquired Teasel.

'It *seems* to be,' he replied prodding at the bird, which unexpectedly made a strange gurgling sound. Raising an eyebrow Lance lifted the crow to discover Eyebright underneath. He'd been following Lance and had hoisted himself under the dead scout to escape the hunting party.

'Eyebright! How disgusting!' scowled Orchis. To which they all laughed.

Then Lance's face lit up. 'Wait a minute, Eyebright's given me a brilliant idea!' Eyebright flew up hovering excitedly as Lance continued. 'Woodruff read us a story once, do you remember Teasel, about a wooden horse, in which an army of Greek men hid to enter a city called Troy.'

'Yes, I recall it.'

'We could conceal at least two Orbs in the crow. Disguised they could get on board the ship and search out the contract.'

'Do you think it would work?'

'It's got to be worth a try! If we hurry they can go now while Arvensis is in the forest. I need two *brave* volunteers!' Lance called out.

Eyebright immediately hovered forward. The terrified Orbs looked at each other. As Orchis went to speak Brier flew forward, followed by another and then another. Suddenly finding their courage they all came forward to volunteer. Last of all was Dodder, who cowered his head saying, 'I feel it is *my* task as *I* am responsible for all the trouble.'

'That is *not true*, Dodder. But if you want to go, then it shall be yourself and Eyebright,' concluded Lance. Orchis smiled as Dodder's face proudly lit up.

The dummy crow was ready in no time and they prepared to leave.

'Take care; there will still be lots of crows around. Good luck!' said Lance as they departed.

Everyone waited anxiously. As the hours dragged on, Lance began restlessly pacing the floor. 'They've been *too* long. Something *must* have gone wrong!' he remarked. Just as he spoke Cracked Ice let out a warning growl and the dummy crow zoomed in.

'Well? Did you find it?' asked Lance, apprehensively. They threw off their camouflage to reveal their downcast expressions.

'We truly searched *everywhere*, Lance, but there was *no* trace of it. Then Miles came back. We just managed to escape as he entered the cabin.'

'Did he see you Eyebright?'

'Well – yes-'

'We kind of clipped his head as we left,' added Dodder.

'Don't fret, you did your best but Arvensis is not stupid. If he thinks you were searching for the contract, he will suspect I am still alive and may have had you followed. We'd better find somewhere else to hide, just in case.'

'But where Lance? They'll turn into ice balls if they're exposed to the cold for too long!' declared Teasel.

'We'll head for the camp. I've a feeling Arvensis will be keeping Miles with him for a while. I have a plan to get all the

Orbs safely off Echoco in the next storm. Once through to Earth time they can enlist the help of the Kindreds.'

'But there's thousands of crows, they won't stand a chance!' argued Teasel.

'Ah, but you haven't met my other new friend!'

'Tell me more?'

'His name is Cumulus, a buffalo cloud. He couldn't withstand the hurricane but he *could* mask their flight out to it.'

'Fantastic, where is he?' asked Teasel excitedly.

'He'll be there when I need him.' Lance addressed the Orbs and told them all to wait in the cave till he sent Eyebright back for them.

Cracked Ice and Blizzard led the way, followed by Lance, Teasel and Eyebright. Cautiously they made their way out, vigilantly looking all around.

Making their way towards a clearing and confident the coast was clear, Lance signalled to Eyebright to return. But just as he zoomed forward, they heard a deafening 'CRAAAAAAH!' followed by a thunderous rumbling.

Eyebright hovered as Lance and Teasel stared horrified at each other.

'Arvensis!' cried Lance.

'AVALANCHE! RUN!' yelled Teasel.

As the snow cascaded down the cliff they ran and jumped, diving under a fallen tree that was suspended on another.

When the rumbling stopped, they kicked their way out to discover the face of the cliff completely buried, entombing the Orbs. They were still in shock when alerted by the sound of snow crunching; they turned to face Miles, the boys and a mass of crows that were swooping down behind them.

The hair went up on the nape of Blizzard who bared his teeth and began to snarl. The boys gawped at Lance and Teasel whom they'd presumed dead. Miles stared dumbstruck, in disbelief.

Cracked Ice leapt in front of Lance twisting his head growling and pawing the air.

'ATTAAACK!' commanded Arvensis, as he landed behind them.

Lance drew his cutlass. Miles brandishing his sword swiped towards Lance's head. Cracked Ice reared up taking the force of the blow to his chest. As he fell aside Miles lashed forwards again; Lance blocked the sword but took a cut to his shoulder.

The boys joined ranks and punched the crows while Blizzard attacked Arvensis. But this canny crow was giving up nothing but feathers.

'WE'RE OUTNUMBERED,' shouted Lance. Just then a shadow fell upon them and a dense fog suddenly engulfed them. 'CUMULUS! RUN FOR IT! SPLIT UP!' yelled Lance.

They all ran leaving Arvensis, Miles and the crows trying to fight their way out of Cumulus who smothered them until everyone had escaped.

'SOON, LANCE, SOON!' bellowed Miles.

Blizzard headed off with Teasel and the boys. Eyebright followed Lance and Cracked Ice who, finding a stream overhung with dense trees, waded into the freezing water to disguise their bloody trail.

Lance tore some cloth from his clothes with which to tend their wounds. Eyebright was very quiet. 'Are you OK, Eyebright?' queried Lance.

'Yes! I'm fine, just worried for the others.' But he wasn't fine. He'd been slightly pierced during the skirmish and didn't want to worry Lance who had more serious issues to deal with.

Presently they heard Blizzard whining close by. Shivering and shaking they got themselves together and ran to find him.

Blizzard wagged his tail as they approached then led them to the boys, whose spirits now lifted, were having fun playing in the snow at their old camp.

'What are we going to do now, Lance?' asked Teasel.

'Well, if we're going to stand our ground and fight we might as well do it here.'

'What about the Orbs?'

'There's nothing we *can* do at the moment, at least the crows can't get to them.' Lance looked up to the sky where lightning warned of an incoming storm. He spied Cumulus stationed above. *Hurricane!* he thought and knew what he had to do.

Beckoning to Blizzard he took Cracked Ice inside the camp, concerned about the severe wound he had sustained. 'Listen my good friends, do you think you could hold the fort while I go for help?' They both nodded. Teasel came in overhearing him. 'Teasel, I fear we are too few to beat them and well - *Arvensis!*'

'I know Lance, he's indestructible. Don't worry; we can hold them off for a while. There's plenty of supplies, Miles had us store them here.'

'Good. Here, take care of my cutlass. Use it well.'

'But Lance, where will you go?'

'When I was in Cragga my sister's spirit came to my aid, she told me to seek out one in Earth time called Margaret as a last resort. Hopefully she'll know the whereabouts of the Kindreds. Somehow I'll get help!'

'But how will you find her?'

'Eleanor told me where she'd been buried. I'll start there.'

Lance prepared to leave, torn between staying to fighting a useless battle or risk the journey to Earth time for help. Patting Blizzard and silently choking back a tear he turned to Teasel. 'Don't worry, remember what Woodruff told us about the Cup of Destiny, we all drink from our own.'

'Yes, I remember, C.U.P.' 'Yes Teasel, they *will* get their ComeUpPance!'

Lance walked up to Cracked Ice who was licking his wound, stroked him on the head and then hurried out.

He whistled to Eyebright who swiftly flew over. 'Thank goodness I still have you, my little friend, I couldn't do this without you. Do you think you can take my weight?' Eyebright nodded. Lance held onto him with both hands and they slowly ascended up to where Cumulus was waiting to camouflage their flight out to the storm.

Everyone looked on apprehensively as they disappeared from sight.

- CHAPTER TEN -

A Chance Encounter

Earth time had now progressed to October and the start of the half term holidays. Jill and her family were preparing to leave for Cornwall, taking two cars, as John had to return a day earlier due to work commitments.

Margaret was arriving at the end of the week to spend a day with them, as she wanted to visit the graves and inspect the repairs. Bob was dropping her off, as he needed their car, so John offered to drop her back on his way home. Pamela had already set off with Ritchie and Simon. Jill was travelling with her father, who'd loaded the car but had since mislaid the keys.

The Surf gang unexpectedly arrived to see Jill off. Waiting outside they began to fool around. Podge decided to climb a tree in the front garden but unfortunately got stuck and boys being boys instead of rushing to his assistance, Matt and Jack hid from sight, leaving him distressed. Jack climbed into the boot of the car, squeezing in with the luggage and Matt hid round the side of the house.

John came out ahead of Jill, shouting. Spying the keys in the car door, he stormed over to retrieve them, went back, slammed and locked the front door then ordered Jill into the car. Due to his mood the Surfs decided to stay in hiding, except for Jack, who, on hearing the car's engine start, tried to push the boot-lid open but it was shut tight.

As they drove away Matt ran over to the tree. 'Podge, guess what, Jack's still in the boot!'

'JUST GET ME DOWN FROM HERE!' he shouted.

Jack began to panic but was frightened of drawing their attention in case he caused an accident.

After about three hours the car came to a halt at a service station. Jack was in agony as cramp had set into his legs. Jill and her father got out and were just starting to walk away when they heard banging and yelling coming from the boot. Frowning, John went to investigate.

He was horrified to discover Jack and began ranting and raving. (He knew of Jack as he'd visited the house on occasions.) Jill called to her father to stop, as she could see Jack was stressed and in pain. He huffed, then told Jack it was too late to take him back so he'd have to come with them and he'd decide what to do later.

Jack felt really uncomfortable and just wanted to go home. But as soon as John realised he'd stayed silent with regard to their safety, the air cleared and everyone began to relax.

They arrived in Cornwall later that afternoon. After a heated discussion with Pamela and her parents it was decided Jack could stay as long as his foster parents consented. After phoning and explaining the situation it was agreed. It was also decided that he would travel back with John a day earlier. The children were delighted. Jack was to share a room with the boys where he would top and tail with Ritchie.

Sensing his awkwardness the family made an effort to make him feel welcome. John took him to a local market and bought him a few items of clothing. Jack soon relaxed and began to enjoy his stay in which time he would get the chance to surf, which he couldn't wait to brag about to Matt and Podge. Ritchie had a new surfboard so he gave Jack his old one.

*

The time passed quickly. Margaret arrived at the end of the week and the whole family set off to the coast for the day. It was cold and windy but the sun was shining.

When they arrived Ritchie and Jack hurried into their wet suits and were soon out on the surf. Jill's nan and granddad set off for an amble along the coast. Pamela took Simon to investigate rock pools and John went off to buy some refreshments.

Jill sat with Margaret on the beach. She was desperate to tell her aunt the whole story of the notebook but wasn't sure how she'd react and couldn't risk her mother finding out she'd lied.

'Jack seems like a nice lad,' commented Margaret.

'Yeah, 'e is.'

'Jill! Don't talk while you're chewing gum.'

'Sorry Auntie Margaret,' she replied, quickly removing it.

'I've noticed a big change in you, especially the way you talk.'

'You 'ave?'

'See you're doing it now, talking in Essex slang with a Cornish accent.'

They both began to laugh.

'How long has Jack been in foster care, Jill?'

'I'm not sure, but I think he's had quite a few foster parents.'

'That's a shame, still he seems to be pretty level headed, considering.'

'Auntie Margaret, while we're on the subject is it true you had a son adopted?' Margaret began to frown and remained silent. 'Oh, I'm *so* sorry, I didn't mean to pry. *Please* don't tell mum, she'll be *really* angry with me!'

Margaret sighed a big sigh. 'It's all right Jill, it was a long time ago now, but yes - I did.'

'Have you ever tried to find him or heard from him?'

'Oh no! I've had *no* contact whatsoever; I felt it was best. Look at Ritchie and Jack, they're really showing off,' she said, quickly changing the subject.

Jill looked out to sea, knowing in her heart it was useless to pursue the issue. 'I don't think they should be in that area,' said Jill, looking worried.

All of a sudden Jack's surfboard somersaulted and he disappeared from sight. He'd got caught in an undercurrent and failed to resurface.

'JACK!' screamed Margaret, jumping to her feet. 'PAMELA, IT'S JACK!' she yelled, frantically pointing.

Ritchie began diving under in a panic searching for him. The lifeguards had seen them in difficulty and were already swimming out towards them.

John returned and ran down to join the others who were waiting anxiously at the water's edge. One lifeguard had hold of Ritchie, shortly after another surfaced with Jack. They carried them onto the beach. Ritchie was shaken and unharmed but Jack was unconscious.

A small crowd, who had gathered, stood back and waited with baited breath as the lifeguard tried to resuscitate him. To everyone's relief, Jack coughed and spluttered. Margaret knelt down beside him. He looked into her worried face and smiled. She gave him a little hug as she helped him up.

An ambulance was already on its way and although Jack insisted he was fine, they thought it best he was checked out. He asked them not to worry his foster parents and said he'd ring them from the hospital where Margaret accompanied him.

John drove the family back to the cottage and then made his way to the hospital to collect them.

Jill had been keeping watch at the window. *'They're here!'* she called out, running to the door. Jack had been given the all clear and was in good spirits.

After supper John and Margaret prepared to leave. It was decided that Jack should stay the extra day to make up for his bad experience. Everyone gathered on the drive to wave goodbye.

Jill noticed that her Auntie Margaret had grown quite fond of Jack as she hugged him saying, 'Don't forget, if you want a new foster mum, just ring!' He smiled and thanking her for everything kissed her on the cheek. 'Oh, the flowers, I left them in the kitchen!'

'I'll fetch 'em - I mean - them, Auntie,' said Jill hurrying inside. On returning she passed them to Margaret, who kissed her good-bye and winked that familiar wink.

It was nearing closing time when they arrived at the cemetery, which is probably why they were the only ones there. John carried some water down for Margaret and after paying his respects said he'd wait for her in the car.

Kneeling down, Margaret began to arrange the flowers. Assuming no one could hear her she spoke openly out loud. 'Lily of the Valley for you Grandma and roses for you Granddad … I met with a young boy today who had a lucky escape, lovely lad. Guess someone's looking after him. Just as you watch over us … Well the repairs look good. Those vandals will get their comeuppance, aye Granddad. I recall the day my purse was stolen, containing the money I'd saved for nan's birthday present. Remember? You said; *Margaret, they will loose more than there was in your purse throughout their lives!'*

Just then she heard a gasp and caught sight of a figure out of the corner of her eye, behind a nearby tree. Assuming it was vandals she gathered the flower wrappings and casually walked to a bin on the other side of the tree, from where she intended to surprise them. But it was Margaret who was surprised when a voice said, *'Margaret - are you* Margaret? Eleanor said you would know me.' Lance stepped into view.

Totally shocked and taken aback by this strangely dressed little ruffian, she glanced over to see if John had noticed but his head was buried in a newspaper.

'*Please* hear me out. I am Lance! I believe we are related!' Margaret began to tremble.

'How *dare* you, what sort of sick child are you!' she cried.

Lance realising things were about to go pear shaped quickly replied, 'I'm Lance, brother of Eleanor and Miles.' He then reached up into the tree.

Margaret thought the crazed child had concealed a weapon but as she opened her mouth to scream, Lance pulled Eyebright down from the branches. Gasping she covered her mouth with her hand, then lowering it slowly she stared in sheer, dumbstruck awe.

'So it *was* all true!' she declared.

'We don't have much time. We urgently need to find the Kindreds and Orbs. There is *serious* trouble on Echoco!' said Lance desperately, with eyes bulging.

John stepped out of the car but could not see Lance who was obscured by the trunk. 'ARE YOU ALL RIGHT, MARGARET? WE HAVE TO LEAVE SOON. THEY'LL BE LOCKING UP SHORTLY.'

Pulling herself together she called back, 'YES JOHN. JUST COMING!'

She didn't know if to laugh or cry. 'Oh look at the cute little thing!' she said smiling at Eyebright. 'But what can *I* do Lance, I - I've never met a Kindred. I remember granddad told me they held meetings at the ruins of Tintagel Castle. The only two he really talked about were Ulex and Furse. Ulex supposedly lived somewhere in Cornwall and Furse in a grand castle on the cliffs at Southend-on-Sea, which coincidentally is where my sister and her family live now. I always told him I *believed* his stories but I didn't *realise* they were true!'

Suddenly Eyebright fell to the ground.

'Eyebright! Whatever's wrong?' said Lance panicking.

'I'm sorry Lance, I - I'm - injured I didn't want to worry you - I-' Eyebright passed out.

'Oh my!' cried Margaret. Lance quickly scooped him up. 'Is he ill?'

'I'm afraid so, I *have* to find them soon! Which is the way to Tintagel?'

'You'll never find it and it will take you ages on foot - Wait a minute I have an idea. *I* can take care of Eyebright. He'll be safe with me. Does he need medication?'

'No, just total rest, out of the light.'

'Good. Now listen carefully and then do as I say ...'

Margaret put Eyebright carefully into her bag then ran back up to the car acting alarmed pointing and shouting, 'VANDALS! JOHN, OVER THERE, QUICKLY!' Whilst John ran off to investigate she signalled to Lance, who hurried over unnoticed.

Opening the boot she quickly hugged him so tightly his arms and legs were all akimbo. Lance winced as his shoulder wound pained him. Margaret thought he was just showing his affection.

'Here, you may need this,' she said, putting some money into his hand, and then hid him in the boot.

John returned saying he couldn't see anyone and they set off.

Margaret was unusually quiet on the journey. When they arrived at her house John popped in to use the bathroom. He noticed she seemed anxious for him to be on his way as he chatted with Bob. They were discussing a hurricane currently building in the Pacific Ocean that had been named Dylan. It was anticipated to reach a whopping fifteen on the Beaufort scale and predicted to evolve any day.

The instant John left she went up to a little attic room where she made Eyebright comfortable.

John travelled straight home.

When he opened the boot to get his suitcase Lance leapt out and run off into the night. Flabbergasted, John removed his case and checked the boot thoroughly to make sure no *more* boys were going to suddenly appear. Shaking his head he went indoors.

Lance was totally bemused by all the sights he encountered. Finding himself on a cliff-top, he viewed the seafront that was lit by a thousand fairy lights snaking their way as far as the eye could see. Voices in the distance screamed and laughed amidst an array of music and all manners of strange mechanical sounds. 'Wow!' he blurted, catching sight of a great illuminated wheel rotating as it towered in the night sky.

Exploring, he happened upon a bandstand where an elderly couple were sitting on a bench eating a fish and chip supper wrapped in newspaper. Enticed by the wonderful aroma he approached them, taking the opportunity to inquire about the castle. 'I seek the *grand* castle.' At first they appeared a little startled. 'Castle?' he repeated. Frowning they pointed down the coast in the opposite direction to the bustling arcades.

'That way. It's that way,' muttered the man. Perturbed by Lance's presence, they threw the remains of their food into a nearby bin and hurried off.

Lance retrieved their leftovers and after sampling them, ate every last scrap before lying under the bench and drifting off to sleep, confident of finding Furse in the morning.

CHAPTER ELEVEN

A Twist of Fate

Early the next morning Lance awoke to the cooing of pigeons that were pecking at the crumpled newspaper in search of crumbs. Pulling himself together in the brisk and chilly air, he looked about and discovered a drinking fountain. After working out how to use it he continued on his way along the cliff-top. He'd seen pictures of castles in Woodruff's archives so he knew what he was seeking.

After walking a few miles Lance became concerned, as there were no signs of a castle. He was beginning to feel desperate when he overheard a group of people mention they were going to the castle, so he discreetly followed them at a distance.

Eventually, the group headed down a beaten track from where a turret loomed into sight. Lance stared at the castle that stood on a mound in view of the sea. He was alarmed to find it lay in ruins, but for a crumbling tower, surrounded by broken walls. Not quite the grand fortress he'd envisaged. But allowing for the ravages of time, unperturbed he began to explore, searching every nook and cranny for any giveaway signs, but found nothing. Deciding that the Kindreds would not show their faces till nightfall he explored around its perimeter to pass the time.

It seemed as though the sun was never going to set. When it eventually did, Lance resumed his search. He repeatedly called out for Furse hoping he would come out to inquire who should know of him, but there was no response.

He sat crumpled in a heap and was near to breaking point when an animal like one he'd never seen before ran up to him barking. Lance smiled at the friendly beast that proceeded to lick his face. 'Hey you! What are you doing there?' called a man, carrying a leash.

'I'm sorry, I was just visiting the castle!'

'What, at this time of night? It seems Bones likes you. You're honoured, he doesn't normally take to strangers.'

'What is he?'

'Don't tell me you've never seen a Great *Dane* before?'

'Oh – well - Yes – I think he's a - wonderful warrior,' replied Lance, recalling a history lesson with Woodruff. The man looked totally bewildered.

'It's a bit late for you to be out isn't it? Where do you live lad?'

' … *Here* in Southend-on-Sea!'

'Well you're obviously lost. This is Hadleigh. Southend is that way!' he said pointing in the direction from which Lance had come. Lance looked shocked and before another word was spoken, he ran off.

'Strange kid,' commented the man.

Running as fast as he could and feeling somewhat stupid, an idea came to Lance. If he could get onto the giant wheel, surely he'd be able to see for miles and spy the castle from there. With that thought in mind he made his way down to the coastal path.

Before long Lance reached the theme park, noticing that there weren't as many lights and noises as the previous night. He spied a majestic galleon afloat in a watery compound behind locked gates. Looking about, no one was in sight so he quickly climbed over.

Once on board he found every cabin door was also secured. As everything appeared to be closed down for the night, he found a large hollow barrel on the deck, tucked himself inside and safely concealed, fell into a deep sleep.

*

The morning of Halloween dawned and as the sleepy seaside town began to stir Lance slept on. In fact it was the last day the theme park was going to be open for some time, as winter had strengthened its icy grip on the town.

Later that morning he was wakened with a start by a bang that rocked the barrel. 'Don't do that, you naughty boy!' a woman scolded.

'Try and stop me!' came the obnoxious reply.

'Right, no candy floss for you my lad.' There followed a defiant scream, accompanied by a barrage of footsteps on the wooden deck, blending into the fairground sounds that filled the air.

Stiff and aching Lance twisted round to peep out of a tiny hole in the side of the barrel but couldn't see much at all, just parts of people's legs. Suddenly, his injured shoulder gave way; he jolted causing the barrel to topple onto its side. 'Oh no!' he cried as it began to roll.

Stopping abruptly, the lid popped open and a disgruntled man peered in. 'OUT!' he barked. Lance scurried out and ran down some wooden steps into the hustle and bustle of the park.

He wandered around staring in awe at all the rides. Upon spying the giant wheel and making his way there, he heard loud bursts of laughter coming from inside a crooked house. Curiosity momentarily got the better of him. Intrigued, he joined the queue of children waiting to enter.

In front of him was a girl with long blonde hair, wearing dark blue jeans and white boots that matched her leather jacket. A strong aroma of perfume filled the air around her, which was probably a good thing, as Lance didn't smell at his best.

A rather shabbily dressed plump boy with bright ginger hair and a multitude of freckles came up behind him, pushing his stomach *hard* into Lance's back, squashing him into the girl in front who quickly swung round.

'Sorry!' said Lance. She looked over his head.

'PODGE!'

'Wot?' said the boy smirking.

'You know what!' she scowled. 'You don't have to apologise,' she said to Lance. *'Podge* was just being his usual *rude* self. My name's Jill,' she smiled.

Podge pulled a sweet face and mimicked her. 'My name's Jill!' he said in a silly girlie voice. She glared at him, screwing her lips into a pout.

Lance looked at her icy blue eyes that were caked in bold blue makeup, set off with shimmering pink lipstick. 'My name's Lance.'

'Nice to meet you - Lance.' Jill paused for a second, then continued. 'That's Roger by the way. Podge is his nickname.'

'I *can* speak!' he butted in as they neared the turnstile. 'Yeh, can't dodge the Podge,' he proudly announced, protruding his stomach once again.

Jill handed in her ticket and walked through. Lance looked a little bewildered as the ticket man held out his hand. 'Ticket?' he asked. Lance reached into the pouch tied around his waist to find the paper money Margaret had given him had *gone.*

'Lost somethin'?' asked Podge cockily. Jill guessed he'd been up to no-good and glaring at Podge quickly handed in a ticket for Lance.

Podge smirked as he came through but got stuck in the turnstile.

'Serves you right!' she blurted.

The ticket man pulled and tugged eventually freeing him. Podge turned crimson with anger and embarrassment.

Lance overheard Jill whispering sternly to him. 'If I find out.'

'Find out wot?' he snapped. Jill huffed and went inside.

The crooked house was great fun. The floors and ceilings went the opposite way to which they appeared. They came to a wall of mirrors. Lance became a bit unearthed by these strange reflections of himself, looking short and squat in one, then tall and skinny in another. Jill was laughing at Podge's reflection, in which he looked as though his waist had been pinched to a point.

They walked down the crooked steps that led back outside. Jill, feeling sorry for Lance, handed him her last two tickets. 'Here, have these,' she said smiling.

'Oh - thank you!' he replied gratefully.

'Bye, Lance, take care,' she added, flicking her handbag over her shoulder and walking off swaying her hips.

'Yeah. Take care,' mimicked Podge, taking hold of Lance's cheek and spitefully squeezing it, to which Lance began to snarl and bare his teeth.

'Weirdo!' called Podge, walking off a little perturbed.

Lance looked over to where Jill met up with two other boys before disappearing from sight amongst the crowds. He then headed in the direction of the towering wheel.

'The Big Wheel!' he read out loud, as he approached a display board. The queue had already got onto the ride and the attendant called Lance forward as the next empty cradle swung round.

'Two tickets a ride,' said the man. Lance handed them to him. The attendant snapped the safety bar in place and the wheel began to turn.

Amidst the cries of the other riders Lance could be heard shouting 'STOOOOP!' every time the wheel reached its peak, as he wanted time to scan the cliffs.

When the wheel eventually came to a halt, Lance's cradle was at the top, creaking as it swayed in the salty breeze. He could see for miles, but there were no signs of a castle.

Feeling deflated he made his way out of the park and across the road to the arcades. His mind was in a cloud when Rocky and his gang on their skates unexpectedly encircled him.

'What clever transport!' remarked Lance, snapping out of it and trying to make polite conversation.

'Are you takin' the mickey?' spoke one of them abruptly.

'Got any dosh?' demanded Rocky.

'Dosh?'

'Money!'

'If I don't have it then I obviously don't need it,' replied Lance.

'Get real. Dressed like that yeh gotta be kiddin'!' All the boys began laughing.

'My clothes have little to do with *who* I am.'

'*Oooo, get you*, so who are you?' said Rocky cockily, turning up his top lip.

'I am Lance!' he replied indignantly.

'Lance oo don't need a lot. Ha! Yeh must be Lancelot!' The gang began to laugh hysterically. 'Well Sir Lancelot yeh better find yerself an 'orse an' a suit of armour. You'll need 'em if I come across yeh again. Now get goin' before yeh get me stoppers to give yeh a lift,' threatened Rocky raising a skate in the air.

'Go on - scoot!' said another of them, seemingly feeling sorry for Lance, as he patted him on the back. 'Leave it,' said the boy to the group, who skated off, mocking him.

Lance wandered back towards the park where he came across a boating lake. He was sitting for a while watching the children having fun, when without warning a boy came over and kicked him in the back. 'Ouch! What the?'

'You *asked* for it!' said the boy chuckling and pointing. Lance totally bemused put his hand behind him and grasped hold of a piece of paper attached to his jacket that read: Kick Me!

'What is it with people round here?'

'Can't apologise, not done. The name's Jack.'

'Mine's Lance.'

Jack took the note from him. 'Yeah, thought as much, The Rocks, they always sign the back.'

'Who are The Rocks?'

'They're a nasty piece of work!'

Jack, whose black hair was styled in curtains, was wearing a white T-shirt, black baggy trousers, trainers and had a silver puffa jacket tied around his waist. He placed a large radio cassette player on the pavement. Switching it on he turned up the volume and began dancing.

Lance stared in amazement as Jack finished by spinning on his back, jumped to his feet, and then landed in the splits.

'Wow! What kind of dancing is that?'

'Break dancing.'

'I'm not surprised, did you break anything?' Jack looked at him puzzled for a moment, then smiled and sat down beside him.

'So, Lance, why the long face?'

Lance suddenly felt he needed to talk to someone and Jack just had one of those listening faces.'Well, I've got a *huge* problem with birds!' he said glumly.

'Totty?'

'Whatever, anyway, there's *thousands* of them.'

'Thousands! Wot - all after you?'

'Yes, one nasty one in particular and my brother who thinks *I* killed our parents.'

Jack pondered, raised his eyebrows then replied, 'No kiddin'.'

'No, no kidding. They're trying to kill everyone and my friends are in grave danger. I've *got* to get back to them, I've been away too long as it is. I left to get help but I can't find the Kindreds.'

'Kindreds?'

'You know, oh you probably don't. They're the little people.'

'Right,' slurred Jack, thinking Lance was a bit bonkers.

'I was injured in the last fight.'

'Where?'

'My shoulder.'

'No where was the fight?'

'Oh sorry, on the island.'

'That's funny, I 'aven't 'eard about it, then again I've bin away,' replied Jack referring to an island further down the coast.

'Anyway there's going to be a *big* fight soon and unless I find the castle I can't get back. Do *you* know where it is Jack?'

'Castle? The only castle round 'ere is on the cliffs.'

Lance leapt to his feet. 'That's it! That's the one I seek! Where is it Jack?'

Jack thought Lance was a lunatic but feeling sorry for him and worried he was being targeted by the Rocks, decided to keep an eye on him for a while. 'I'll take yeh there presently, besides if there's gonna be a fight - yeh've found yer man.'

'Seriously, you'd help?'

'Count me in!'

'Thanks Jack, but I'm afraid it will take more than just us.'

'Noooo problem, I'm meetin' up wiv the Surfs tonight.'

'The Surfs?'

'Yeah, it's our gang, well, Matt's gang. I'm sure 'e'll be up for it. We're going trick or treatin' then ghost huntin' in The Haunted House in the park.'

'Won't it be closed?'

'Of course, but not to us. Fing is, Lance, we don't 'it girls.'

'Girls?' queried Lance, looking confused.

'Yeah, yeh know, totty; birds.'

'Oh no Jack, not those birds. Crows!'

'Crows? Right! Hey, no sweat, we can tackle them for yeh!' he reassured him, now convinced he was cranky, but liked him anyway. 'Come on,' he said, picking up his cassette player. 'It's gettin' late. I'll show yeh where the castle is. We can grab some chips on the way.'

Lance felt happier having made a friend.

'How old are you Jack?' asked Lance, as they walked along.

'Me, thirteen, same as Matt. 'E's me best mate.'

'Have you always lived here?'

'Nah, all over the place. I'm wiv me fifth set of foster parents now, probably be six soon.'

'How's that?'

'Recently finished me time in a prison youth wing.'

'What's that?'

'A place for *bad* boys.'

'What did you do?'

'Don't do braggin'. 'Ow old are you Lance?'

'I *think* I'm nine but Eyebright said I'm nearer to one-hundred in your time!'

'Ha ha, I knew it, yer an alien,' laughed Jack.

Lance came to a sudden halt. 'I've just realised something!'

'Wos that?'

'I haven't been away as long as I thought!' Just then the aroma of fish and chips hit their nostrils.

'Good. So we've got time to eat. Come on, this one's on me,' replied Jack as they entered a seafront cafe.

'Two bags of chips, please mate.' Jack got the chips and they sat down at a table outside.

They smothered the large chunky portions in salt, vinegar and tomato sauce, before tucking in. There were so many chips it seemed the more they ate the more grew on the plate.

'So, exactly *where* on the island is this fight gonna take place?' asked Jack, licking his salty fingers.

'I'm not really sure, probably at the camp.' Lance picked up the sauce bottle and squirted out a map of Echoco on the table. 'It might be here - or here,' he said dipping a chip into the sauce.

'NOOO!' screamed Jack, knocking the chip from Lance's hand as he put it to his mouth. Startled Lance jumped back in his chair that toppled backward crashing to the floor. Wide-eyed and shocked he stared up at Jack. 'Don't eat the map, Lance! We might get lost!' For a moment there was silence, and then they both burst into fits of laughter.

After eating their fill they continued along the coastal path adjacent to the cliff.

'Shouldn't we be *climbing* the cliff?'

'No need, It's there!' said Jack, pointing to the grassy landscape that donned the cliff-face, that housed many larger than life fairy-tale figures.

As they crossed the road Lance spied the castle, hidden amongst the trees. 'It's small - but grand!' exclaimed Lance.

'It's a model. Will that do?' inquired Jack as they walked up to it.

'Yes, I must have run straight past it last night. How stupid of me!'

It was amazing. The main castle with its pointed turrets, led down to a moat with a bridge that led to a keeper house. Lance peered in all the little windows. It appeared deserted. He guessed the Kindreds probably wouldn't come out with Jack present.

'Are they in?' asked Jack, humouring him.

'No, they don't seem to be, never mind I can call back later,' he replied cheerfully.

'Well, it's gettin' late. Come on Lance, let's go an' view the cruisers.'

'Cruisers?'

'Yeh know, cars!'

As dusk settled on the town, the streetlights surged to full power and the colourful lights by the arcades danced as they flashed. A steady stream of pristine cars revved their engines as they travelled back and forth along the seafront.

They reached the arcades and leaned on a side rail, from where they admired the shiny cars. Every so often the drivers would sound their horns and wave out of the windows, to which Jack waved back.

'Do you know them Jack?'

'Nope, but it looks cool,' he replied.

'There's lots of girls around,' commented Lance.

'Dun I know it. Their interest is in the drivers, who are more interested in the cars. Don't get me wrong, they wanna impress the totty as well. Wot could be nicer than cruisin' along in a mean machine wiv a beautiful girl by yer side.'

'Playing conkers with the boys?' Jack raised his eyebrows smirking.

'Oh, masks! I nearly forgot. We'd better get 'em now. We'll be meetin' up wiv the gang soon.'

Lance followed him into a shop that sold all sorts of novelties.

'Why are you called the Surfs, Jack?' asked Lance as they browsed.

'Well, when the tide's comin' in we run along the sand in front of the waves and dodge the surf. The first one to get wet 'as to do a dare, which is chosen by whoever is still dry at the end, so then we all race in to get wet. Whad'ya fink?' he asked mysteriously, donning a mask of Count Dracula.

'I think it suits your blue eyes but your teeth seriously need trimming.'

The boys had great fun trying on the various masks. Lance settled for a Werewolf and Jack, sticking with Dracula, bought them both a black cape and some tiny balloons.

'What are they, Jack?'

'Water-bombs, they're for tricks. Yeh look dressed to kill,' laughed Jack, at which Lance playfully growled at him.

Wearing their disguises they headed off towards the theme park to meet up with the Surfs.

CHAPTER TWELVE

New Recruits

Jack and Lance had really bonded. It was around 6.00 p.m. when they arrived at the theme park.

Jack called out to two young boys leaning on the railings in front of the galleon. 'Yo! Dapper, Simon.'

'Are they in the gang?' asked Lance, who thought they looked familiar.

'Yeah, they're brothers. We nicknamed Ritchie, Dapper 'cos of the way 'e dresses. Simon's too young to be in the gang but tags along sometimes. 'E's a cute kid but boy can 'e rabbit.'

Dapper was wearing a blue silky jacket and white jeans that had triangles of paisley material sewn into the flares. Simon was wearing a green puffa jacket and trousers with trainers.

'Wow! Can I have your mask Jack?' called Simon, running over to them.

'In a nutshell? No!'

'Who's the werewolf?' asked Dapper.

'This is Lance. 'E's gonna hang around wiv us tonight.'

'Hi,' said Lance, lifting his mask.

'All right, I'm Dapper, this is Simon.'

'I like your shoes,' commented Lance.

'Me Wallabies? They're my favourites,' replied Dapper, smugly pointing a shoe forward showing off the beads threaded onto the laces.

Simon lifted Lance's cape. 'Does your jacket bite?' he asked inquisitively.

'Oi! Don't be rude,' scolded Jack.

While Simon barraged Lance with questions. Dapper pulled Jack to one side. 'Does Matt know he's here?'

'No, but 'e'll be all right about it. The kid's 'avin' a tough time, 'e's bin hallucinatin' about the little people.'

'You're too soft Jack. He won't be happy.'

''E'll 'ave to live wiv it then. I like Lance and right now 'e's wiv me.'

'Chill Jack, I was just saying.'

Jack walked back over to Lance.

'Where's Jill?' he asked Simon.

'Up the hill, painting her face in the toilets!' chanted Simon.

'I should 'ave guessed and cut it wiv the Jack 'n Jill jokes!' Just as he spoke Jill came clicking over.

Lance, recognising her, recalled where he'd seen the boys. They were the two she had met up with earlier.

'Hi boys. Oh Lance! What a nice surprise. I like your getup, it goes with your jacket.'

'It does?'

'Yeah, you look like a wolf in sheep's clothing,' she laughed. Simon fell about giggling, although Lance didn't quite understand the quip. 'I see you've met my brothers.'

'Your brothers?'

'Yes. I didn't know you knew Jack?' she said adjusting her fringe.

'Well, only just,' he replied.

'Dapper, do us a favour, go down to the toilets 'n' fill these,' said Jack holding out the water balloons.

'Yippee!' cried Simon, grabbing them and running off. Dapper casually strolled along behind him.

'Oh look, Matt's coming!' beamed Jill. Quickly turning away she rummaged in her handbag and taking out a mirror, discretely checked her makeup.

Matt was dressed in black clothes similar to Jack's. He looked apprehensive as Jack walked over to meet him. They had a heated conversation just out of earshot, apart from the odd word that was shouted. Matt, making sharp hand gestures was pointing into Jack's face and glaring over at Lance, who, feeling uneasy pulled his mask back down over his face. Matt put his hands in his pockets, tossing his head of mousy brown hair he turned his back on Jack and began kicking the ground with his trainers.

'Oh, I see! He wasn't expecting you Lance. Don't worry, he can be quite brutal at times but I know there's a soft side to him somewhere. He's just finished working a community service order.'

'What for, Jill?'

'He got in another fight.'

'Another?'

'Well, he does have rather a short fuse. Jack says he's got a chip on his shoulder.'

'I can't see one?'

'Oh, you are funny,' she replied and on noticing Matt looking over, hugged Lance giggling loudly, to which Matt didn't blink an eye.

Matt and Jack walked over to join them.

'Lance, this is Matt. 'E said it's OK for you to 'ang around wiv us tonight.' Matt glared at him adversely.

'Thanks Matt.'

'Matthew to you!' he replied sharply.

'I won't be a minute,' said Jack. 'I'm just gonna hide me cassette deck on the ship till later.' With that he climbed over the railings and ran on board.

Matt leaned in towards Lance. 'You're only 'ere because I owe Jack one. After tonight I don't wanna see yer face again, is – that - clear?' said Matt maliciously, giving him daggers.

Lance nodded but feeling unwelcome and realising he probably wouldn't be getting any help from the gang decided not to hang around.

Jack returned.

'I think it's time I headed off,' said Lance, turning to walk away. Jack put his hand on his shoulder stopping him.

'It's all right, trust me,' he said reassuringly, guessing that Matt had upset him.

'GIVE THEM BACK!' shouted Simon angrily. Podge was holding a water bomb high above his head. Dapper was following behind, chuckling.

Lance immediately recognised Podge.

'Don't tease him Podge, you're twice his age,' called Jill.

'D'ya want it?' asked Podge.

'Yes!' demanded Simon. At which Podge dropped the balloon onto his head. 'ARGH! YOU STINK!' yelled Simon punching him.

'Yer lucky it wasn't a stink bomb,' laughed Podge. Jill joined in, whacking him with her handbag. ''Oo's the big bad wolf then?' he asked, dodging out of their way. 'Wot big teeth you 'ave, Mr Wolf!' Lance lifted his mask. 'YOU! Wot's 'e doin' 'ere? 'E tried to *bite* me this afternoon!'

'Oh p-lease,' huffed Jill.

'Wot's the matter, Podge, scared 'e's got rabies?' smirked Jack.

'RIGHT, THAT'S ENOUGH!' shouted Matt, 'Let's go if we're goin'.'

'Matt? Can we stop off on the way? I've left Simon's outfit at home.'

'Oh, wot?' complained Matt.

'I'll only be a minute,' she whined. 'Besides there's some posh houses nearby we can knock at.'

'Whatever,' he replied moodily.

Eventually, they came to a park where the boys waited for Jill and Simon.

'Jill, nick us some eggs!' called Podge, as they walked off.

'Go lay 'em!' she shouted back. To which Podge began to cluck, imitating a chicken.

After a while Matt became impatient. 'Wot's she doin', makin' it?' at which point they reappeared. Simon was dressed as a monster.

'Phwoar! Wot's that pong?' asked Matt scowling, as Jill walked past him.

'That's her Eau De Toilet!' said Dapper.

'Smell's like it too,' he sniffed.

'Wow, look at you, yeh little monster,' laughed Jack as Simon growled at him.

'Can we *go* now?' said Matt, abruptly.

'Let Simon knock, 'e'll get more treats than us, won't ya my little fiend,' said Podge smugly, as they headed off.

'I haven't forgotten the water bomb yet,' said Simon frowning, knowing that Podge would be after pinching his treats. 'And don't try picking my pockets either or I'll tell Matt!' he added. Podge laughed at him.

'Don't worry, I'll sort him out if he does,' smarted Dapper.

'Yeah? You and whose army,' snapped Podge.

'Oh, he doesn't need an army!' commented Lance. Everyone fell silent. 'He'll just get his comeuppance if he does. You see, if someone does a bad deed of any kind, it will come back on them ten fold, sometimes the same day, sometimes a week, month or even *years* later!' Jack lowered his head as everyone stared at Lance.

'Right, let's make a start at that house over there, shall we,' said Jill, quickly changing the subject.

Strangely, nobody made comment to Lance's outburst, yet the boys all seemed to be deep in thought.

After an hour or so they'd collected quite a few treats. Of course nobody actually asked for a trick so they had a water fight amongst themselves.

'Wot time yeh gotta be in, Podge?' asked Matt.

'When I feel like it!' came the cocky reply.

'Wot *time*, Podge?'

'Ten, at the latest,' he replied glumly.

'That goes for us as well,' said Jill. 'Mum said Simon can stay out a bit longer as it's Halloween.'

'I think 'e should go in now, in case there's trouble,' said Matt, firmly.

'NO! NO! PLEASE JILL, TELL HIM,' shrieked Simon.

'I'll tell you what, you can have *all* my treats if you go home now,' suggested Dapper.

'Not if I get to 'em first!' threatened Podge.

'Shut up, sawdust brains!' blurted Dapper scowling. Simon thought carefully then half-heartedly agreed. 'I'll take him back. I won't be long,' said Dapper, taking Simon by the hand.

''URRY UP, THEY'LL BE CLOSIN' SOON!' yelled Matt, after them.

'Jack, I may have to go soon,' said Lance as they tucked into their treats.

'Just give it a bit longer. I know Matt'll come round. 'E's really pent-up at the moment, probably 'ad a row wiv 'is dad. If there's gonna be a fight, 'e'll be up for it. I pity anyone who rubs 'im up the wrong way at the moment. Anyway, I'll walk yeh back to the island whatever happens.'

'Thanks Jack, but I was planning on flying.'

'And exactly *how* do yeh plan to do that?'

'Orb it.'

'Orbit? Sounds good to me,' laughed Jack.

Dapper soon returned and they hastily made their way back to the theme park.

''Ow much money did we collect Dapper?' inquired Matt, as they reached the gates.

'Enough to get two of us in.'

'Better 'urry then. Jill, you stay 'ere wiv the Werewolf till we get back. Jack, I'll need yer disguises.' Jack took Lance's cape and gave it to Matt. 'Podge, you wear that one. I'll wear Jack's.'

'Do I *'ave* to wear 'is?'

'Leave it out, Podge. When we get near, Dapper you hide under Podge's cape and Jack can get under mine,' instructed Matt.

As Jack pulled his cape over his head his T-shirt came up with it.

'JACK! THERE'S A SPIDER ON YOUR BACK!' screamed Jill.

'Wot? Oh that, it's *just* a birthmark,' he laughed.

'Do we have to wait here?' she complained. 'Don't start Jill, we 'aven't got time for it,' rebuked Matt.

The boys hastily headed off.

'What's happening Jill?' inquired Lance.

'They're sneaking Jack and Dapper in so they can hide inside The Haunted House. When they lock up, Jack will unlock the door from inside. He knows how to deactivate the alarm and needs Dapper to hold the torch.'

'I see, then we hunt for ghosts?'

'Oh, I forgot to mention. *We're* the ghosts. You see there's a gang called The Rocks.'

'Yes, I encountered them earlier.'

'Oh really! Well, Rocky, their leader, told Matt he had an appropriate name and threatened to walk all over him. Matt hates him. He says Rocky thinks he's hard but he's all mouth and trousers. There are six of them who pick on smaller groups.'

'So they're all cowards, not their own person.'

'Oh, I suppose.'

'Believe me Jill, when fate catches up with them, they will be on their own. Comeuppance has a funny way of doing that.'

'You know, I believe there's some truth in what you say.'

'More than you know. There are some things in life that you can never hide from.'

'Well - anyway, Matt's been informed that they're going to break into The Haunted House tonight and we'll be waiting for them, we just make scary noises. They're going to get such a fright!'

Just then Matt and Podge returned laughing hysterically.

'Are they in?' asked Jill.

'Yeah went like clockwork. Come on, we'll wait over by the boatin' lake,' said Matt, sniggering.

'What's so funny Matt?'

'Oh - your brother, 'e nearly gave the game away.'

'How?' Podge began to laugh so hard he was hugging his stomach. 'What?' demanded Jill.

'Oh, it was Podge, 'e'd eaten too many of those liquorice treats,' chortled Matt, with tears streaming down his face.

'Podge, you didn't! Not while he was under the cape?' she gasped. This made Podge hysterical, even Lance started laughing. It was the first time he'd seen Matt happy.

On hearing a loud clunk they silenced and turned to see the whole park fall into darkness.

'We'll give it ten minutes,' said Matt.

They watched as the staff, chatting, left the park and waited till they were out of sight.

'Come on, quick!' said Matt. Taking a small torch from his pocket, he led them over to a side fence that had loose planks, which he held aside while they climbed through. Quietly, they all scurried across to The Haunted House.

'Psst, Jack!' whispered Matt, gently tapping on the door. Jack let them in and then locked it behind them.

'You lot stay 'ere. Quick, follow me Jill,' said Jack, shining a torch ahead of her.

He directed her to the witch's cavern. 'AAARGH!' she screamed, as a large spider caught the top of her head.

'It's not real,' chuckled Jack, as he positioned her behind a cauldron.

'I don't *like* it. Don't leave me in the dark!' she winged.

'Oh all right, but as soon as yeh see us signal wiv the other torch, turn this one off.'

'I will. Thanks Jack.'

'Now shine it back that way for me.'

Lance and Dapper were put in the bat cave and Podge was positioned behind a six foot cut out of a ghost.

'Right!' called Matt. 'Everyone keep quiet. When yeh see the torch flash start wailing.' Then he joined Jack behind a black curtain by the entrance.

'This is gonna be such a laugh!'

'Yeah. Er Matt?' whispered Jack. 'If you thought a friend was in trouble and needed backup, would yeh help?'

'Of course, yeh shouldn't even 'ave to ask me that. Why, are you in trouble?'

'Well, I might be - indirectly.'

'Whad'ya mean - indirectly?' said Matt frowning.

'It's Lance.'

'*Lance!*'

'Sssh! Keep it down.'

'Wot's 'e got to do wiv anythin'?'

''E's been involved in a fight on the island.'

'Well that's 'is problem,' snapped Matt.

'Well it's kinda mine too Yeh see I promised I'd 'elp 'im. The Rocks were picking on 'im earlier 'n I think they're involved.'

'I don't believe I'm 'earing this. You're saying that you're gonna back 'im, so will I back you,' said Matt sharply in a loud whisper.

'Er, yeah.'

'Leave it out Jack, the kid's weird.'

'I admit 'e does come out wiv some strange things.'

'I don't wanna know!' snapped Matt.

There followed an uncomfortable silence.

Presently, Matt huffed and reluctantly said, 'Yeah, all right if it involves The Rocks. I'll be there for *you*, not 'im!'

'Listen! Did yeh 'ear that Matt?'

'What?' listening they heard footsteps outside. Matt quickly turned on the torch, which gave out a dim orange glow. 'Oh no!' he cried shaking and bashing it on his hand. 'The battery's goin'! Quick Jack, yeh torch!'

'Jill's got it!'

They heard voices outside.

'Yes sir, I saw 'em go in!'

'All right lad, run along now, I'll take it from here.'

'Rocky! We've bin set up!' scowled Matt.

A key turned in the lock. Suddenly the door swung open with a bang, kicked by a huge burly security guard who stood in the doorway. He flashed a torch into the house, which the others saw as their signal. The guard caught sight of the light from Jill's torch, which she'd forgotten to turn off. Jill began to cackle and the boys began to moan and groan. Matt and Jack stared at each other horrified.

The gang gradually fell silent, as they hadn't heard any reactions. Then a chain rattled and a snarling growl filled the air.

'Blimey! That was life like, bet that was Matt,' whispered Dapper.

'I've got a feeling that was for real!' replied Lance apprehensively.

'RIGHT, YOU LOT. COME OUT. THE GAME'S UP!' bellowed the guard in an angry gruff tone. His Alsatian dog began to jump up and down barking loudly.

Dapper and Lance slowly emerged from the bat cave and Jill ventured out of the cavern. Podge stepped out from behind the cut out. Fumbling his way towards Dapper he tripped and fell on top of Lance, pinning him to the ground.

The guard dog with saliva dripping from the sides of its mouth lunged towards Podge barking fiercely. The choke chain around its neck snapped tight as the guard pulled the dog back inches from his face. Podge quickly jumped to his feet, leaving Lance squashed on the floor.

The dog unexpectedly pricked up its ears and pulled towards Lance whimpering. 'WHAT'S WRONG WITH YOU, YOU STUPID ANIMAL?' shouted the guard as the dog wagged its tail, then lay down on all fours with its nose pressed against Lance's.

Matt, on hearing the distraction, burst out from behind the curtain shouting, 'EVERYBODY SCRAM!'

They all made a dash for it except for Lance who held the dog's attention. The guard let go of the leash and pursued them.

'Thanks old Chum. I think it's time I found the Kindreds and headed home,' said Lance, fussing the dog who yapped and licked him on the nose. Lance swiftly made his way out.

Podge and Dapper scrambled through the fence and headed for the pier. Jill and Jack ran towards the galleon. Matt scaled a wall, and ran off towards the arcades.

Lance, now confident of finding the Kindreds, made his way to the galleon, hoping Jack had gone to retrieve his cassette player, as he wanted to say goodbye. But there was no sign of him so he scaled the gates and headed off.

Jack and Jill were submerged in the freezing water at the bottom of the galleon. They'd heard Lance's footsteps but thought it was the guard so they stayed silent.

'I think this t-torch has had it,' said Jill, shaking the water out of it.

'Just lob it,' said Jack.

Jill dropped the torch into the water. 'I w-wish I was h-home in my nice warm b-bed,' she said, with her teeth chattering.

'Your mum's gonna hit the roof when she sees the state of you!'

'What happened to your p-parents, Jack?'

'Mine?'

'You know before you went into foster care. Oh s-sorry, that's a bit r-rude of me.'

'No problem Jill. I didn't get on wiv me adopted parents. *Long* story.'

'Adopted? I didn't realise you were adopted!'

'No, neither did I till a couple of years ago. I made some enquiries but it's 'ard getting information out of the authorities. All I discovered woz me mum lived in Cornwall and was called Margaret. Your auntie from Devon was so nice to me I almost wished it was 'er. That's all they knew, well so they said. I don't think they'd 'ave told me that if I 'adn't insisted, still I've put it all behind me now - Jill are you all right?'

Jill's mind began buzzing; knowing her Auntie Margaret lived in Cornwall at the time of the adoption. *Could* Jack be her cousin who still bore his birthmark? She *dare* not make any assumptions on such a delicate subject. 'Yeah but I'm f-f-freezing! Do you think the coast is clear now Jack?'

'Even if it isn't we've gotta get out of this water. Come on!' Shivering, they clambered onto the lower walkway and then made their way up.

Podge and Dapper were waiting on the other side of the gates. 'Quick! Up 'ere. 'E's gone!' called Podge.

'Jack, your cassette player!' Jill reminded him.

'Don't worry I'll get it tomorrow.' Quickly, they climbed over the gate.

'Podge, Where's Matt?' asked Jack.

'I didn't see which way 'e went.'

'Knowin' Matt 'e'll be after Rocky. Wot about Lance?'

'Oo?'

'Leave it out Podge, did yeh see 'im get out or not?'

'No, I didn't Jack, 'onest!' declared Podge.

'He's not lying,' added Dapper.

'Poor kid. 'E's really mixed up. 'Is brother thinks 'e killed their parents. 'E's probably gone to find the little people to 'elp 'im fight the crows! 'E's gotta go to the island tonight.'

'What did you say Jack? - Crows! - What little people?' inquired Jill, her face screwing into a tight frown.

'Kin – somethin'.'

'KINDREDS!' she blurted with her eyes blazing.

'That's it! Oh, you've 'eard of 'em. I thought 'e'd lost the plot. Still they ain't real, are they? Well - anyway, apparently 'e can't get back without 'em, so I promised I'd 'elp 'im.' Jill's mouth slowly fell open and she nearly passed out.

'JILL!' cried Dapper.

'Whoa, I gotcha! We'd better get you 'ome.' said Jack catching hold of her.

'I should have known!' she cried pulling herself together.

'Jill, calm down. Wot's wrong?' asked Jack.

'There's no time to explain. Do you think you can find Lance?' she said quickly.

'I was gonna try anyway.'

'*Find* him Jack. Hurry! Then meet me back here. Dapper, Podge, stay here in case he returns. I'll be two minutes!'

'Jill, wait!' cried Jack. But she was already running like the wind.

There were no more ifs, buts or maybes, this time she knew. But Jack didn't get the chance to hunt for Lance as Matt called him for back up after finding Rocky and his gang.

*

126

Jill burst through the front door of her house. 'Jill? Is that you?' called her mother from the front room.

'Yes Mum,' she replied nervously, trying not to sound breathless.

'Is Ritchie with you?'

'No - I'm just going to meet him.'

'It's a bit late to be going out again, isn't it?'

'I know Mum, but I've got to meet Ritchie. I just came back for a warmer jacket. Won't be long!' Jill was dreading her mother coming out.

'Guess who's here!' called her mother, as Jill stepped onto the stairs. Just then her Auntie Margaret leaned around the corner of the doorway. She was shocked at Jill's appearance. Jill *pleaded* silently with her to stay quiet.

'Auntie Margaret! What a nice surprise,' she said, pulling all sorts of faces at her.

'I'll come upstairs with you,' replied Margaret. Frowning she followed Jill to her room.

'*Jill,* what on *earth's* going on?'

'Sorry Auntie Margaret, can't explain. *Promise* me you won't tell mum,' she blurted, as she frantically emptied a drawer. On finding the photographs of the birthmarks she went to rush past her. Margaret, sensing something was seriously wrong, grabbed hold of her hand.

'What are these?' she demanded, taking the photographs from her. Jill began to panic. Margaret looked her straight in the eyes. 'You *read* the notebook, didn't you!' Jill squeezed her mouth tight. '*Lance,* You've met him haven't you!'

'It's *true* isn't it! The notebook, everything!' Jill cried, snatching them back.

'Yes!' said Margaret with a worried expression.

'Then *cover* for me Auntie Margaret; I've *got* to help him. I *promised* Great Nana!' Margaret's eye's widened. 'I don't even know what I'm doing, but he may need these.'

'But Jill, they're no good without the- Jill?'

'No time!' she blurted, hurrying out.

'Jill, it's too dangerous!' But Jill was already halfway down the stairs. Margaret ran out onto the landing. 'Wait!' she called in a loud whisper. Pausing Jill glanced back. 'Tell Lance, Eyebright is slowly recovering.'

'Eyebright? You mean!'

'Yes, now go! Take care!' Jill rushed out.

'Margaret?' called Pamela, coming out. 'Where's Jill? And what's all this water on the carpet?' Margaret came down the stairs as white as a sheet.

'Do you have any brandy, Pamela?' she asked.

Meanwhile, Lance had returned to the castle. 'They *must* be here!' he muttered in frustration, knocking on all the turrets and calling out for Furse. There was no response and Lance broke down. 'NOTHING! NOTHING!' he cried clawing his hands across the drawbridge in despair.

Walking a little way up the cliff-face, he sat, tucking his knees under his chin and stared out to sea. He was so upset he couldn't think straight.

His attention was drawn to a squirrel that scurried past him with an acorn in its mouth. It paused momentarily, to see if Lance posed a threat. Sensing all was well it hurried over to the castle and proceeded to push the nut through one of the windows. *The Kindreds would be really angry with you if they* had *lived there,* he thought to himself, at which point he felt an itch on the palm of his hand. As he went to scratch it he saw a faint glow, following which a tiny grain of what he thought was sand, suddenly zoomed towards the castle and exploded like a firework, sending the squirrel on its way. 'WHOA!' he shouted, jumping to his feet. 'KINDRED GRAINS!'

He hastened back over to the castle, realising he must have picked one up on the drawbridge. Peering into the gatehouse he spied some minute mining tools tucked away in a far corner. He tugged at the little door till the lock gave way, reached inside and pulled them out, but there were no traces of the grains. Reaching in again he felt a slight cavity in one of the walls. Scratching at it with his nail, a part of the wall fell away revealing a tiny door.

Using one of the tools he managed to prise it open and pulled out a tiny drawstring bag, no bigger than a bee. 'Sorry about the mess, Furse,' he said, then desperately tried to recall what Woodruff had told him about the powerful Kindred grains. *What was it? Think - think! Yes, they track your thoughts and … That was it! Be careful of what dwells in your subconscious!* He wasn't sure what to do with the grains or how they could get him back and was debating what course of action to take when he heard someone frantically calling.

'LANCE! LANCE!'

It was Jack, running towards him in a blind panic.

'Jack! What's wrong?'

'Lance. Come quickly! It's the Rocks!'

'What's happened?' puffed Lance as they ran.

'They tied up the security guard an' broke down the gate at the galleon. They've barricaded Podge 'n Dapper in a cabin. Two of 'em have got 'old of Jill and Matt's gone ballistic! I need yeh 'elp,' he panted.

As they drew near to the galleon they heard raised voices.

'Jack, wait!' said Lance pulling him to a halt. 'I have an idea. Follow me.' They sneaked round to the front of the galleon and quietly began to climb. Lance peered over the top.

The whole Rocks gang was on the deck. Jill was struggling to break free from the two boys. Three others were holding Matt face down. Rocky, wearing his skates was standing by him.

'So! 'Ow does it *feel* to be a *mat!*' jeered Rocky.

'LEAVE HIM ALONE!' screamed Jill.

'You're gonna pay for this!' scowled Matt, who already had a bloody nose.

'Pay? Oh I don't think so. You're one mat that's as cheap as they come. I'm gonna 'ave to wipe me feet on yeh,' he smirked, rolling a skate across his back, to the amusement of his gang.

'Jack?' whispered Lance. 'Can you make your way round the side?' Jack nodded. For some reason he felt Lance knew what he was doing. 'Good, when I confront them get ready, then when I nod, jump over, grab Jill and take cover.'

'*You* confront 'em? Are yeh mad!'

'Trust me.' Jack took a deep breath, nodded and then proceeded to the side of the vessel.

'Now let me see. Wot else do we do wiv mats?' continued Rocky. 'Ah, yes we walk all over 'em and *beat* 'em to remove the dirt!'

'NO!' shrieked Jill, as he stood on Matt's back, digging in his stoppers.

Matt gritted his teeth in anticipation as Rocky stepped off and swung back his skate to kick him, at which point Lance pulled himself up and leapt onto the quarterdeck.

'ROCKY, LOOK!' shouted one of his gang.

'Well, look 'Oo's dropped in, Sir Lancelot!' sneered Rocky. To which his gang burst out laughing.

Matt raised his head to see Lance leaning on the mast. Lance had to lure Rocky away from Matt.

'LANCE! Be careful!' called Jill.

'Oh, 'ow sweet, me 'eart bleeds,' jeered Rocky.

'Sir Lancelot at your service!' mocked Lance taking a bow and spying Jack in position.

'Well pay attention, Lancelot, and you'll see 'ow we clean a mat!'

'Oh, I'm afraid you can't do that, Rocky. You see we're just about to leave!'

'You ain't goin' nowhere!' snarled Rocky, glaring at him. 'Or maybe I'm mistaken? Maybe yeh've found an 'orse to escape on!' he mocked, walking threateningly towards him, angry at his insolence in front of his gang.

'Why how perceptive of you, but first I will do as you suggest. But instead of beating Matt, I'll beat you!'

'You must 'ave a screw loose kid!' Jack was beginning to think so too.

'Really? But it's easy I just remove the dust,' said Lance, removing a few of the grains and nodding at Jack. 'And then the dirt!' he smirked, casually flicking a grain. BANG, the grain exploded.

They all hit the deck with their hands on their heads. 'Wot the-?' before Rocky could say another word, Jack jumped on board, grabbed Jill and pulled her out of harm's way. 'Fireworks? They don't scare me!' scowled Rocky, getting up.

'Can't stop, got to fly!' said Lance as he flicked a further two grains.

'RUN!' shouted one of the gang. They all jumped from the ship except Rocky, who nervously stood his ground.

BOOM – BOOM, the grains exploded, blasting a hole in the deck by his skates. 'AAARGH!' he shouted, stumbling off the galleon and then he ran off.

'Nice one, Lance,' said Jack as he helped Matt up. He then went to let Podge and Dapper out. Jill, almost in a trance like state walked over to Lance.

'I *know* who you are - Lance Pearce, son of Henry and Edwina and brother to Eleanor and Miles. Auntie Margaret said to tell you Eyebright is slowly making progress. I am your Great - Great Niece, Jill, and unless I'm mistaken Jack is your Great - Great Nephew as are Dapper and Simon.' Lance stared at her stupefied.

'Don't push it, Jill,' said Jack. 'It's all right Lance,' he continued, 'Take no notice of 'er. Before the Rocks caught up wiv us she came back wiv some photographs 'n told us a ridiculous story. The cold water must 'ave got to 'er.'

Jill removed the photographs from her bag. 'Here Lance, look! Each birthmark has a dark spot on it. If I'm not mistaken these and the one on Jack's back, map the co-ordinates of a star constellation. When it's above the Pacific Ocean during August, the centre spot, which is Jack's, marks the entry to Echoco Island.'

'August?' queried Lance, still trying to take it all in.

'Yes! Lance, if my calculations are correct it should be August, *your* time not ours, and that's *now*!' Jill stared at him wide-eyed in anticipation.

Realising Jill was telling the truth, Lance quickly pulled himself together. Besides, he had nothing to loose, his friends were in grave danger and every second counted. 'I think I can use the photographs to get back!' he replied anxiously.

''Old up! Wot are yeh saying Jill? We're - cousins!' blurted Jack.

'Yes!'

'Yeah right! Go on then prove it, cos, if your ludicrous, absurd, *laughable* story is true, then I will go wiv Lance *right* now, as I promised 'im and fight for 'im. Cos that would make us *family* which means you, Dapper and me owe it to 'im!'

Jack proceeded to remove his cassette deck from inside a barrel and waited for the reply with an inquisitive expression on his face.

'And, me. I owe 'im one too,' added Matt, going along with Jack.

'Well you ain't leaving me out,' declared Podge.'

'Show me your birthmark, Jack,' she said taking a pen and paper from her bag. Jack huffed but knowing he'd set her the challenge, he had to go along with it and lifted his T-shirt.

Jill copied it onto a piece of paper and placed the photos around it. 'See, Lance, Jack was third born so he'd be in the centre!'

Lance turned to Jack. 'If you come with me you *must* understand that there are *thousands* of crows including Arvensis, who's *huge* and currently indestructible!'

'Lance, yeh don't *seriously* fink I could show me face in Southend again if I ran away from a load of birds, d'yeh?

132

Don't get me wrong. I know some of the two-legged variety that are scarier than a thousand crows. If I said no, I'd never live it down.'

'What about you Matthew?'

'Er - that's Matt to you Lance. Well I need to exert some anger, so bring 'em on!'

Just as Jack and Matt exchanged a ridiculing glance, Podge shouted out; 'MATT, THEY'RE COMING BACK AND THEY'VE BROUGHT REINFORCEMENTS!' Rocky was heading a huge gang, running down past the arcades.

'Well, ya better do yeh stuff Lance, cos if it don't work we're done for anyway!' said Jack.

'*Hurry* Lance, what do you need?' asked Jill anxiously.

'Transport - the galleon won't withstand the hurricane, we'll all be killed … Wait! I have it! Everyone follow me.' Taking the photos and sketch from Jill, he ran into the park. 'I don't even know if this will work Jill.'

'Now 'e tells us! At least we're running,' said Jack.

'Did he say – 'urricane?' panted Podge. Dapper just looked at him sideways.

Lance ran to The Big Wheel. 'QUICKLY, GET ON!' he yelled.

'It won't take 'em two minutes to find us 'ere,' said Matt. Jill got into a cradle with Lance, Jack with Matt and Podge with Dapper.

'THERE! THEY'RE OVER THERE!' bellowed Rocky, leading the gang towards them.

Lance took out some of the grains, thought positively and threw them to the base of the wheel. 'HOLD TIGHT!' he hollered.

There was a blinding flash of golden light in a haze of smoke, followed by a loud SNAP as The Big Wheel broke free from its holding. Hovering in the air it slowly began to spin. The gang below dived for cover and were staring mortified. As the wheel gathered momentum Lance blanked everything out around him, concentrating his thoughts on the co-ordinates.

'BLIMEY! It was all *true*. The crows, the little people!' cried Jack stupefied.

'OH MATE, TELL ME THIS AIN'T 'APPENING!' shouted Podge.

'AWESOME!' yelled Dapper.

Matt, gob smacked, looked down to where the seafront lights now resembled a starlit sky as spinning, they rose higher and higher. 'Wot Ocean did Jill say we're 'eaded for Jack?' he slurred.

'She said somethin' about the Pacific,' he mumbled, still in shock.

'I think we're about to get the ride of our lives!' said Matt turning to face him. 'That's where 'urricane Dylan is! I read about it on me fish 'n chip paper.'

'Oh,' replied Jack vacantly.

Lance dropped a few more grains into the spinning wheel, squeezed his eyes tightly shut then, BA-BOOOOM, the Big Wheel circling upright propelled out to sea.

CHAPTER THIRTEEN

A Date is Set

Lance had only been away for one night of Echoco time. During his absence, Arvensis had sent out flock after flock that had constantly and callously attacked the camp till the early morning hours, wearing down their prey.

The Three Great Whites had done everything in their power to protect the boys who had sustained painful pecks and were all exhausted. Cumulus warned of the crows' approach and hindered them as much as he could. Cracked Ice, still ailing from his injury, fought side by side with Blizzard. This strong, proud animal tried to disguise the weakness and pain that was consuming his whole being.

Morning broke to a dark and murky sky. The attacks had stopped due to a threatening storm enabling them all to get some sleep, apart from Teasel, who was keeping watch from a platform, high up in a tree above the camp.

Teasel was becoming increasingly anxious as the storm approached. The lightning was wilder than he'd ever seen. Fierce winds were rapidly gaining strength and Cumulus was blown from sight.

Meanwhile, The Big Wheel with its dizzy occupants was spinning above the Pacific Ocean and fast approaching hurricane Dylan. Lance, concerned that the bulbous black clouds would obscure the constellation, hoped that his concentrated thought had been sufficient.

'Look! Lance, Look! Up there!' cried Jill, pointing.

He stared up at the night sky through shifting clouds and just managed to make out the five points. 'We're nearly there, Jill! Now all we need is a *hurricane* ... I wonder if the grains would start one?' he quizzed, fumbling for the tiny pouch.

'Er, Lance. I don't think you're gonna need the grains,' said Jill sheepishly, looking ahead.

Jack nudged Matt. 'How big did yeh say hurricane Dylan was gonna be?'

'I didn't!' he replied. They stared ahead with their eyes bulging from their sockets. Podge and Dapper began frantically shouting as panic set in.

It came from nowhere. Spiteful hailstones bombarded them. They were deafened by the wrath of a raging storm as the waves that were far below suddenly swelled up to meet them. The Big Wheel began to shunt as it battled with the fierce winds.

Straight-ahead, lit by vicious bolts of lightning appeared a colossal swirling funnel. Lance was worried, as he'd never seen one *this* big before. The winds became so savage he had to grab hold of Jill as she almost got sucked out underneath the bar. It was so dark they could neither see nor hear each other as they clung on for grim life.

The wheel hit the wall of the hurricane and was flipped onto its side. Spinning at tremendous speed, the force of gravity pinned them back into their cradles. Their faces contorting with the pressure as simultaneously they all screamed, 'AAAAARRGGHHHHHH!'

Back on Echoco the increasing winds caused the platform to sway dangerously. Teasel decided it would be wise to climb down. As he descended he could hear Blizzard howling at the base of the tree. 'On my way!' he called. Blizzard became agitated, growling and spinning in circles. 'What is it boy?' he asked as he twitched and dropped the last few feet.

Whining, Blizzard pushed his nose into Teasel's leg. 'I'm pleased to see you too,' he smiled, but as he bent to stroke him, Blizzard veered away and began to jump up at the trunk barking excitedly. 'No boy, you can't climb up there!' With that he bit into Teasel's clothing and pulled him towards the tree, growling. 'Oh I see. You want me to go back up!' A little confused, Teasel began to climb to the delight of Blizzard, who barked his approval.

Cautiously pulling himself onto the platform he began to look about. 'Nope, no sign of anything?' Hanging on tightly, he continued to survey the area. 'Nothing,' he muttered. His nose began to run. Sniffing he wiped it with his arm, and then froze, with his arm suspended under his nose. Frowning, he slowly raised his head. 'Wait a minute!' As the lightning flashed he caught sight of a tiny black dot in the distance.

As it drew near he spied the giant mechanical wheel, which had slowed its pace, spinning in the direction of the lake. 'WHOA! What's that?' He looked down at Blizzard then back to the wheel. 'Lance? No it couldn't be - could it?' Blizzard barked loudly. 'LANCE!' he yelled, almost falling off the platform, and then shimmied down as fast as he could.

This strange daunting phenomenon had not gone unnoticed by Arvensis who was observing from the galleon with Miles.

'Well, well. It would appear that Lance has been away on a little trip. I thought it strange there had been no sightings of him.'

'Let me take him out now before he gets back to the camp!' cried Miles.

'No, stop, not so fast, he's obviously been to get help. We'll wait awhile till we know what we're up against.' With that Arvensis summoned some of his finest crows and sent them off to investigate.

*

Following their terrifying ordeal, the children were shaken, but they were all safe.

'We were so lucky to get through before the hurricane changed course!' remarked Lance.

'Oh, how beautiful! It's just like a Christmas card,' exclaimed Jill as they spun over the forest.

'Did you see 'em?' blurted Podge, nudging Dapper.

'See what?'

'Birds, thousands of birds!'

'No!' he replied with his eyes squeezed tightly shut.

'LANCE 'OW YOU GONNA LAND THIS FING?' shouted Jack.

'I'M WORKING ON IT,' he yelled back.

As they spun over the frozen lake, Lance accidentally dropped a grain. 'Oops!' he remarked. The grain hit the ice. CRACK. A network of jagged lines creaked across the lake, followed by a rumble. Suddenly a huge mushroom of water surged up stopping the wheel in its tracks. Retracting, it cushioned the wheels descent as it plunged into the freezing lake.

The children quickly released the bars and frantically swam to the embankment, which was luckily close by. Shivering and shaking they stared at The Big Wheel which slowly sunk to the depths.

Arvensis's spies, who'd been observing from the nearby trees, flew swiftly back to report their findings.

On seeing them leave Arvensis's cabin, Miles hurried in. 'Well Arvensis, what news?'

'Laughable! It would appear he has rallied the help of a handful of children and judging by his mode of transport he couldn't have found the Kindreds.'

'Do we attack now?'

'Have I taught you nothing, Miles?'

'I'm sorry, it's just that my blood boils at just the thought of Lance!'

'I understand and rightly so. But you must learn patience and wisdom. Besides - we are ready to add the finishing touches. It makes the final kill that much more enjoyable,' he said gloating.

'What did you have in mind?'

'Torment and tease. We shall set a date for their doom and let them sweat it out. Now come, I need you to write a note.'

Meanwhile, Teasel, his fear overridden with excitement, had woken Cracked Ice to keep watch as he and Blizzard raced towards the lake.

The gang anxiously jumped to their feet, as Blizzard suddenly appeared bounding towards them.

'WHOA, BIG DOG!' cried Podge.

'Blizzard!' called Lance. 'It's all right, he won't hurt you,' he reassured them as Blizzard jumped up and licked Lance's face.

'That is one *stunning* wolf!' commented Matt.

'Lance! Yahooooo!' yelled Teasel, as he hurriedly approached. 'Thank goodness you're safe! We were beginning to worry. Have they come to help?'

'Yes, Teasel. I'll tell you all about it back at camp. How is everyone?' he asked anxiously. Blizzard whimpered. 'Cracked Ice?' he queried apprehensively.

'He's very weak. He fought so bravely and hardly rested. He'll probably pick up now you're back. We haven't lost anyone yet. Hi, I'm Teasel,' he said, twitching nervously.

'Hello Teasel, I'm Jill. My, what lovely hair you have.'

'I have?' he said blushing.

'Oh, give me a bucket!' remarked Podge.

'Actually Podge, for your information I wasn't flirting, I was trying to take his mind off his twitch!' she whispered sharply in his ear.

Lance introduced the rest of the Surfs. 'We'd better get back and dry off!' he said, leading the way.

They were unusually quiet as they made their way through the forest, still numb from their epic journey, especially Jack.

When they reached the camp, Dapper, so intrigued, ran in ahead of them. 'WOW! What a wicked Den,' he called out.

'GRAAAH!' snarled Cracked Ice, threatened by his intrusion.

'AARGH!' screamed Dapper.

'NO CRACKED ICE. IT'S OK! He's a friend!' called Lance, running in to shield him. 'Hello boy,' he said, kneeling down and stroking him. Cracked Ice looked up at him contentedly through tired eyes. Lance was a little shocked to see his once pristine coat, bedraggled and spotted with blood.

Once everyone had been introduced they all sat together around the campfire and Lance told the boys of his exploits.

*

For the next few days the Surfs explored their new surroundings, during which time they bonded with their new friends.

One night they sat discussing Arvensis and how strangely quiet it had been. Jill revealed her findings in the notebook, after which Lance informed the Surfs of the events that had recently occurred on Echoco and how he wished he had a sack full of Kindred grains.

'Can we see the grains?' asked Teasel.

'Yes,' replied Lance, carefully removing one.

Unexpectedly the grain began to glow. 'OUCH!' Lance cried, dropping it. 'Look out!' he yelled grabbing back hold of it. 'UCH, EECH, OUCH!' he cried, tossing the hot grain up and down. Swiftly he ran out and threw it into the forest. 'GET DOWN!' he yelled as he dived back in. BOOOOM.

The explosion caused a tree to fall on the camp, loosening the mud in the roof that showered their heads.

'What happened?' spluttered Teasel, as they got to their feet.

'I - I don't understand!' frowned Lance. 'It must have been my subconscious, when I was talking about Arvensis.'

'But Lance wot if you 'adn't run out in time?' queried Matt.

'I know. I have to learn how to use them and fast!'

'Dangerous little mites,' commented Jack.

'More like dynamites!' smirked Matt.

Blizzard began to sniff towards the entrance, snarling. 'What is it boy?' asked Teasel.

'Stay here, I'll take a look, I heard a thud after the explosion,' remarked Lance. Still a little shaken and confused he went out to investigate with Blizzard following close behind.

He returned clutching a scrunched up piece of paper.

'What's that?' asked Teasel.

'I found it wrapped around a rock.'

'What does it say?'

Lance straightened out the note and read out loud. *Today is the first of five days. Enjoy every minute of them, for on the fifth day you will all be annihilated!* Lance looked up. 'It's been scribed in - blood!'

Everyone remained silent for a few moments.

'Does this mean - we could - die!' gasped Podge.

'Afraid so!' replied Lance.

Jill grabbed hold of Dapper's hand. All of a sudden everyone began cringing and moaning, falling over each other, in a race to get outside.

'PHWOAR! PODGE!' barked Dapper.

'It wasn't me! Who smelt it, dealt it!'

'YOU'RE DISGUSTING!' yelled Jill, covering her nose.

'That's rank!' blurted Jack, running out with his T-shirt pulled over his face.

Cracked Ice and Blizzard hastily ran around marking the camp with their scent.

They all lay on the ground outside, gasping for air.

'Is he a secret weapon, Lance?' asked Teasel.

'Not quite, but he could come in handy!' Everyone burst out laughing.

The snow clung to their warm clothes as they lay, staring up at the sky where the sun began to break through the remaining storm clouds.

'What's that noise?' queried Dapper. Suddenly there was a deafening 'CRAAH, CRAAH.' The sky above them blackened as a mass of crows flew over above the trees. 'They're enormous!' cried Dapper.

'Don't worry, they're just taunting us,' Lance reassured them as they disappeared from sight.

'It could 'ave bin worse,' uttered Podge. 'They could 'ave pooped on our 'eads!' Chuckling, they all got to their feet and went back inside the camp.

Lance stayed outside on his own for a moment, where Cracked Ice joined him.

'We haven't got long to come up with a good plan,' said Lance sighing, as he stroked him on the head.

Knowing their chances of survival were slim, he decided to take the Surfs to meet with Myosurus and seek her advice. Cracked Ice, pre-empting his intentions, sat up on his haunches, pleading. 'I know my friend, I wish you could come too, but it's a long walk and you need to rest. Besides, who else could I trust to guard the camp?' Cracked Ice lowered his proud head, and then playfully leapt up knocking Lance down and pinning him to the ground. 'It won't wash with me.'

Blizzard bounded over and tussled with Lance. 'That goes for you too!' he laughed, pulling himself up. 'I don't trust Arvensis. I need you both here.' They brushed against him and followed him back inside.

'Teasel, I'm taking the Surfs to Crowfoot territory. While we're gone I need the boys to muster food supplies and sharpen as many branches as they can. The snow looks set to thaw. Tomorrow, take Blizzard and go over to the green wall. We need to monitor the thaw so the crows can't get to the Orbs.'

'Consider it done. Here's your cutlass,'

'Thanks Teasel. Blizzard, if there's any sign of trouble you know where to find me. We'll be back as soon as we can.'

Bidding the boys farewell, Lance and the Surfs set off.

*

It was late in the afternoon when they passed the lake. Lance wanted to get across the canyon before nightfall but knew it would probably be unlikely. A pack of wolves had picked up their scent and were following at a distance.

'Will they attack us at night Lance?' asked Jill, who'd been feeling uneasy since first spying them.

'No, don't worry, they can probably smell Blizzard's scent.'

They continued into a sparse wooded area when a freezing fog began to sweep in. Suddenly Jill tripped, twisting her ankle as she fell. 'Ouch!' she cried. While Lance inspected her ankle, Matt kicked at the snow to see what had tripped her.

'Ere, Jack, look at this!'

'Whoa! No way!' he exclaimed, as Matt pulled his cassette deck out of the snow. 'It was behind me in the cradle. It flipped out when the water 'it us!' he declared. They turned it on, but it wasn't working. Jack was about to launch it into the trees.

'Wait! The batteries might just be damp. 'Ang on to it for now,' advised Matt.

Just then Podge and Dapper began arguing. 'Oi! You two, leave it out!' rebuked Matt.

'It's his fault,' shouted Dapper. 'I'm freezing and sawdust brains just shoved a load of snow down my back!'

'That does it!' snarled Podge, lashing out.

Matt caught his fist mid-air and pulled him to his knees.

'I'm sick of people callin' me that!' yelled Podge.

'Now chill! That goes for *both* of yeh. Don't you fink we've got *enough* to worry about!' shouted Matt, sharply letting go of him.

143

''Ow's she doin'?' asked Jack.

'She's sprained it quite badly, it'll slow us down.'

'The wolves will get me now, won't they!'

'Stop whinin' Jill,' said Matt frowning.

'*You* could carry me Matt,' she suggested coyly.

'You're 'aving a laugh ain't cha!' he huffed.

'We're running out of daylight. We'd best set up camp for the night,' suggested Lance.

'But we'll freeze!' declared Podge.

Just as he spoke they were engulfed by dense fog. 'Where'd that come from?' queried Dapper as they fumbled around bumping into each other.

Lance began to smirk. 'Stand still everyone,' he instructed. 'Now walk towards my voice ... Right all hold hands.'

'Do we 'ave too?' winged Podge as Dapper took his hand.

'Matt, help me lift Jill,' instructed Lance. Jill smirked as they cradled her in their arms. 'Now hold tight!'

'What's 'appening Lance?'

'Well Jack, you're about to get a ride on a cloud.'

'A wot?'

Before they knew what was happening, their feet lifted and they rose in the air.

'This ain't natural!' squealed Podge.

Jill laughed hysterically.

'We're flying!' exclaimed Dapper.

'Wicked!' blurted Matt.

Cumulus bounded across the canyon. 'Brace yourselves, we're coming in to land!' called Lance as Cumulus thundered downwards and then gently settled them on top of the mount. 'Thank you my great fluffy white, I was beginning to think you'd evaporated,' chuckled Lance. Cumulus playfully kicked him and then disappeared into the fog.

'It - It's!'

'That's right Podge. It's a buffalo. Come on everybody. Myosurus will have a potion for your ankle Jill.' With that he led them down the hill. Jill was so enjoying being carried by Matt, she wasn't sure that she wanted a potion.

'Welcome!' called Calyx, running to greet them.

Lance introduced his friends. 'Myosurus?' he inquired.

'She's in her teepee Lance. She hasn't been very well, but her mind is strong. You'd best go in alone. I'll find your friends somewhere to sleep for the night. My mother can treat the lame one. You can share with me.'

'Thank you Calyx.'

While the Surfs followed Calyx, Lance made his way to Myosurus's abode. Lingua who was just coming out bowed his head; Lance nodded back and then entered.

Myosurus was huddled in a corner, wrapped in a blanket. Her complexion was grey and she'd lost weight since he last saw her.

'Welcome my little brave.'

'I'll come back tomorrow if you'd prefer.'

'No, no, I'm glad you are here.'

'I brought some friends with me. Some of them are my *family*. I hope you don't mind?'

'Of course not.'

'Calyx is taking care of them.'

'He is such a good papoose. He keeps my spirits high. I don't know what I should do without him.'

'The girl, Jill, has a sprain. His mother is attending her.'

'Ficaria! Yes, she has powerful medicine, but the winds took her voice after Hellebore's death and she has not spoken a word since. Now, tell me, what news?' she asked eagerly.

'It doesn't look good Myosurus,' he said, lowering his head.

They powwowed till the early morning hours.

'When the sun rises I shall consult with the Elders. Do not lose hope, Lance. Now you must go and rest.' He lifted the flap to leave. 'I shall look forward to meeting Jack and your friends in the morning, Lance.'

'OK … How did you know one of them was called Jack?'

'Let's just say a big bird told me.' A little confused he smiled and left. Myosurus contentedly closed her eyes and fell asleep.

CHAPTER FOURTEEN

Time to Powwow

Day two dawned. Lance woke to the sound of Jack's cassette player blasting throughout the camp. 'Myosurus! What is he *thinking* of? … JACK! JACK!' he yelled, running out, but was stopped in his tracks.

'Lance! Over 'ere. We got it workin'!' called Jack. He and Calyx, both sharing a passion for music, had hit it off immediately. Jack was showing off his dancing skills as Calyx drummed. Myosurus was dancing alongside Dapper, Podge and the braves, while Matt and Jill looked on.

When the music stopped a rapturous applause erupted. Lance ran over to Myosurus. 'Myosurus! You really shouldn't be-'

'Oh, but I really should!' she smiled, interrupting him. 'Strange music but it does mix well with the tom-toms, don't you think?' Lance noticed her cheeks had acquired a rosy glow. 'I've become acquainted with your friends Lance. Come; let them have their fun. I want you to sit in council. There is much to discuss,' she said, leading the way.

Later that afternoon, Matt found Jill sitting alone. 'So, 'ow's yer ankle doin'?'

'Oh Matt, I didn't know you cared. Well, apart from being green from the potion, it actually feels much better thanks.'

'Good.'

'Matt, I'm worried,' she said in an undertone.

'Wot about?'

'I'm scared of what could happen, aren't you?'

'It might sound crazy but no. It's like I'm livin' a dream in which everythin' is so far fetched 'n unbelievable it can't possibly be real. So I feel as though nothin' can 'urt us!'

'Basically you're living reality in a fantasy.'

'Yeah, I guess.'

'I suppose that's one way of dealing with it.'

Matt realised it was first time he'd actually conversed with Jill. Just then Dapper came running towards them in a panic. 'Matt, come quick, it's Podge!'

'Wos up?'

'It's the braves, they're gonna *scalp* him!' he declared.

They quickly followed Dapper to where Podge was being led by one of a group of braves with his wrists bound. 'Matt 'elp! I ain't done nothin'!' squealed Podge.

'Alright, keep yer 'air on!'

'That's not even funny,' commented Jill.

'OI MATE, whad'ya think yer doin'? Let 'im go!' demanded Matt, stepping in their path. The brave pushed Matt to one side and continued to drag Podge along. Matt saw red and leapt onto his back, following which a fight broke out.

'STOP! STOP!' yelled Calyx, running over with Jack. Together they fought to pull them apart.

'What's going on?' asked Jack.

'They're gonna scalp him!' declared Jill.

'Don't be silly? But you're lucky Lingua is out hunting. He would *not* have stood for this behaviour,' said Calyx, who then spoke with the brave while Jack calmed Matt.

'It would appear your friend *stole* something from one of them. It will be dealt with by Myosurus,' stated Calyx.

'Sawdust brains!' blurted Dapper. Podge dived at him but was pulled back.

'You too must join him, Matt. It is our way,' cited Calyx.

'Goin'! But don't even fink about puttin' a rope near me!' he threatened.

'Well that's put the dampers on everything,' sighed Jill.

'Only if yeh let it. Calyx and me 'ave bin workin' on a wicked song. Come and listen,' suggested Jack.

'What about Podge and Matt?'

'They will be reprimanded, that's all,' Calyx reassured her.

'OK. Coming Dapper?' she called, as they walked off.

Lance and the Elders were coming out of the meeting. 'Matt, what's happened?' Biting his lip and a little red faced Matt walked past Lance.

A brave went in ahead of them and spoke with Myosurus, after which two others escorted Podge in.

'Podge, It has been brought to my attention that you had *taken a hunting knife* from one of my braves!' Podge stared at the ground defiantly. 'Well Podge? You know that it is not only a *dangerous* implement but bears *sharp* retribution.' Still he remained silent. 'By simply *doing* the deed you have condemned yourself. It is in the hands of fate now. Maybe - if you change your ways the spirits will look kindly on you.'

Podge slowly raised his head. 'I'm sorry Myosurus,' he said, sheepishly.

'I *accept* your apology, but as I said, you have to *really mean it* and *adjust* your ways.' She ushered the braves to untie him and leave. 'Tell me, is Podge your *real* name?'

'No it's Roger.'

'I see, and who named you Podge?'

'I did, before anyone else did.'

'So why do you steal, Roger?'

'Cos everyone calls me fick or sawdust brains. Then I found I was good at picking pockets. I've only bin caught twice!'

'It seems you are missing your *true* vocation in life!' He looked at her, bewildered. 'If you have slight of eye and speed of hand, amongst other things you would surely make a *marvellous* magician.'

He pondered for a moment. 'Do yeh really fink so?'

'Oh, I know so! Just think how people would applaud your cleverness.' His face lit up. 'Go now - Oh and Roger, remember this. If someone says your heads of wood, with sawdust in great heights, thank them for the compliment. Inform them that they're right. Then, when they ask with great despair, explain please if you could. Say, books hold knowledge a million fold and paper's – made - from wood!'

'Wow! fanks Myosurus.'

'That's OK Roger,' she smiled, ushering him out.

Next it was Matt's turn. Lingua had returned and escorted him in.

'Matt.'

'Myosurus.' Standing with his hands in his pockets he stared arrogantly around the teepee.

'What are we to do with that temper of yours? It seems you leap before you look.'

'Myosurus, I 'ave the utmost respect for you, but yeh don't even know or understand me!'

'Then let me try.'

'It won't wash; you're wastin' yer breath. I've bin lectured 'undreds of times.'

'Then you have closed ears and deep-rooted problems.' Matt screwed his lips into a sideways pout and blew down his nose. 'Would I be correct in assuming that every time you lash out, you see another image before you?' Matt half nodded. 'Tell me about your parents?' At this, Matt turned to walk away but Lingua blocked him with his arm. 'You know when children leave the nest they are not always ready to fly,' she continued.

'All right!' he huffed, turning back. 'Me mum ran off when I was a baby and me dad's a drunk! He finks 'e's so cool but everyone just humours 'im. Then 'e turns verbally nasty wiv me.'

'I *see* and words can sometimes hurt *more* than physical pain. It's been hard for you. Some children want to grow up too quickly. They miss out on the wonders of childhood. But you, Matt, had no choice! You see your mother's unknown face and your father's weakness in the face of your enemies. Would I be correct?'

After a pause Matt replied. 'Yeah, I guess.'

'Then don't let yourself become bitter and twisted. You have no respect because you've had no discipline or guidance.'

'Well it's a bit late now!'

'It's never too late Matt. You must first learn to discipline and respect yourself. You chose to join Lance and fight. But whom will you fight? Your father, mother or yourself? Or *maybe* you will fight for your friends … Think on it. Now be off with you.'

Matt felt as though she'd seen straight through him.

Meanwhile, Jack and Calyx were sitting by the tom-toms, discussing Podge. 'So why does he do it Jack?'

'Look, don't get me wrong. Podge is a mate. But I disagree wiv 'is way of thievin'; it's a bit lowlife. Me, I'm different. I only rob companies!' Calyx looked at him alarmed. 'Wot's wrong?' asked Jack.

'You! You think what you do is any different?'

'Er -Yeah!'

'And I thought you were clever!'

'Well I am! Unless I get caught, then I get locked up and pay me dues!'

'But all the things you do now set a precedence for your future. Why don't you pursue your musical talents?'

'You're startin' to sound like my foster parents! It's not bin easy for me.'

'Whatever your upbringing, Jack, you've got a brain in your head, how you use it is down to you. Grandmother says, don't live with excuses or you'll go through life blinkered. Aren't you scared of what lies ahead?'

'No! I'm not scared of anythin'. Teachers, police. You name it!' Calyx got up and turned to walk away.

'Hey! Where yeh goin'?'

'I'm not sure who you are, Jack.'

'So now yeh don't like me?'

'It's not that. I feel sorry for you.'

'Oh, spare me *please*. I suppose this is that comeuppance thing Lance goes on about! Well wot about the good people that 'ave rotten luck?'

'That's different, that's life. You affect your own destiny by the path you tread. But be scared Jack, be *very* scared, because the shadows that haunt you, will be your own!'

Jack stood up and pushing past him, stormed off.

A feast had been laid on for the guests, who were seated and anxious to tuck in. 'Has anyone seen Jack?' inquired Lance.

'He went for a walk,' said Calyx in an undertone.

Myosurus looked at him inquisitively. 'Is he alright?'

'I think so - I'll - go and look for him, Grandmother.'

Hop flew about ahead of Calyx and quickly locating Jack's whereabouts, landed on a tree nearby and tapped at the bark till Calyx arrived.

Jack was sitting on a log, deep in thought.

'Jack?' He didn't reply.

'Look I'm sorry if I upset you. If I didn't care I wouldn't have said anything.'

'Don't apologise, Calyx,' said Jack, turning to face him. 'Everythin' yeh said made sense. I guess I've never 'ad to face myself before. Then it dawned on me that I might *die* soon. I suddenly realised that yeh don't 'ave to be old for that to 'appen. You made me fink about my life. If I come through this, I'm gonna make somethin' of it!'

'I'm glad to hear it,' said Calyx smiling. 'Hey Jack, let's give them some entertainment. Let's perform our song!'

'Can we eat first, I'm starvin'!'

'Of course!'

They both hurried back.

'Lance? Can we 'ave some of that stuff they're drinkin'?' asked Podge. Lance looked to Myosurus.

'Well, under the circumstances, I suppose *a little* wouldn't hurt.' Podge helped himself, taking a big gulp he coughed and spluttered to everyone's amusement.

The brave that Matt had fought with brought a ladle and offered some to him. 'I'll oblige if you'll forgive me for attackin' yeh.' The brave smiled, but whilst filling Matt's cup, he became distracted and it overflowed. 'Hey!' shouted Matt, jumping to his feet with his fist poised. The brave anticipating a punch, leaned back. Matt hesitated, 'Just kiddin',' he jested. The brave nodded. Matt sat back down and glanced at Myosurus.

'How does it feel Matt?'

'Good, Myosurus. A little wet, but good!'

Podge suddenly belched, loudly.

'Oi! Pig breath!' shouted Dapper.

'Good Boy. Well done!' applauded Myosurus, causing a silence. 'Now remember children, when you were babies you were bounced on knees and patted over shoulders for hours on end, then congratulated when the great wind broke! So why do you think, Dapper, when you've been trained this way, it is classed as disgusting when you are older?'

'I - Well - I?' Dapper was lost for words. Podge grinned at him smugly.

'However, *Roger*,' she continued. 'You are now older and in control, therefore a polite excuse me would not go amiss.' Podge lowered his head sheepishly.

There followed a drum roll to which Myosurus stood up. 'Great tribe of the Crowfoot, today the Elders and I have sat in council with Lance, to discuss the issue of Arvensis and his threatening onslaught. If Arvensis is the victor it will not be long before we become his prey and our territory an extension of his own. The blood of your fathers' fathers, still runs through your veins. Should the situation arise, your instincts would bring the war paint to your faces. It is against our spiritual laws to fight the pending battle, but it is *not* written that we cannot offer our support. Therefore we have come to this decision; tomorrow all skilled hunters will join Lingua to help train these children to fight. Women braves, you will prepare medicines and food. Calyx, take what help you need and carve as many weapons as possible. Once these tasks are fulfilled all able-bodied braves shall return with Lance and his friends to construct a fort in the clearing by the lake. So enjoy this evening and keep a clear head, for our guests, who are truly *brave* warriors will need *all* your strength and wisdom. Now I believe we have some entertainment.' She clapped her hands to which Hop began to tap the drums.

Jack and Calyx walked into a clearing near the campfire. Jack stepped forward and addressed them. 'This song was inspired by a flight on a cloud and is called Cloud Nine.' Calyx stood behind a row of tom-toms and played as Jack rapped to the beat.

'Where am I, the people say, on cloud nine and far away.

Always on the move, I've got a dream to prove.

People's business I ignore, few but good friends grace my door.

All around they say 'e's on cloud nine and far away.

Great to be up there and free, far from life's reality.

Hurts to take life in, cloud nine is where I've bin.

Careful not to turn my back, on life's cruel and rear attack.

Mock me down then say, Oh not again 'e's gone astray!'

(Calyx somersaulted forward and together they rapped
the chorus.)

'That's where we would rather be, far
away from sanity.
That's where all our dreams come true, if
we really want them to.
Cloud nine you're so light and free, all
our visions you can see.
Come wrap around our shoulders bare,
let's disappear amidst the air, cloud nine.'

(Jack began to dance as Calyx rapped the next verse.)

'Silver linings, no mistake, on them you
can roller skate.
Cosmic sparks do fly, shooting stars into
the sky.
Turbulence up here is fun, as the clouds
go soaring on.
All kinds of shapes evolve; a face can
change from smiles to scolds.
Right between the grey clouds shone,
rays of gold vermilion.
Unto no man's eyes, a colour artists all
despise.
When the cloud begins to break, into
mystery snowy flakes,
Then I head for home, tomorrow I will
roam.'

(Together they repeated the chorus, finished with the splits
and received a standing ovation.)

It was the early morning hours of day three. Jill came out of her teepee stretching and yawning. Upon spying Matt, she quickly ran back inside to apply her make-up.

Lance was conversing with Myosurus. 'Then it is decided. Jill will stay here!'

'Thank you, Myosurus. What if?'

'If the worst happens, she will be a welcome tribe member.'

'I'd better go and speak with her.'

Lance entered Jill's teepee. Shortly after which she began yelling. 'NO! *NO WAY* LANCE. I'M COMING WITH YOU AND THAT'S FINAL!'

'But Jill, it's going to be *far* too dangerous!'

'I don't care!'

Dapper went in to find out what all the fuss was about. 'What's going on?'

'Try and talk some sense into your sister, will you. I can't be doing with tears and tantrums right now!' he said angrily, storming out.

The camp soon became a hive of activity, as preparations got under way. Even the young papooses helped by binding the spears Calyx carved into little bundles, pausing every now and then to playfully fight as warriors.

Lingua took the boys into a clearing where all manner of targets had been set up. Their weapons consisted of spears, catapults, bows and arrows.

Hop reluctantly obliged to help train the boys. Posing as the enemy, he would fly overhead, displaying his prominent white spots as targets. As the boys' aim improved, the braves resorted to catapulting wooden discs into the air. (Needless to say, Hop was more than relieved).

Jack and Matt were good. Dapper was fair, but Podge was a total natural, shocking everyone with his precision. With a little coaching, it wasn't long before they all began to excel.

'Just a word of warning boys.'

'Wot's that, Lance?' asked Jack.

'Don't stand in front of Teasel when he's armed!' They all chuckled.

'So, did you manage to knock some sense into Jill?' asked Lance as Dapper fired an arrow.

'No joy, sorry Lance. Her mind's made up!'

'I thought you were going to say that.' Jill was standing nearby with Myosurus. 'JILL!' he shouted, beckoning her over. She slowly approached.

'Yes?' she asked, with attitude.

'You know, sometimes an observer can learn more. I'll tell you what; let's put it in the hands of fate. If you hit the target with your first shot, then you can join us!'

'Guess she'll be stayin' 'ere then,' whispered Podge.

'What about the best of three?'

'No Jill, one shot! Take it or leave it,' he replied, holding out his bow. Taking the bow, she positioned an arrow.

'Ready?' he said to her and then signalled to Lingua. Jill nodded. 'Aim ... FIRE!'

The disc shot into the sky. *Twang* went the bow. As the arrow disappeared from sight, Hop zoomed in on the target and caught it mid-air.

'Sorry Jill, it's still in one piece.' Hop flew over their heads and dropped the disc to the ground, where it fell into two halves.

'YYYYES!' she yelled elated, punching the air.

'Pretty impressive. Guess it's meant to be then,' said Lance, raising his eyebrows.

Podge and Dapper were gobsmacked.

'Good shot!' remarked Jack.

'Beginner's luck,' said Matt.

'Open your eyes, Matt,' whispered Myosurus under her breath.

By midday, everything was ready and the entourage began to leave. The Gang were thanking Myosurus and bidding her good-bye. 'Be brave my little warriors. May the spirits guide you,' she called after them as they set off.

Calyx came running over. 'May I go and help, Grandmother?'

She looked to Lingua, who nodded. 'Very well. But don't wander off anywhere!' she said firmly.

'I won't, I promise!'

*

The snow had continued to slowly thaw and there were no signs of frost as dusk drew in.

Back in the forest camp, Cracked Ice and Blizzard simultaneously raised their heads with ears pricked.

'TEASEL!' called one of the boys from a lookout. 'LANCE IS COMING!'

Teasel ran to meet him. 'Lance! Where are the others?'

'At the lake. Most of the Crowfoot tribe are with them. They've come to help us build a fort!'

'Really?'

'Really! How have things been here?'

'Quiet, we haven't sighted *one* crow.'

'What about the Orbs?'

'They're still well barricaded in.'

'Come on then, let's rally the boys, there's no time to lose. It'll be dark soon.'

Once everything they needed was gathered, they set off.

The shadows of the teepees danced in the light of a healthy campfire. Lance had returned with the boys and after everyone had eaten they retired for the night.

Jill, feeling restless, came out to the lake where she came upon Jack. 'Are you OK?' she asked, sitting down beside him.

'Yeah I'm fine. I was just tryin' to weigh things up.'

'What things?' she asked, removing a chewing gum packet from her bag and offering him a piece.

'No thanks - I was thinkin' about Margaret. I *still* can't believe I was right there wiv 'er. If only I'd known!'

'Margaret knows.'

'She does? How? When?'

'Oh, not till just before we left. She doesn't exactly know it's you, although she probably has her suspicions. But she knows I've found you.'

'She was just as I'd want my mum to be. Warm, carin' 'n a bit mad,' he smiled.

As the campfire burnt down, Lance approached, carrying a lighted torch. 'What are you two still doing up?'

'Couldn't sleep,' said Jack.

'Oh, Lance, I just had a thought. Do you know where Eleanor buried her brooch?'

'No Jill, I didn't know she had till you told me. I found a little cross made of twigs.'

Jill's eyes lit up. 'Where?'

Lance looked about. 'Somewhere over there, I think.'

They both joined her as she searched the ground.

'Jill, why don't yeh leave it till mornin'. You'll be able to see better,' said Jack. But just as he spoke she uncovered a tiny mound under the snow.

Lance used his cutlass to break up the hard soil. Pulling out a tattered cloth, he handed it to her. In anticipation, she carefully unwrapped it to discover the brooch inside. 'Wow! It's beautiful!' she declared, holding it up to the flame … 'If you don't mind I'd like to be alone for a little while.' The boys smiled and securing the torch in the soil, went back to the camp.

She sat pondering at the brooch then stared out at the lake, which shone like silver as it reflected the moonlight.

After a short while there was a ripple in the water, which went unnoticed, as Jill was so deep in thought. Another followed. This one caught her attention. Looking about she caught sight of a large shimmering tail skimming the water towards her. Almost too scared to breathe, she bit into her chewing gum.

Bubbles appeared on the surface following which the head of a slimy creature surfaced, so that just its eyes were visible. As she gasped she kicked her handbag, causing her make-up purse to fall down the bank. Her heart raced in her chest but she didn't scream, as it seemed the creature was smiling at her. Quickly recalling the stories Lance had told her she removed the gum and softly called out, 'Peony?' Peony slowly lifted her head and looked at her inquisitively.

Retrieving the purse Peony held it forward with her spindly webbed hand, at which point a lipstick fell out. Picking it up Peony marvelled at the pretty casing. 'It - It's a lipstick. Here let me show you.' Jill nervously took it from her, removed the lid and swivelled the case to reveal the bright red lipstick, then demonstrated on her own lips. Peony's face lit up with excitement. 'Would you - like - to have it?' she said, holding the lipstick out to her.

'Yes!' replied Peony.

Jill, startled at hearing her speak, flinched as she handed it to her. 'You can talk!' she said heartily. 'Are you - Peony?'

'Yes.'

'I'm Jill.'

On hearing someone approach, Peony quickly disappeared from sight.

'Jill! Lance told me to check on yeh,' called Matt. Jill was a little flustered.

'Wos up?'

'Nothing,' she mumbled, shrugging her shoulders.

'Are yeh comin' or wot?' snapped Matt impatiently.

'Yeah, Oh Matt, hold the torch for me.'

Wrapping the brooch she carefully placed it back then patted the earth around it. 'She'd have wanted it to stay here,' she said warmly.

Following Matt, she glanced back over her shoulder at the still lake.

CHAPTER FIFTEEN

Joining Forces

Before dawn had touched the horizon, light drizzle dampened the air, but not the spirits of the work force.

Trees were already disappearing from the skyline. Blizzard and Cracked Ice were back and forth with lengths of twine. Jill was running around like a headless chicken keeping everyone supplied with water. She also used one of the teepees to treat all the cuts and bruises.

Matt had sustained a rather bad gash to his leg but, being proud and stubborn, refused help, till Lance insisted it was treated, as there was a large splinter in the cut.

Jill hadn't told anyone of her strange encounter the previous night and was feeling quite excited by it.

'Oo put a spark in your smile?' asked Matt, as she tended his wound.

'No-one,' she replied naively.

'Jill?'

'Yes Matt?'

'You 'aven't got any make-up on.'

'I haven't? It must have worn off!' she said, looking down and tossing her hair across her face.

'Yeh look a darn sight better without it, I mean - when yer - Ouch!'

'There, that's got it!' she said grinning, holding the splinter up. She applied some ointment and wrapped a cloth around the wound.

Every time she passed the lake, she glanced over in the hope of spying Peony, who at one point peeped out from behind a bush near the water's edge. Jill smiled as Peony dived below, waving the tip of her tail before disappearing.

Everyone worked relentlessly. By nightfall the fort was all but completed. Lance decided it was time to call a halt.

It was too dark to see the finished product. The braves attached some torches around its exterior.

'Lance, do you wish us to stay and help in the morning?' asked Lingua.

'No, that won't be necessary, we can manage now. Besides tomorrow is – well - you know.'

'Then, we shall depart when the birds sing.'

'How can we *ever* thank you?'

'By winning!' he replied smiling and then bid them goodnight. Lingua retired but his smile masked his anguish, as he wished with *all* his heart to stay and fight.

There was an eerie calm that night, apart from the occasional snores from the tired work force.

In the early morning hours, Lance, unable to sleep, walked out to the lake. His heart was heavy as he wandered along the bank.

Eventually, he came upon a rock pool secluded by some trees where he sat tossing stones into the water.

Reminiscing over the past weeks, he thought of the poor frightened Orbs, Woodruff and the Lavaights, knowing that their supplies must now have run out, the grave danger his friends and newfound family were in. Then visualising Miles trying to kill him, his mind became overwhelmed and his strong pretence of courage crumbled as he sobbed, uncontrollably.

His thoughts turned to Arvensis. Anger and hate consumed him. He stood up, stared in the direction of the coast and wished him dead. But was too upset to notice the grain that flew out of the tiny pouch on his person. Strangely, no explosion followed to alert him of the fact.

Staring at the nearly full moon that seemed to wear a frown he cried out in desperation, 'Was it *true? Did I kill* our parents? Is this *my* comeuppance? … How can I save them? If there is a man in the moon or *anyone* out there. Please, *please* help us!'

He stood silent, listening, almost expecting a reply. But none came. In frustration, his whole being wanted to lash out. 'If you won't answer my plea, at least give me the strength I feel *now* when the time comes!' With a rush of adrenaline, he picked up a large rock. 'AAARRGH!' he shouted, throwing it into the pool. SPLASH *Splash*.

He made his way back to the camp, oblivious of the fact that there were two splashes. The second had come from Scelaratus, who, searching for Peony, had been submerged beneath the water and had had to dodge the rock. She overheard everything Lance said. Slowly and silently she swam back to the swamps.

*

The fifth day dawned. Miles was stirring from his sleep. 'Today … Die Lance … Mother? NO! NO!' Gasping, he sat bolt upright, his eyes bulging as sweat dripped from his brow.

Lighting a candle he lay back down, gazing at what he thought was the flame reflecting in the porthole. The light began to retract, assuming it was going out, he glanced at the candle but the flame was still strong and bright. Turning back he saw an orange glow forming around the perimeter of the porthole.

Startled by this strange phenomenon, he jumped to his feet. Then a familiar voice boomed out, 'MILES! DON'T BE ALARMED. IT'S MY EYE!'

Miles stared in bewilderment. 'Arvensis?' he called, warily.

'CAN'T BELIEVE YOUR EYES OR EARS? COME OUT ON DECK.'

On hearing the crows croaking outside and fearing some trickery by Lance, he grabbed hold of his sword.

Bracing himself, he kicked the door open and leapt out to find himself up against a black feathery wall. 'WHAT IS THIS? WHERE ARE YOU?' he shouted, lashing out with his sword.

'NOW, NOW, CAREFUL WITH THAT! LOOK UP, YOU FOOLISH BOY!'

The great mass of feathers backed away from him.

'Arvensis! How? What magic is this?' he queried, staring up at the gigantic monster that was *indeed* Arvensis.

The crows shuffled nervously.

'SILENCE! YOU MISERABLE EXCUSES FOR BIRDS!' bellowed Arvensis.

'I - I don't understand?'

'Neither do I, Miles? Strangest thing. In the early morning hours, feeling restless, I came out for some air. Suddenly a golden shooting star, a gift from the spirits, came straight at me. Hit me, bang! On the head.'

'What did you do?'

'Not much I could do. It knocked me out, cold! When I came round, I thought the island had shrunk. But it was *I* that had grown!'

'How mysterious!'

'Yes! I think I'll fly about this morning, just to let them know what they're in for. Then we'll let them sweat out the day. In fact you can ride into battle on my neck.'

'One problem.'

'Problem?'

'Yes, what are we going to feed you with till then?'

'Oh, I think I'll wait till we *feast* on our prey, CRAAH, CRA, HA, Ha, Ha!' he laughed to which Miles joined in.

The children were all admiring the impressive fort as they bid farewell to Lingua, Calyx and the braves.

'Wot on earth was that?' said Jack frowning, as the raucous laugh sounded in the distance.

'It doesn't sound like anythin' on Earth to me,' commented Matt.

'Bad medicine!' remarked Lingua.

Calyx, looked concerned.

'Hey, Calyx,' said Jack. 'We'll start workin' on a new song as soon as it's over.'

Hop, flew onto Jack's shoulder.

'He's going to hang around with you. On his leg is a binding. If you need anything urgent just tuck a note into it,' said Calyx, trying to be positive.

Lingua stroked Hop and patted Jack and Calyx on their backs, avoiding eye contact, lest they see the tears that dwelled in his eyes.

The braves set off, waving as they went.

Lance broke the sullen atmosphere. 'Right! Let's get the weapons and supplies in.'

As the boys set to work, Jill went down by the lake to where the brooch was buried to mark it with a cross she had made. She was deep in thought when suddenly, Peony surfaced, startling her. 'Oh!'

'Ssh. Jill, I have come to warn you!'

'Why? What is it?'

Just as Peony opened her mouth to speak, Blizzard began to howl. Cracked Ice reared, growling fiercely and swiping the air. Then as the sky blackened, Peony grabbed hold of Jill and pulled her under the water.

Podge let out a terrifying scream. Everyone looked up to see the monstrous figure of Arvensis approaching, Craahing a thunderous 'CRAAAAAAAAAH!'

'QUICK, EVERYONE INSIDE!' yelled Lance.

They all ran, falling and stumbling, except for Dapper, who had frozen on the spot, staring in disbelief.

'DAPPER! *DAPPER!*' they all shrieked. Snapping out of it, he ran towards them, but his legs turning to jelly gave way and he fell, flat on his face.

As Arvensis made a B-line for Dapper, Jack and Matt grabbing their spears ran out yelling. Cracked Ice lurched himself forward in an attempt to shield Dapper, causing his previous wound to open. Twisting in pain he rolled onto his back. Arvensis diverted his attention to Cracked Ice. Quick as a flash the boys launched the spears, striking his bill, lessening the blow as he struck the open wound.

Snarling, Blizzard leapt up and catching hold, dislodged a tail feather. Arvensis glared at Blizzard with his evil beady eyes as he began his ascent, deafening them with an elated 'CRAAH!' as he flew from sight. Blizzard fiercely shook the feather in frustration.

'CRACKED ICE!' screamed Lance, running to where he lay, panting in a pool of blood.

Jill pulled herself out of the water.

'That's what I was trying to tell you. I saw him this morning; eating a seal!'

'JILL! JILL! FETCH THE MEDICINE BAG, QUICKLY!' yelled Lance.

'I have to go, Peony!' she blurted and hastily ran off.

Stunned and speechless, everyone gathered round Cracked Ice.

Jill hurried over. 'Stand back. Give him some - Oh! Cracked Ice!' she cried falling to her knees.

'Will he be all right?' asked Lance, through glazed eyes.

Jill became positive. 'Right, let's get him inside. I'll need fresh water. Hurry, everybody. Go, go, go!'

Calyx had made them a stretcher with which they carried him into the fort. Jill found a strong potion, mixed by Ficaria, for extreme wounds. She applied it, and then set about stitching him up. 'Sorry Cracked Ice. This is going to hurt me as much as it will you.' When she'd finished, Blizzard, licked every stitch, knowing his saliva had its own antiseptic.

Jack and Teasel began to wander towards the forest.

'I know Lance said 'e was huge, but I didn't reckon on that!' exclaimed Jack.

'He wasn't that size before!' replied Teasel.

'Don't go far!' called Lance after them as he and Matt walked over to the lake.

They sat on the bank. For a while, they remained silent. Eventually, Lance spoke. 'I don't understand. How on earth did Arvensis get that size!' Matt shrugged his shoulders.

'We don't stand much chance now do we?' he said sullenly.

'No Matt. And what if …?'

'Wot?'

'What if *all* the crows are that size?'

'*That* would be disastrous, *wouldn't* it!' said a raucous, loud voice.

They both stared at each other, bemused.

Suddenly, Scelaratus reared her head out of the lake.

'WHOA!' yelled Matt, jumping to his feet. Lance stared with his mouth wide open.

'It's *rude* to stare!' she snapped, flipping her tail, showering them with water and swimming closer. 'It would appear you have created a *bigger* problem for yourself and consequently one for *us*, Lance, as big birds like *big* fishes!' she scowled.

'Created? What do you mean?' asked Lance, totally baffled.

'The golden grain that flew from your pouch. Oh, and by the way,' she sneered, stretching forward. 'You only *just* missed me with that rock!'

'You were there? The grain! Oh no! I wished - What have I done?'

'A Crowfoot contract is binding. To go against it caused it to backfire.'

''Ow bad's yer luck!' commented Matt.

'It *only* affected Arvensis. The problem is what are we going to do now?' she snarled.

'Without the contract, it's hopeless, Scelaratus. Today, they attack and Arvensis alone could take us all out in minutes.'

'True, but he'll bide his time, it will give him more pleasure. He timed this well; with the number of crows at his disposal it's not going to be easy for you. Already as the snow thaws he has a mass of them waiting at the green wall.'

'That's why I went through to Earth time, to muster the help of the Kindreds. They are good fighters. I hoped they'd distract him to give me enough time to find the contract.'

Scelaratus, pondered for a moment, then, a twinkle appeared in her eyes. 'How long would it take to find the Kindreds?'

'I - I don't know. The only place I *didn't* try was Tintagel in Cornwall. Apparently, they hold meetings at a castle there. If I were there now, I'd have at least two days, during which time only four to five hours will have passed here. But, one, I can't get back and two, there's no time!'

'There's always time Lance, but none to waste. Did I spy the tribal bird earlier?'

'Hop? Yes, he's with Jack.'

'Good, then it is possible. Now, do just as I say. I need seven of you to make it work. Meet me back here - Well don't just stand there *gawping*. I can't stand this clean water as it is. Be quick!' she barked. Swinging her sleek body back into the lake, she sped off.

Lance and Matt ran towards the fort.

'Whad'ya think she's gonna do, Lance?'

'I don't know Matt, but *anything's* worth a try.' Jill was standing at the fort's entrance. 'Jill!'

'Ssh, Lance, you'll wake Cracked Ice.'

'How is he?'

'Not too good, he's lost a lot of blood. All we can do now is keep him quiet and wait. Blizzard hasn't left his side.'

'Jill, round up Dapper and Podge. We'll track down Jack and Teasel. Meet us at the lake. Hurry!'

'Why? What's happening?'

'Just do it!'

Lance and Matt ran swiftly into the forest.

Jack and Teasel were pulling conkers out of a tree hole. 'This one's a corker, Jack. It cracked another clean in half.'

'Yeah?'

'JACK, TEASEL, COME QUICK!' yelled Lance, on spying them. Jack and Teasel looked at each other anxiously and then ran back, following close behind.

Hop flew overhead and landed on Jack's shoulder as they reached the lake where Jill and the others were already gathered.

'Wot's goin' down, Lance?' asked Podge.

Just as he spoke, a wave the width of the lake, suddenly swelled up and surged towards them. As it broke, Scelaratus, Peony and six other Newteleons the same rainbow colours as Peony, burst out of it. As they stared mesmerized at the Newteleons, a harrowing cry sounded in the distance.

'Ranunculus!' uttered Lance.

'Ran who?' asked Jack.

'You don't want to know!' said Lance.

'He is angry. His pride ails him,' stated Scelaratus, crawling onto the bank. At which the gang took ten paces back. 'Do not fear, I shall not *eat* you, till this is over!' she jeered. Swinging her great lizard body round, she signalled to the Newteleons, who somersaulted backwards into the depths. Then she tapped her claws impatiently on her scales.

When they resurfaced, each held up a piece of glistening gemstone. Peony was last, holding up a bright red ruby but keeping her other fist clenched tight. '*Well* Peony? Do you have it?' scowled Scelaratus. Peony nodded. With her head bowed submissively, she handed Scelaratus an object. Jill half smiled at Peony. 'This is *your* colour I believe!' snapped Scelaratus, handing Jill the lipstick that now matched the colour of her face.

'Jill?' queried Lance.

'Her colour is red! Now all we need is a rainbow,' stated Scelaratus.

'A rainbow?' said Jack, totally bemused.

Lance began to smile. 'Of course! That's why the gems are a separate colour.'

'Help me out on this one, Lance, yer not makin' any sense.'

'Well Jack, as you know it is *impossible* to reach the end of a rainbow. Only a *Newteleon* can!'

'Exactly!' intervened Scelaratus. 'All the colours have to go in for it to work. However, only *three* of the shafts will act as a passage.'

'Brilliant, which three?' asked Lance.

'Nobody knows, they change every time. Therefore you will all have to be prepared. We'll rescue those that don't go through.'

'Go through! Whad'ya mean?' asked Matt frowning.

'A passage to Earth,' she replied.

'But 'ow do we know it'll reach Tintagel?' he queried.

'As you travel through you just keep chanting your destination. In this case; Tintagel, Cornwall.'

'Yeah but 'ow do we get back?' said Jack sceptically.

'The Kindreds!' declared Lance. 'Scelaratus, what if the three that go through can't make contact?'

'That's your dilemma, Lance. It's the only chance you've got. Take it or leave it!'

Lance turned to the others who nodded. 'Take it!' said Lance quickly.

'Very well. Time is of the essence! We need to get a message to Calyx,' she said, looking up at the white clouds.

'No sweat,' said Jack, stroking Hop.

'Tell him we need sun and rain.'

'Jill? Pen, paper?' said Jack, prompting her.

'Oh, right,' she flummoxed and ran off to fetch some.

Jack wrote a note and fastened it to Hop's leg. 'Be swift, my little drummer,' he said, lifting Hop into the air.

'Newteleons, line up!' ordered Scelaratus. 'Now, you must all catch a colour. THROW!' she ordered the Newteleons, who tossed the gemstones towards the boys.

'Time to get wet,' said Lance, as he caught a yellow citrine.

Jill, being red, went first. She waded out to Peony and climbed onto her tail. Matt was next with orange, carnelian. Lance followed and then Jack carrying a green emerald. Dapper took a dubious step forward, clutching a blue sapphire, closely followed by Podge who had caught an indigo tourmaline. Podge's Newteleon didn't look too impressed as he tried to clamber on. 'Just my luck!' she muttered under her breath, as he weighed her tail flat in the water. Lastly came Teasel, with violet, amethyst.

'Keep hold of your gems, they secure your passage into the tunnels. Once inside, release them as they will disintegrate,' instructed Scelaratus.

The other boys ventured warily over.

'Lance? Where are you all going?' asked one of them, sounding worried.

'It's all right. Some of us will be back soon,' he assured them.

They all waited anxiously.

'LOOK SMOKE, there's smoke!' cried Dapper.

'Right, everyone,' said Lance. 'Whoever goes through, find the castle and just keep calling for Furse. If you don't make it - I mean-'

'Don't worry, Lance. We all know the score,' said Matt.

'Listen! The drums ... It's Calyx. Go boy go!' said Jack, egging him on.

The drumming got louder. A fluffy blanket of grey clouds drifted into sight and a white sun, peeped through the gaps. Its shafts of light splayed out through the shifting clouds, flowing like chiffon. Then the drums beat faster and the shafts of sunlight became bright spotlights scanning the lake. Suddenly, the sun broke through in all its glory. Calyx changed the rhythm to one that was heavy and war-like.

'Good luck! And remember what to chant,' called Scelaratus, signalling to the Newteleons, who slowly began to move out.

'I can't swim!' cried Podge, clinging on.

'Don't tell them that, if you fall back in they may leave you there!' said Lance laughing, knowing the Newteleons were really quite callous.

'Lance, look!' called Teasel, pointing.

They looked up, to see Cumulus, asserting all his might, pushing a thick black cloud over the lake. Suddenly, there was a CRASH of thunder, followed by a fierce *bolt* of fork lightning. The wind picked up and torrential rain began to fall.

They clung on tightly as the Newteleons tails became even more slippery.

'*THERE* EVERYONE, OVER THERE!' shouted Jack pointing, as the biggest, brightest rainbow they'd ever seen, arched into the lake.

'OH MY. SIS!' cried Dapper.

'IT'LL BE ALL RIGHT, RITCHIE!' yelled Jill. 'MATT! MATT!' she shouted. But the words blew back in her face. Sensing her anxiety, Peony, waited for Matt's Newteleon to come alongside. 'Matt. What if I go, or you go, or - what if we - never see each other again?' she cried.

Suddenly the water swelled, tilting Peony. As Jill slid sideways, Matt stretched across and grabbing hold of her hand, pulled her back upright.

'Calm down Jill. Everything will work out fine!' Matt reassured her, seeing how frightened she was, but disregarding the loving look in her eyes.

They approached the end of the rainbow.

The Newteleons lined up at the relevant shafts, and then sucked a ray of colour from the huge tunnels that lay dauntingly open. Ducking their heads under the water they began to blow, causing huge coloured bubbles to envelop their riders.

'SEE, PODGE, IF YOU HIT THE WATER, YOU'LL FLOAT!' shouted Dapper.

'Y-e-s, till someone bursts his bubble,' sneered Podge's Newteleon.

'HEY, JACK. WE'RE LIKE GIANT ORBS!' yelled Lance.

'YEAH? NOW I KNOW WOT YEH MEANT BY *ORB IT*,' laughed Jack, nervously.

'RIGHT THIS IS IT, HOLD TIGHT EVERYONE!' shouted Peony.

A short spiky crest, flashing a neon rainbow of light, emerged on the Newteleons' heads, then travelled down to the tips of their tails, gripping the bubbles. They skimmed backwards through the water to the far side of the lake, where they came to a halt. With baited breath, everyone waited nervously.

Suddenly, Scelaratus screamed a piercing shrill cry at which the Newteleons lunged forwards. Rapidly accelerating they sped through the water. When they reached the rainbow's end they simultaneously stopped abruptly and flipping their tails, catapulted them into the shafts.

There were screams of fear, shock and elation. Jill's bubble, dropped from the sky, knocking into Lance's. Podge's bounced off Teasel's.

As their bubbles floated in the water, they quickly looked at each other to find that Matt, Jack and Dapper had gone through.

Jill's heart sank. 'Don't worry. They'll be back,' said Peony heartily, as she popped her bubble and scooped her out of the water.

Podge was being tormented by the Newteleons, who were playing ball with him, as the others rode back to the bank.

'Thank you, Scelaratus,' said Lance, as he helped Teasel onto the bank. Her attention was diverted to Podge. Quick as a flash she slithered into the lake and sped towards him at the same time as Ranunculus, who was about to assert his anger.

Ranunculus burst Podge's bubble with his spiky crown. ''ELP!' gasped Podge in-between gulps of air and water.

'Oh no, you don't!' scowled Scelaratus, grabbing Podge by his arm at which Ranunculus swiped his tail across her head.

The others watched helplessly from the bank as Podge sank below.

Ranunculus dived with jaws gaping. Podge stared goggle eyed at Ranunculus as he zoomed in on him, but Scelaratus was faster and reached Podge in the nick of time. Scooping him into her tail, she tore to the surface and flipped him as far as she could.

Podge swam like mad.

'I thought he said he couldn't swim?' commented Jill.

'Amazing how fast you can learn,' replied Lance smirking.

Coughing and spluttering Podge dragged himself out of the water and sat, shaking on the bank, nursing his bruised arm, which Jill inspected.

The Newteleons, fighting amongst themselves, headed back to the swamps. Peony waved and then followed.

As the rain stopped, the children's attention was drawn to the rainbow that faded from sight.

'I hope they make it,' sighed Jill.

'We'd best get inside,' suggested Lance, knowing it was now just a waiting game.

CHAPTER SIXTEEN

Mystic Tintagel

'TINTAGEL, CORNWALL - TINTAGEL, CORNWALL.'

'JACK, JACK! Are you all right?' asked Matt, shaking him. 'It's OK; yeh can stop sayin' it now. We're 'ere!'

'We are? We made it?'

'Spot on! Well I think it's Tintagel. It's a bit dark but I saw some ruins in the distance.'

'But everything's *green* at the moment, even you're green Matt!'

'Don't worry; it'll wear off in a minute. Bright, weren't it.'

'Blindin'! Beats any ride I've ever bin on!' remarked Jack, rubbing his eyes.

'Wot, even The Big Wheel?' chuckled Matt, raising his eyebrows as he helped him up.

''Oo else came through?' queried Jack.

'I dunno. Come on, we'd better scout around and find out.'

Dapper had lost consciousness whilst exiting the tunnel. 'Oh, my head!' he groaned. Opening his eyes he focused on huge waves crashing on the rocks below. 'WHOA!' he cried, falling sideways. Reacting swiftly he grabbed hold of the ledge on which he was perched high up on the face of a cliff. 'AAARRGH! HELP! SOMEBODY *HELP* ME!'

'Dapper! Come on Jack, it came from that direction.'

Quickly, they ran off to find him.

'DAPPER! WHERE ARE YEH?'

'MATT? THANK GOODNESS. I'M HERE, DOWN HERE!'

''ANG ON, WE'RE COMIN'!'

They hurried to the edge of the cliff and peered over.

''E's only a stone's throw away. 'Ang onto me feet, Matt,' said Jack, as he lay face down and leaned over the edge. 'DAPPER! Give me yer 'and!'

'Jack! I can't move!' he cried, petrified.

'Yeh've *gotta* get onto yer feet or I won't reach ya!'

''URRY UP JACK! YER SLIPPING!' shouted Matt.

'Come on Dapper, or we're *all* goin' over!' said Jack, pleading with him.

Dapper pulled himself onto his knees, and then clinging to the cliff face, clawed his way upright. 'That's it, you can do it,' said Jack, coaxing him. Stretching up, Dapper caught hold of Jack's hand. 'Right, now 'old tight and *don't* look down!' said Jack, trying not to himself. 'OK MATT. *PULL!*' Matt dug in his heels as Jack heaved.

As soon as they were safely on terra firma, Dapper clung round Jack's neck, sobbing. 'It's all right mate, it's OK to cry,' said Jack, smiling at Matt and remembering that Dapper was only eight.

Deciding it was too late to look for the castle, they headed inland towards a village that was lighting up in the distance.

On their approach and much to their relief they found *Tintagel* signposted.

'I'm starving!' winged Dapper, as they passed a shop window dressed with Easter eggs.

'No way!' cried Matt.

'Of course. The time difference, it must be nearin' Easter. Look, there's a chippy down there. 'Ang on,' said Jack, rummaging in his pockets. ''Ere, I've got some change. That'll do us.'

'Oh, smell that aroma!' said Matt blissfullly, as they walked into the shop.

There were only two ladies at the counter. 'That's a rather pungent fish smell, isn't it?' said one of them turning around, holding her nose. The boys all smiled politely, to which they tutted and left the shop.

'What do you lot want?' asked the proprietor in an undertone.

'Chips!' they replied in unison.

The man quickly piled loads of chips into some paper, doused them with salt and vinegar then ushered them out with no charge.

'That was very friendly of him,' said Dapper.

'Can't think why?' commented Matt, holding his nose and chuckling.

'Yeah, right, gotcha. Don't exactly smell like a bouquet of flowers, do we!' said Jack, smirking.

Venturing into a park they sat on a bench and tucked into the chips.

'Guess we'll be kippin' 'ere tonight,' said Jack.

'Good a place as any,' replied Matt, scrunching his chip paper into a ball and tossing it into a nearby bin.

'Dapper? Ere, Matt, 'e's fallen asleep eatin' a chip!' laughed Jack, removing it. They laid him down on the bench and then squatted on the ground in front of it.

Matt, putting his hands on his head, rubbed his tense scalp.

'Are you OK?' asked Jack.

'Yeah. It just feels a bit *weird*, being back 'ere. Everythin' seems so normal. If we were on the island I would expect to find the - wot they called?'

'Kindreds.'

'Yeah, them. But now we're 'ere, well, it doesn't seem possible!'

'I know wot yeh mean. It's like Echoco never existed.'

'Right!'

'But Jill and Podge are still there, so it is real. That means the Kindreds must be 'ere!'

'I 'ope so, Jack, for all our sakes.'

Jack jumped to his feet.

'Where yeh goin'?'

'Back in a minute.'

He soon returned carrying some cardboard boxes. 'Found 'em behind the chippy.' Matt laughed. Breaking them open they covered Dapper, and then making themselves as comfortable as they could, drifted off to sleep.

*

The next morning, Jack was first to wake. He went off to find a sweet shop, where he spent his change on some drinks and then went back to rouse the others.

Once they'd got themselves together, they set off towards the castle.

The ruins were housed on two separate divides of the cliff. They decided to split up. Matt took one side, Jack and Dapper the other that jutted out from the mainland. After climbing the steep steps, they searched every nook and cranny of the sparse remains, calling out for Furse.

At one point a middle-aged couple approached Jack, inquiring who Furse was. Jack told them they'd lost their dog. Matt looked across, scratching his head on hearing the couple calling for Furse, as they joined in the hunt. Jack threw his arms up in the air and Matt began to laugh. After a while they wished the boys luck and continued on their way.

At midday, the boys met up at the bottom of the steps, unsure of where else to search. Dapper told them of Merlin's cave below, which he'd visited with his parents. Undeterred they spent the afternoon exploring the magical cave, repeatedly calling his name. Matt became so frustrated he raised his voice each time, till he was shouting.

As the wind picked up and the tide drew in they made their way back up the cliffs where they searched the outskirts.

'This is 'opeless! Come on we'd better 'ead back. It's gettin' dark,' suggested Matt.

They eventually reached the park.

'Do you think that guy will give us some more chips?' asked Dapper, whilst rubbing his rumbling tummy.

'Nope.' replied Jack bluntly.

'We could go to my nan and grandad's, they'd feed us!'

'It's a bit far to walk, Dapper. But yeh know - you could stay 'ere. I mean - go home - if you wanted to,' suggested Jack, to which Dapper frowned.

'Wot are yeh talkin' about Jack? *We* ain't exactly goin' anywhere, are we! It looks like we'll all be stayin' 'ere!' barked Matt.

'OH RIGHT, SO YEH'VE GIVEN UP?' shouted Jack.

'WELL *YOU* TELL ME WOT WE'RE SUPPOSED TO DO?'

Nerves frayed and tempers flared. As Jack and Matt argued, Dapper became distressed and hid amongst some bushes. He picked up a Chinese lantern from the ground and twiddled it nervously in his hands.

Eventually the boys, realising they'd upset him, calmed down and went off to find him.

'DAPPER? DAPPER? Oh there you are!' said Jack, crawling under the bushes. Dapper stared po-faced at the little lantern.

'It's all right, Dapper, me 'n Matt 'ave sorted it. We're just really tense at the moment. Wotcha got there?'

'It's a Chinese lantern. Mum decorates the table with them on Halloween,' he muttered.

'Yeah, they do look a bit like pumpkins. Bit out of date then, ain't they?' he replied looking at the fragile orange lanterns that lay all about. 'Come on, we'll see wot scraps we can find behind the shops. Don't worry. We'll find Furse tomorrow.' But Jack's heart was not in his words.

'Jack!' whispered Dapper.

'Wot's up mate?'

'*Behind* you!' he squeaked.

Jack slowly turned his head. There on the ground glowed one of the lanterns. Suddenly, two beady little eyes lit up within as two tiny legs popped out of the bottom. A layer peeled away from the point of the lantern, splayed out and down, curling up at the tips, dressing the legs in a beautiful veined skirt.

As they stared in disbelief, Matt popped his head in. 'Are you two comin', or-' Just then, a little head and arms burst out. Matt gawped, speechless.

'*Who's* out of date?' said the tiny figure, indignantly, as she shook her red curls and looked up at them with piercing green eyes. 'You mentioned Furse?'

'You're – Y-You're a - Kindred!' cried Jack. Nodding she snapped her fingers. Following which, all the lanterns on the ground began to open. Before they knew it, they were surrounded by Kindreds.

Dapper's face lit up as the one he held evolved into a little boy, whose lantern unfolded into puffy trousers. Gently, he placed him on the ground.

Tears of relief welled up in Jacks eyes as she spoke. 'I am Vicia, Granddaughter of Furse. He is aware of your presence and sent us to investigate. We saw you arrive. A Newteleon rainbow shines brighter than any other does, so we knew you came from Echoco. We just had to make sure you were not Newteleons in disguise. Then Furse recognised your faces as the missing children.'

'Wot! We made the papers?' declared Matt.

'Oh, yes, your means of transport caused some concern. Furse is convinced you raided his castle.'

'Oh, but, that was Lance!' said Jack.

'You can explain everything later. Now we must away before we're seen. Follow us.' Vicia ran under a thick bush, and then stopped abruptly. 'Oh, silly me! Of course you can't, well, not that size anyway.'

Removing some grains from her pocket, she handed them one each. 'Pop them down,' she coaxed.

'WHOA! No way. I've seen wot they can do!' declared Matt.

'In the wrong hands, they *can* be *very* dangerous.'

'Tell me about it!' he remarked.

'Don't worry; they're quite reversible. Trust me,' she smiled. The boys knew they had little choice and warily swallowed them. 'Now close your eyes and think small thoughts.' A little bemused, they did as Vicia asked. Jack thought of chips, Matt visualised ants and Dapper, the beads on his laces. 'Good. Now, open them.'

'WOW! WE'VE SHRUNK!' cried Dapper.

The Kindred girls giggled at Matt and Jack, who turned crimson.

Just then an owl hooted. 'Come. Follow quickly. He has yet to feed!' said Vicia, leading the way.

Presently, they came to a sawn off tree stump where a frilly petticoat of mushrooms circled its base. A number of Kindreds climbed up and stood in circles within the age rings on its surface.

The boys looked on in astonishment, as some of the rings swivelled clockwise and others, anticlockwise. 'Impressive, isn't it,' said Vicia, as it clunked to a halt, causing a door to open in the side of the stump.

They hastily followed her inside, as a wood lice ambled past.

It was very spacious, with an array of stairs that travelled into the roots. At its centre, seated at a table laden with food, was an aged little Kindred, dressed in a royal blue robe trimmed in gold. His full head of curly gold hair stuck out in every direction and his matching beard was so thick it covered most of his face.

He looked the boys up and down through a monocle lens as they approached. 'Welcome, I am Furse.' The boys introduced themselves. 'Be seated,' he said, ushering them to sit opposite him. 'Eat, drink, then we shall talk.'

'Thanks!' they replied and with no hesitation, tucked in.

Vicia seated herself next to Furse. Those that couldn't be seated, squatted on the floor.

When they had eaten, Furse wiped his mouth with a napkin. 'Now,' he said. 'You must tell us everything! Please pay attention to the smallest of details as they may have the biggest significance.'

Matt and Dapper looked at Jack, volunteering him to speak. Jack began. Dapper and Matt butted in whenever they thought he'd missed something. Vicia had to keep slowing him down, as he anxiously told the story. The Kindreds listened intently, reacting with gasps and squeals as the drama unfolded.

'Well I'll be darned!' exclaimed Furse, as Jack finished. 'Tell me, did Lance speak of Ulex?' The boys shook their heads, bewildered.

Frowning Furse stood up and paced the floor, stroking his beard muttering. 'Bless my soul. Bless my soul.' Then he summoned Vicia and taking her to one side began to talk quietly with her. Pausing, he called over to the boys. '*How* many crows, did you say?'

'Thousands!' replied Jack.

Furse nodded to Vicia at which she turned to face all the Kindreds and seemingly communicated with them, by moving her pupils in an agitated fashion. Quick as a flash, the Kindreds rushed outside. Vicia followed them, locking the door behind her.

'Wot's goin' on?' asked Matt.

'Never you mind,' said Furse. 'We have much to put into place before tomorrow night.'

'TOMORROW! But, that might be too late!' cried Jack.

'Trust me, what has to be done *will* take time. I know you're worried, but you *must* understand. We only have *one* shot at this, if we go in unprepared, we don't stand a chance. Besides, we can't go in without a natural hurricane. That's why I am here for a meeting with the Kindred Leaders, scheduled for midnight tomorrow at the castle. We know of one that is currently building in the Pacific, which should peak in the early morning hours. A group of us were already planning to visit Echoco, to find out what lies amiss there. Our grave concerns were the *only* reason we made contact with yourselves. Now I know, it changes things. Come, I'll show you to your quarters.'

The boys could see that Furse was very uptight and anxious. They followed him down some steps to a room, where great fluffy feather and down puff balls beckoned their weary heads.

Meanwhile, outside, the Kindreds were hastily making their way to the castle ruins.

Once there, they closed their eyes and concentrating, began to hum incessantly. After a short while, tiny lights appeared in the night sky, dashing about like fireflies. It was their Orbs. Swooping down they hovered by the Kindreds who climbed on and zoomed off in all directions.

'My, what a busy night for the electricity companies,' smirked Vicia, as she climbed onto her Orb and then headed out to sea.

Within an hour, a train of flashing streetlights began their journey. Starting in London, down to the South coast, simultaneously, out to the East and West, through the North to Scotland, across to all the little islands and finishing in the largest, Ireland, of course.

The pilot of an aircraft was beginning his descent towards Heathrow. 'Hey, Bob, look at that!' he remarked, to his co-pilot.

'What on earth! Are the runway lights flashing?' asked Bob.

'No, they look stable. Three short, three long, three short. That's an SOS! They're flashing for miles,' puzzled the pilot.

'Oh, of course, got it! What's the time?'

'One minute past twelve.'

'April Fools!' declared Bob.

'What will they think of next?' said the pilot, shaking his head.

They both laughed.

*

The boys woke the next day to find all the Kindreds had returned and were busy with preparations.

They were feeling restless and anxious. Vicia, sensing their unease, went over to them, carrying a cockle. 'Would you like to help?' she asked. They nodded eagerly. Handing them each a thorn she asked them to steady the shell as she demonstrated how to dislodge the cockle. 'There's loads more over there you can do,' she said, pointing.

'Wot yeh gonna use these for - Dinner?' asked Matt. Vicia laughed, and placed the empty shell on her head.

'Ha, ha. They're helmets,' chuckled Dapper.

The time passed more quickly as they became busy.

Sometime during the afternoon there was a loud rapping on the door. Vicia looked to Furse, who nodded. She opened the door, at which Dapper let out an almighty scream. 'AARGH, VICIA LOOK OUT! IT'S ARVENSIS!'

Matt and Jack, stopped in their tracks as a huge bill protruded through the doorway, followed by a loud, 'PRUUK.'

'Don't fear. It's Waldron, he's a raven,' Vicia assured them.

'I - for a minute – I …' blubbered Dapper.

'I can't blame you after all you've been through. He's a scout for Grock, the Head Raven at the Tower of London.' The boys looked at each other and remembering they had been miniaturised, sighed with relief.

Furse went over to talk with Waldron.

When Waldron left, Furse addressed them all. 'Grock is aware of the distress signal and requests an audience. We'll call by after the meeting.' The boys seemed a little confused.

'Distress signal?' inquired Jack.

'Yes, we sent out a message via the streetlights,' said Vicia.

'Wot message?' queried Jack.

'Save Our Souls,' stated Furse.

'Oh, SOS!'

'That's correct Jack. Grock has to be informed if there is any pending threats as they guard the Tower,' Vicia informed him.

Eventually, the time came to set off. All the Kindreds dressed in tiny suits of armour and holding their spears, with their cockle helmets snugly on their heads, filed out.

Furse and the boys followed them out and then waited as Vicia locked up. 'Stay close,' she warned, wrapping a black cape around her shoulders. 'Keep your eyes to the ground. If the owls spy the whites, you'll be on their menu tonight.'

It was a long trek to the cliffs for their tiny legs. Eventually they arrived.

They came to the steps that led up to the ruin that jutted out to sea. Climbing onto each other's shoulders they scaled up to the top.

Jack gazed up at the moon that shone brightly in the sky, where all the stars were visible in the crisp blackness. He was suddenly taken aback. 'Amazing, isn't it,' commented Vicia.

Everyone looked up. 'It's called a moonbow. Normally, you'd be very privileged to see one as they're very rare.'

'It's magical. It's the same colours as a rainbow, isn't it?' inquired Jack.

'Yes, and normally a little fainter, but this is no normal moonbow, watch!'

The boys stared mesmerised, as it began to sparkle and snake a path towards them. Closer and closer it came, glistening, with smiley faces all aglow.

'The Orbs!'

'Yes, that's right Dapper,' said Vicia. 'They will be transporting us to Echoco.'

Some of them were mounted by little Kindred Leaders wearing their national dress.

'Look at that one, Jack. 'E's wearin' a kilt!' smirked Matt.

'Ssh! For goodness sake, don't upset *any* of them!' warned Vicia.

Once the Leaders dismounted, the Orbs flew down into Merlin's cave.

Furse greeted his friends. 'Now come, it is nearly midnight,' he said, checking his fob watch.

Making their way to the far end, they all turned back to face the ruins, looking expectantly.

'Wot are we waitin' for?' asked Matt.

'The drawbridge of course!' stated Furse.

'Is 'e feelin' all right?' said Matt turning to Vicia. She smiled and raising her eyebrows, beckoned Matt to look back.

A haunting grey mist swept up from the sea and surrounded them. Covering the whole of the ruins it began to shift and shape. Then before their very eyes, the ghosting image of the castle reappeared, in all its former glory, its turrets standing tall and proud, silhouetted by the full moon. Their mouths dropped open as the drawbridge fell across to the other cliff-top.

Furse led the way. 'Now take heed,' he announced. 'Just because it looks transparent, it doesn't mean you can walk through the walls. Please use the doors like the rest of us. Oh, and don't show any fear to any apparitions, only the *strong* will be ignored.'

They made their way into a courtyard and clambered up some steps to an enormous door. Furse knocked and two burly, bearded guards, dressed in long red robes, opened it. Their shoulders and joints were plated in metal and great swords hung on their hips. 'Greetings,' said Furse, hurrying past them.

They continued through a network of corridors, passing arches and stairways where apparitions appeared, taunting them. The boys kept their heads down, afraid of showing their fear.

At one point they could hear drumming and marching. As the footsteps got louder the boys looked up to see a group of gigantic knights standing in front of them. 'Look away!' said Furse quickly. But Jack had made eye contact with one of them and they all came to a halt.

The apparition placed the point of his broadsword under Jack's chin and lifted his head. Jack stared at his rugged face, where his soulless eyes showed no emotion. Furse became anxious as he slowly lifted the sword, to the side of Jack's head. A tense silence followed as Jack and the knight stared at each other. Unexpectedly the knight smiled and lightly tapped the point on Jack's shoulders, almost as if knighting him after which they continued marching on their way.

Furse was amazed. 'Come, don't dally!' he said, smiling at Jack.

'Are you all right Jack?' asked Matt.

'Yeah –Yeah I'm fine,' he replied, feeling somewhat elated.

Eventually they entered the great hall, draped in curtains with all manners of shields on the walls. But most stunning of all, at its centre was the huge, famed Round Table.

They climbed a mesh net of sticky cobwebs that hung to the floor. Once on top, Vicia seated them.

'Pretty impressive!' commented Matt.

'Cor! Just fink, King Arthur could've eaten right where we're sittin'!' remarked Jack.

'What if we'd been this size *then*. I mean - they could have been eating - us!' said Dapper, to which Matt and Jack smirked at each other.

Furse took centre stage, from where he conveyed the important factors of what had come to light, during which there was much muttering and tutting from his audience. The Kindreds would occasionally stand and ask questions. Furse was a good negotiator and always put forward a strong argument knowing he needed their full support.

Eventually he rounded up with a final statement. 'If we don't go in, it will be the *end* for the Orbs. It is *their* birthplace. With them dies our spirit and consequently our existence! *Yes*, many of us *may* die, maybe all! But, if there is a chance that our cups will overflow and Arvensis's will run dry, then it will be proven this night that the CUP of destiny is a truth!'

The Leaders all stood up and raising their fists shouted unanimously, 'ECHOCO!'

'Then let it be so!' declared Furse. Apart from the children and infirm, we meet in one hour in the skies over John o' Groats! Bring all the grains you can spare,' he concluded.

Within minutes, the hall was empty.

They left the castle and watched as it faded from sight. The Orbs flew up from the cave and the Kindred Leaders departed.

'Well, we'd best find you each an orb,' said Furse, to the boys. 'Here, take these grains. When we arrive at Echoco, choose your moment and pop them down. Think big and you will return to normal size.' But as he summoned the Orbs forward, Vicia looked suspiciously inland. 'What is it, Vicia?'

'There, Grandfather, it's a - stray Orb.'

The little Orb flew up to Furse. 'Forgive me for joining you so late. I saw the alarm, but only now am I well enough to travel. My name is Eyebright.'

'Eyebright!' blurted Jack.

'Oh, you know of me?'

'Tell me Eyebright, were you on Echoco when my brother Ulex visited?' asked Furse, anxiously.

'Ulex? Yes. I didn't see him myself but Dodder told me he came and left the same night.' Furse almost fainted.

'GRANDFATHER!' cried Vicia.

As his legs gave way, Matt and Jack grabbed hold of him. 'Are you OK?' asked Jack.

'Y-e-s, yes,' he mumbled, the words sticking in his throat. Holding his brow and trembling, he straightened himself up. Choking back his tears he summoned Eyebright to be his steed.

Once mounted, they flew off towards the Tower of London.

*

'Whoa! clock the view!' exclaimed Jack, as they homed in on the Tower. Waldron joined them as they began their descent.

Silently, they flew up to the raven's enclosure, which housed six birds. The largest of them was Grock. Regally, he moved his head, inspecting the visitors as his partner preened his tail feathers. 'That will do, Zelia,' he pruuked, walking up to the bars.

'Zelia, nice name,' commented Jack.

'It means zealous; one who is true to duty. Grock is tactical and wise,' said Vicia, as she and Furse dismounted.

'So, Furse, what is your course of action?' pruuked Grock.

'Ninety per cent, going in.'

'Odds?'

'Slim!'

'Hum, Damn that infernal crow and all that fly with him. I refuse to be associated with such oversized cousins. No doubt, if he succeeds in this barbarism, it won't be long before he sets his sights on London?'

'I'm sure he'll spare some of the Orbs to use for transportation! Of course, I'd appreciate any strategic advice you can give me. I know you can't leave the Tower - Can you?' queried Furse.

As Grock, pondered, Zelia glared at him. 'Don't start that, woman!' he pruucked.

'Why, would you have us all dismissed?' she spat.

'Would you rather Arvensis dismissed you!' argued Grock.

'I don't wish to hurry you, but time is precious,' said Furse.

'It would take a good squadron to keep him busy … I'm sorry Zelia, but on behalf of our ancestors, we *have* to go. It is our duty!'

'But, the Kingdom will fall!'

'It *won't* fall. They'll replace us tomorrow,' he pruuked and then turned to the others. 'Well, ravens, are you all with me?'

'Yes!' came the·unanimous reply.

'Then what are we waiting for!' he cried.

'To get out?' said Zelia, cockily.

'Uhum. Of course. Do your stuff, Vicia.' Waldron suddenly became alarmed as someone approached. 'Hurry!' pruucked Grock.

'Stand back!' said Vicia, throwing a minute grain at the bars, causing them to part.

'Who goes there?' barked a gruff voice.

Vicia and Furse quickly threw some grains, which the ravens caught in their beaks. Immediately, their lifting feathers, which were clipped to stop them flying, grew back.

All together they soared up into the night sky.

On reaching John o' Groats, the Orbs hovered and the ravens flew about as they waited.

'*Come on*, where are you?' muttered Furse, impatiently.

'Is that 'em, Vicia?' asked Matt, pointing above a cloud.

'Some of them,' she replied. As she spoke, more and more appeared.

Each Kindred Leader led their group, who were all kitted out in their countries' costume, with shields and all manner of weapons.

Furse began to call a register. The Leaders acknowledged him as they fell in behind. 'Scots, Irish, Welsh, British, Islanders.'

'It's fantastic!' said Jack. ''Oo's that lot comin' in?'

'Where Jack?' queried Dapper, excitedly.

Suddenly, millions of tiny lights swept the skyline.

'NO WAY!' declared Matt.

The boys stared, gobsmacked as Furse continued. 'America, Russia, Africa, Canada, Australia, China …' and on and on he went.

As they lit the sky turning night to day, they prepared to leave. 'I can't *wait* to see the look on Lance's face when we arrive. How long will it take to get there, Vicia?' asked Jack. Vicia remained silent. 'Vicia?'

'Not long,' she replied, tonelessly.

Furse looked at them. 'What she's *not* telling you is that the hurricane has lulled. But don't fear, all is not lost, there is another currently building.' But the boys could see Furse was concerned. 'KINDREDS UNITED, LET'S GO!' he yelled, pointing his spear.

The ravens flew out in front. 'I hope you know what you're doing!' tutted Zelia, as she flew alongside Grock. He looked at her cheekily and blew her a kiss. 'Oh, stop it, you smoothy,' she pruuked, coyly, being won over.

'Oh, to stretch these wings and feel the wind in your feathers!' he pruuked and then began to show off, performing aerobatics, looping a loop around her. 'FOR KING AND COUNTRY!' he loudly proudly, pruuked. Projecting his head from his strong, broad wings he surged forward. His fellow ravens fell in behind him, forming an arrowhead. With Zelia to his right and Waldron to his left, this elite squadron led the way as millions of Kindreds followed.

CHAPTER SEVENTEEN

The Battle

While the boys were away, Lance had kept everyone in the fort, as he didn't want to lose sight of anyone. They had spent the afternoon building a protective shelter for Cracked Ice within its walls. Cumulus was stationed in the sky above, keeping watch.

As the afternoon dragged on, they became restless. Lance was swiping the air with his cutlass. Jill was bathing Cracked Ice's wounds, as Blizzard looked on.

Teasel, who was playing conkers with the boys, noticed Podge had been sitting very quietly in a corner.

'Are you all right, Podge?' he inquired, walking over.

'Yeah, I'm - '

'Scared?' said Teasel, prompting him. Podge nodded and hung his head shamefully. 'There's nothing to be ashamed of Podge. I'm scared too. We *all* are!'

Podge looked up. 'You are?'

'Of course!'

'I wish Matt and the others were back. I even wish *Dapper* were back.'

Teasel smiled at him. 'You two argue a lot, don't you.'

'Yeah, I guess, I didn't realise till now 'ow much I really like him. I actually *miss* our arguments.'

Teasel held up his prize conker and trying to cheer Podge up, cried out, 'You shall be conquered, Arvensis!' To which Podge chuckled. 'Pity, we haven't got a cannon Podge, we could fire conkers at them. We've got hundreds hidden in the trees. Wait a minute!'

'Wot is it Teasel?'

'Come on Podge, I've got an idea!'

'Lance, could we fetch the cannon!' asked Teasel, excitedly.

'Oh, you mean the one that nearly *killed* you!' declared Lance. Teasel smiled, sheepishly. 'What on earth for Teasel?'

'We could use the conkers for ammo!' he said excitedly. 'It's not far from here.'

'It's too heavy. Pity you didn't think of it when the braves were here. Nice thought, Teasel, but they could attack any time now and besides, what would we use as a fuse?'

Blizzard bounded over to Lance and licked his hand. 'What is it boy?' he puzzled. Nuzzling the little pouch of grains Blizzard looked up towards Cumulus. 'So, you think it would work!' Blizzard barked. Lance pondered for a moment. '… OK. If we're gonna do it, let's go! Teasel; find a rope. Boys! Bring some sacks. Podge, you stay here with Jill, in case.'

'But, Lance, I'm probably the strongest!' winged Podge.

'Oh, but *we're* not pulling it. Cumulus is! We won't be long. If we sight the crows, we'll drop everything and get straight back.'

Blizzard panting excitedly followed them out into the half-light.

They soon reached the dip, where the cannon lay. The boys quickly ran to the trees around the camp where they'd hidden their conkers.

Lance and Teasel secured the rope around the cannon. Blizzard taking up the slack ran to the top of the dip and howled softly, prompting Cumulus to descend.

After they tied the rope around his great fluffy neck, taking a big gulp of air Cumulus puffed his cheeks and condensed all the solid matter of his whole being into his shoulders. He then dug his hoofs into the ground and pulled with all his might. Lance and Teasel pushed from behind.

They'd just managed to get it out of the dip, when the boys came running over. 'Got them!' they cried. Blizzard suddenly spotted a scout crow flying towards them. Quick as a flash, Cumulus backed up, hiding them all within him. The crow looked curiously at what appeared to be ground fog, and then continued on his way.

'Phew! That was close,' commented Lance.

They made it safely back to the fort. When released, Cumulus once again stationed himself above.

The boys manoeuvred the cannon inside the doorway.

'Are yeh gonna test it, Lance?'

'No, Podge, we can't risk them thinking we're making the first move. The more time they give us to sweat it out, the more chance we've got of the others getting back.'

The boys began sorting their conkers, venting their hate into each one. 'Hey Lance, the barrel's half-full of shells,' called Teasel, as he inspected it.

'Guess they'll be a bit shell-shocked then!' laughed Podge.

Suddenly, Blizzard began to bark, alerting Lance to Cumulus.

'What is it? Are the boys back?' called Jill, anxiously running over.

They all looked up as Cumulus butting the air, formed a ball, and then assumed the shape of a crow. 'No, Jill. It's the first wave of crows!' said Lance, apprehensively.

Jill gasped and ran to arm herself.

'Quick, close the door!' cried Lance. 'Everyone to the windows. Get those shutters open! We *must* stand our ground here. If they get us out in the open, we're done for! Teasel, cover up Cracked Ice, quickly!'

Teasel ran and secured the lid. Cracked Ice looked up, panting. 'Sorry, Cracked Ice. Lance's orders.'

A mass of crows came into sight. 'I don't see Arvensis with them. Still, that would be too easy,' remarked Lance, as they braced themselves.

Arvensis stood watching from his galleon as the first flock faded into the distance. Miles was in his cabin, polishing his sword. He touched the needle sharp point, stating, 'Today, Mother, Father. Today, his blood will stain this steel. *Then* you can rest, avenged!' following which he joined Arvensis on deck.

'Well, Miles, I see you are prepared. Shall we dine?'

'With pleasure!'

'Oh, not them. Not *just* yet. I fancy them more ... as a desert! We shall wait till they've wasted all their ammo,' he sneered.

The crows CRAAHED loudly as they approached the fort, alerting the Crowfoot tribe, who had congregated around the campfire. Together they chanted to the spirits for the children's safety and victory.

And so it began. Wave after wave of crows bombarded them. They retaliated, by firing at will, with everything they could. Some of the crows managed to get inside, but Blizzard was quick to bring them down.

The relentless attacks ceased at nightfall. Everybody was exhausted, but they were all safe.

'HOORAY! WE'VE WON!' shouted Podge, ecstatically.

'No Podge, we've only just started!' sighed Lance.

'But we killed 'undreds, didn't we?'

'Let's just say, we've removed the icing from the cake. You're forgetting Arvensis and Miles. I think they will be showing their faces in the next assaults. He's just been toying with us up to now.'

'Why couldn't crows be white. It's going to be hard to see them in the dark. At least the moon will be on our side,' said Jill, looking up at the clear night sky.

'The moon isn't enough. Count the ammo; I'll be back in two minutes. I need to light the torches.'

'Isn't that dangerous, Lance. I mean - if they - I mean it's all wood!'

'I know, Jill, and so does Arvensis. He's timed this well, but we have no choice!'

Presently, Lance returned. 'So, how's our ammo?' he asked. Everyone stared at him glumly. 'Like that eh … Right, let's get this cannon loaded!' Just then Blizzard began to growl, warning them of the next onslaught.

Opening the door they heaved the cannon forward.

'Be prepared. More will get inside now!' warned Lance.

The boys quickly loaded the first batch of conkers into the barrel. Lance pulled out the little pouch. 'Damn!'

'Wot is it Lance?' said Podge.

'There's only one, two … *ten* grains left. We'd better make them count!'

The flock approaching was the largest they'd seen. As they came within range, Lance shouted, 'READY EVERYONE!' The crows were now almost on top of them.

'HURRY LANCE!' yelled Jill, panicking.

'Please work, p-leeeease. Think! Think!' *Don't let any harm come to my friends! Ignite the cannon, please.* A grain flew out of the bag, hovered, for a split second in his terrified face, and then zoomed into the fuse chamber.

BOOM. Hundreds of conkers and shells filled the air and the crows began to drop from the sky.

'YES!' They all yelled, elated, and then quickly reloaded.

BOOM … BOOM … BOOM. They made nine assaults, leaving Lance with one last grain. Most of the crows had been taken out. However, another mammoth flock loomed on the horizon.

'QUICKLY, CLOSE THE DOOR!' yelled Lance. The boys struggled to pull the cannon clear of the doorway, but the crows were too quick, overwhelming them they barged in. 'USE YOUR SPEARS!' shrieked Lance, as he drew his cutlass.

They all fought bravely, but were sustaining injuries as the fierce crows pecked at their bodies. Blizzard leapt at a group, pecking the catch off the enclosure, housing Cracked Ice. Then they heard a bellowing 'CRAAAAH.' The crows, acknowledging the command, flew out of the fort, dislodged the flaming torches and tossed them through the doorway and windows.

They battled in vain to quash the flames that licked the walls and quickly spread throughout.

'OUTSIDE! EVERYONE GET OUT! PODGE, TEASEL, HELP ME WITH CRACKED ICE,' screamed Lance. Blizzard was already trying to drag his friend out.

Choking on the fumes of the thick black smoke, they came out into the clearing. They froze in their tracks and stared, horrified, as thousands of crows lit by the moon, appeared, spanning the whole skyline.

Arvensis suddenly emerged, flanked by his best, flying in above them with Miles perched on his neck, brandishing his sword in the moonlight. They didn't stand a chance.

Blizzard growled fiercely, and then shocked Lance by swiftly running away.

The Crowfoot tribe had seen the smoke and flames as the fort blazed. Lining the mount above their camp, they looked on mortified. Calyx began to cry, as he held on to Myosurus.

'Grandmother, can't we-'

'No, Calyx, it is in the hands of fate now,' she stated, trying to compose herself.

Lingua, had to walk away.

'LANCE, WHAT SHOULD WE DO?' cried Jill hysterically.

Quickly removing the last grain, Lance clenched it tightly in his fist. In his thoughts he begged for help, and then flicked his hand open. As his subconscious pre-empted his panic, the grain suddenly shot from his hand and headed out to sea, disappearing amongst the crows.

Lance stared nervously in anticipation. A muffled explosion sounded faraway, followed by an enormous jet of water, spouting up and out, drenching the crows in its path. Arvensis, looked back, 'IS THAT THE BEST YOU CAN DO?' he mocked.

Unexpectedly, the sea began to bubble. Suddenly, lit by flashes of lightning from a distant storm, a forest of gigantic strips of kelp, ascended at speed out of the ocean. Flapping angrily, the green, slimy seaweed slapped thousands of crows into the sea.

'Ugh? I thought help! Not kelp!' uttered Lance.

'Good thinkin', whatever!' said Podge.

Arvensis was not amused, or flustered. As his final reserves replaced those drowned, he signalled his army to slowly advance.

Lance stood proud, as did they all. 'I'm *so* sorry everyone!'

'It was *our* pleasure Lance,' said Podge proudly, as their executioners came upon them and tauntingly hovered above.

As Arvensis began his descent, Miles stared coldly at Lance, his eyes full of hate. Lance brandished his cutlass, to which Miles raised his sword in the air to signal the carnivorous, carrion birds to commence the onslaught. But Lance's focus was suddenly distracted, unearthing Miles, who paused.

Lance watched Cumulus rapidly ascending, shrouding the full moon, as if blindfolding them before their execution. He felt destroyed, as it appeared his Great Whites were deserting him, with two gone and Cracked Ice at death's door.

All of a sudden a shrill piercing howl chilled their bones. Lance's heart skipped a beat as the air filled with the sound of wolves howling, following which, every wolf on the island, led by Blizzard, surrounded the clearing.

Blizzard leapt in front of Lance and stretching his head to the full moon let out a menacing howl. Then the haunting wail of the Newteleons, reverberated from the swamps, followed by the Crowfoot tribe, whooping from the mount. The alarming cries echoed across the whole of Echoco, alerting the Orbs in the cave, where the snow was all but gone.

In the volcano the Lavaights stared up at the summit. Woodruff, with head bandaged, was helped to the main chamber. 'What is it, Woodruff?' asked one of them, as the lightning continued to flash.

'I pray it is the storm that will clear the air. *Drink from your CUP*, Arvensis!'

Cumulus caught Lance's attention, smiled, and then thundered forwards revealing once again the full moon in all its splendour.

Lance stared in total dumbstruck awe, his mouth dropped open, prompting everyone, including, Arvensis, Miles and the crows, to turn their heads. For never had the sky been so bright and never had the moon shone so white, almost crystallised. And, maybe, that's why the face of the man in the moon, was *so* jet-black. They were all mesmerised.

Arvensis broke the silence. 'ATTACK!' he craahed. But nobody moved, for at that precise second, the face of the moon lifted. Everyone gasped as its eyes, nose and mouth came away and headed straight towards them. They were all paralysed by this phenomenon.

Closer and closer it came, still lit by a circle of crystal, which was *indeed* millions of Orbs, mounted by the Kindreds.

The face of the moon formed a V. First the mouth, forming a point, then the nose, split in two and fell in behind, followed by the eyes. As the awesome silhouette of shiny, black ravens came into view, the Orbs burst apart like a giant firework exploding; splaying out across the island.

Grock led his squadron, targeting Arvensis who dropped to the ground, where Miles dismounted.

'EYEBRIGHT!' yelled Lance. Eyebright smiled and Furse saluted Lance as they flew past.

'MATT! DAPPER! JACK!' screamed Jill ecstatically, on spying them. The Orbs dropped the boys at her feet. She gawped at the tiny threesome, who quickly swallowed their grains and resumed their normal height. Jill hugged Dapper and gave him a spear, following which Podge ran up to him. 'Yo mate!' he beamed, thrusting his stomach forward and knocking Dapper backwards. Dapper laughed. The two friends raised their fists, roared ferociously and then charged at the crows with their spears.

'JACK, MATT, CATCH!' shouted an elated Lance, throwing them some spears. They nodded and smiled as they caught them.

The battle commenced and carnage reined.

The Kindreds fought fiercely, blasting the air with grains, before running the crows through and cutting them down. The children, with renewed energy, fought like true warriors. Blizzard ran to protect Cracked Ice, who was trying to claw the crows that were attacking him, where he lay.

Arvensis was grabbing at anything and everything with his giant bill, even the crows that got in his way. The wolves were launching themselves at Arvensis, but he was unstoppable.

Miles, who was seeking out Lance, spied him just as Arvensis made a dive at him. 'HE'S MINE, ARVENSIS!' he yelled, jumping in front of him. Zelia dive-bombed Arvensis who swiped her, tossing her injured to the ground. Grock, enraged, continued to attack him along with the other ravens.

Miles and Lance fought hard. Presently, Miles swiped Lance in his arm, causing him to drop the cutlass, which Miles grabbed as he backed Lance up against a tree. Lunging forwards Miles pinned his jacket to the trunk with his sword and lashed at his face with the cutlass. Lance threw himself sideways, his jacket tore and he pulled himself free.

Miles feverishly tried to dislodge the sword, but the handle broke away from the blade.

'LANCE!' yelled Jack, throwing him a spear.

Miles continued to attack with the cutlass.

Blizzard, who was keeping a close eye on Lance, saw a crumpled piece of paper fall from the handle of the sword as Miles tossed it. Arvensis had seen it too. Blizzard ran swiftly over, picked it up in his mouth and bounded towards Lance.

Arvensis, horrified, craahed loudly and headed towards Cracked Ice. Blizzard, saw him and diverted to Cracked Ice, teeth bared, snarling and growling with the paper held tight. Then he whined a desperate plea through gritted teeth at Lance, who looked across. *The contract!* thought Lance. In desperation he began to edge his way towards Blizzard. Furse caught sight of the predicament and moved in to attack Miles, but he was not being stopped this time.

Arvensis dropped down in front of Cracked Ice and Blizzard. Knowing the loyal wolf would attack and hence drop the contract. He drew back his head, ready to land a final blow on Cracked Ice. His eyes were enraged with evil, as his powerful bill shot forward. Blizzard attacked, barking and snarling fiercely. The contract fell from his mouth, as Arvensis's bill pierced through Cracked Ice.

'NOOOOOO!' screamed Lance. His adrenaline surged, as it did the night at the rock pool. He whacked the spear round Miles' head, knocking him out cold.

As Arvensis went to retrieve the contract, Cracked Ice, with his last ounce of energy, *slammed* his bloodied paw on top of it. Through bloodshot eyes, he looked Arvensis straight in the eyes and with his dying breath; yawned, a big *wide* yawn, then flicked the contract to Lance who was running towards him.

Arvensis slammed his eyelids shut, tight. Cracked Ice smiled contentedly, and then closed his eyes for the last time. Blizzard, whining, fell distraught by his side.

'IT'S TOO LATE, YOU *STUPID* CROW! EVERYONE KNOWS YOU CAN'T *HIDE* FROM A YAWN, IT WILL JUST – GET - BIGGER!' bellowed Lance. Arvensis's beak began to tremble, as he desperately tried to keep it shut.

Miles regained consciousness and seeing Lance holding the contract, yelled out, 'AR - VEN - SIS!' at which everyone stopped fighting.

His huge beak slowly began to stretch open. Lance quickly looked about and spotted Teasel standing nearby. 'TEASEL! YOUR CATAPULT, QUICKLY!' Teasel, gawping horrified at the great monster, began to twitch, uncontrollably. *'TEA - SEL!'* pleaded Lance, beckoning to him.

Teasel concentrated really hard as everyone stared, willing him to gain control. Then he spied Cracked Ice, angered, he took a deep breath and stilling his hand, threw the catapult straight to Lance, who swiftly took aim shouting; 'I LANCE, HEREBY SERVE THIS CONTRACT ON *YOU*, ARVENSIS, FOR DEFAULT!' and then fired the contract into his now wide, open bill.

Arvensis tried desperately to regurgitate it as it slid down his throat, but to no avail. A piercing 'CRAAAAAAAAH!' filled the air. Terrified, Arvensis momentarily froze. His eyes began to glow red and turn to fire. Everyone scrambled from his path, as his gigantic body began circling, deliriously. He caught sight of Miles (who, although a pawn in his game, he'd also grown quite fond of).

Looking on helplessly, Miles began to sob as Arvensis craahed like a thing possessed. His body rapidly aged and shrunk, till all that remained was a skeleton, which suddenly disintegrated in a puff of smoke.

For a few seconds, there was total silence. Following which, all let out a victorious cry.

There were cheers from the Lavaights, who had climbed to the summit of the volcano. Drums beat loudly as the Crowfoot tribe yelled in jubilation. The Orbs, no longer entombed, flew excitedly into the clearing. Orchis rushed over to Eyebright, followed by Dodder and Brier. Then the Newteleons, lined the edge of the lake. Surprisingly, Ranunculus, reared up in front of them scowling. He roared fiercely, raised his head high and then smiling, bowed to them.

The crows panicking dispersed, with the Kindreds hot on their tails.

Grock anxiously followed Jill, who was carrying Zelia.

Lance knelt beside Cracked Ice, stroking him, with tears streaming down his face. Looking up he yelled, 'WHERE'S MILES?'

'THAT WAY, LANCE. HE WENT THAT WAY. TOWARDS THE SHORE!' shouted Teasel. With blood trickling from his arm Lance ran off in pursuit.

Miles too was wounded. Not only from the gash on his head, but also from the pain in his heart.

*

Lance approached the ghosting ship, which stood eerily in the quiet of the night. The only sound to be heard was the distant cries of the crows, as they met their end at the hands of the Kindreds. The air was still pungent from the smell of them and their droppings.

He made his way up to the cabin door that swung banging, gently in the breeze. The dark cabin had only one shaft of moonlight, shining through a porthole. Remaining quiet, he precariously walked in and stood, in the lights beam. Then, he heard Miles, who was huddled in a tight ball, beneath a table, sobbing.

'Miles? You *must* listen to me. *Please* hear me out!' Miles' sobs became quieter and broken. 'Your mind has been manipulated for *so* long by Arvensis. He had this planned from the day he rescued you. *You don't seriously believe I could have killed our parents!* Do you?' Miles became silent. Lance continued. 'Miles, we were *babies!* The children you have just attacked, some of them are our family! *Eleanor's* spirit saved me from Cragga. Do you think she would have if it were true? *Arvensis* killed them. *He* struck the Orbs and just took you, for his own means!'

With that, Miles pounced, eyes ablaze and screaming, he pulled Lance's feet from under him, causing him to crash backwards to the floor. The cutlass flew out of his hand. Somersaulting, it embedded in the wooden boards by Lance's side. But Lance didn't grab hold of it.

Miles leapt on top of him in a wild frenzy. Holding him down by the throat, with one hand and the strength of ten men, he grabbed hold of the cutlass and held it to the jugular vein, which was now protruding from Lance's neck. Gasping for air, Lance rasped, 'If Arvensis had been telling the *truth,* the contract would *not* have disintegrated him!'

Miles hesitated. His eyes shifting as the words penetrated his mind. Frowning, his lips began to quiver and his whole body trembled. Releasing his grip on Lance's throat, he dropped the cutlass and fell limp, as a rag doll.

Lance coughed and spluttered as Miles sat up and blubbered; 'Oh Lance, I want my parents! *And* my brother!' he then wept helplessly.

Lance pulled himself onto his elbows and lifting his brother's face in his hand, caught a tear from his eye. 'This tear represents much pain. I *swear* to you Miles. *No more* shall be shed!' Miles shivered and sighed, as Lance pulled his head to his shoulder and hugged him.

'LANCE! LANCE!' yelled Jack, who along with Matt and Teasel, burst through the door. Lance looked up at them and smiled, reassuringly.

CHAPTER EIGHTEEN

Tell it on the Mountain

A bright, cheerful sun warmed Echoco. Apart from Lance, Miles and Jill, all the boys were using makeshift rafts to ferry the Lavaights to the shore. The Kindreds and Orbs had taken food and water to them during the night. They were weak and feeble, but all had survived.

Woodruff was making his way towards the galleon, with Furse and Vicia perched on his shoulders.

'That's the last of them!' pruuked, Grock, tossing a dead crow on board.

'Miles, would you do the honours?' asked Lance, stretching a lighted torch towards him. Taking hold of it Miles threw it onto the galleon.

They stood and watched as the flames took hold. It wasn't long before it was blazing fiercely.

'What should I do with this?' queried Miles sullenly, holding the sword.

'May I?' interrupted Jill, taking it from him. 'There's a place by the lake where your mother's brooch is buried.'

'Would you show me?'

'Of course!' she replied, smiling.

'She has her great grandmother's eyes,' commented Woodruff, as he approached. Jill smiled.

'Woodruff! I can't tell you how relieved we were to hear you were alive.'

'Well, Lance, from what I've overheard you have been quite *busy*. I shall look forward to hearing the full story.'

'Woodruff – I …' blubbered Miles, shamefaced.

'It's all right Miles, there is a lot of rebuilding to do.' At that moment Eyebright and Orchis flew up to them, with Dodder and Brier following close behind. 'You can make a start now, if you wish!' he added, raising his eyebrows.

Miles apologised to them and asked if they would give him another chance. Brier, consented, Dodder, hesitated, then Orchis smiled, encouraging him, after which he agreed.

'Come on, Miles, I'll take you there now,' said Jill, leading the way. Dodder and Brier followed.

'How is Zelia doing, Grock?' asked Furse.

'She's resting, but she'll survive, she's a tough old bird.'

'What will you do now?'

'Well, I had a discussion with the others this morning. There's no point in returning to the Tower, as we will already have been replaced. They will hardly believe that duty called, so rather than face the humiliation of dismissal, we've decided, if it's OK with everyone, to stay!'

'I can't think of classier birds than yourselves to take the place of the crows,' commented Woodruff.

They were distracted by the sound of drumming, coming from across the canyon. 'I think someone is beckoning us,' said Lance mournfully.

He called to the boys and they all made their way back to the fort, which was still smouldering from the previous night.

Everyone had gathered and remained respectively silent. Cumulus waited above, to escort them to the Crowfoot camp, where Cracked Ice was to be laid to rest. His body had been bound in cloth and was laid on a stretcher. Blizzard had not left his side.

Lance and Jack stood by the front poles, Matt and Teasel, the back. Jill, Dapper and Podge stood behind. Dispirited, Blizzard, walked to the front. The boys lifted the poles onto their shoulders and slowly paced behind him.

A serene tranquillity fell on the island, apart from the sombre beat of the drums, which Calyx sounded for the duration of their journey.

Myosurus, Calyx, the Elders and Lingua, all in ceremonial dress, waited patiently on top of the mount beside a totem pole, which Calyx had spent the night carving. At its top was a head depicting Cracked Ice, underneath, an inscription that read; *To commemorate the Great White Tiger; Cracked Ice, for his loyalty, courage and wisdom but most of all for his friendship.* It stood, tall at the head of the open grave, which was lined with all kinds of objects, to ensure him safe passage to the happy hunting ground.

*

As the group approached, Myosurus bowed her head, acknowledging Lance. The boys carefully laid the stretcher down beside the grave where Lingua assisted them to slowly lower his body, following which Myosurus and the Elders called upon the spirits to protect and care for this great warrior.

As Lingua filled the grave with earth, everyone said his or her farewells and then departed. Presently, only Myosurus, Lance and Blizzard remained.

'He served you well, Lance.'

'He helped to save us all, Myosurus!' he replied, choking on his tears.

'Yes, but he would not rest easy if he thought your heart pained. Come, walk back with me.'

'Good-bye, my friend,' said Lance softly. As they set off Lance slapped his thigh, summoning Blizzard, who was lying at the foot of the grave, with his nose pressed to the ground. But Blizzard ignored him.

'Leave him, Lance, he will come when he is ready.'

The camp was buzzing with talk of the battle. Although a victory celebration had been planned, the proceedings were kept low-key out of respect for Cracked Ice.

Jack was sitting with Calyx by the drums. 'So, I guess you'll all be going home soon,' said Calyx, with a downcast expression, lightly, tapping one of the drums.

'Yeah, I believe a hurricane is forecast for tomorrow.'

'We'll miss you Jack.'

'Likewise,' he replied.

Matt and Teasel, came over to join them. 'Yer grandmother said to tell yeh she's retirin' early 'n wants yeh to pop in 'n see 'er, you too Jack. Jill's with 'er at the moment.'

'OK Matt, thanks I'll go to her soon,' replied Calyx.

*

'Hello, Myosurus.'

'Greetings Jill. I may not be up to see you off tomorrow, as I need my rest. You have shown *great* courage and are *truly* brave.'

'I must admit I was *really* scared.'

'And who can blame you … Matt is a fine looking boy, isn't he.' Jill began to blush. 'Remember Jill, if you want something out of life, don't always refer to it as your dream, or it will stay as one. Call it your ambition!'

'I will,' she replied. Jill went up to Myosurus and gently kissed her on the cheek. 'Thanks for *everything*. Myosurus.' Myosurus nodded and smiled.

On coming out, Jill spied Lance staring up at the mount where the sun had begun to set on the horizon, engulfing the mount in rays of red and gold. 'Are you OK Lance?' she asked, as she approached.

'I took Blizzard up some food, but he just turned his nose at it,' he replied gloomily.

'I wondered where you'd got too. He will be all right, won't he?'

'I hope so Jill.'

They looked up at the mount to see a huge red sun encircling the black silhouette of the totem pole. 'Oh, look there! What's happening?' she asked, pointing, as thousands of Orbs flew about, mounted by Kindreds who were carrying lit torches and sweeping trails of light in the night sky.

'They're writing the names in memory of those they lost in battle.'

Ulex was one name that dominated the skyline.

'That's beautiful. What a lovely thing to do,' she said. Just then they heard Dapper and Podge arguing. 'Hum, thought it was too good to last. I'd better see what the problem is,' she said huffing, and walked off to find them.

'NO! IT SHOULD BE ME. *I'M* THE BEST WIV A BOW 'N ARROW!' boasted Podge.

'WELL, YOU WON'T NEED ONE IN SOUTHEND, *WILL* YOU!' yelled Dapper.

'BOYS, boys. Keep it down. Show a little respect,' interrupted Jill.

'Tell him, Jill, *I* would be best!' blurted Dapper.

'Best at what?'

'Oh, she 'asn't 'eard.'

'Heard what, Podge?'

'Matt's not gonna be our leader anymore. Jack's stayin' an' Matt said, if Jack stays, so is 'e.'

'He's what?'

'You 'eard. 'E's not comin' back wiv us.'

'I don't believe you!' she cried and ran off to her teepee.

'You're *so* subtle, Podge.'

'Wot? Wot'd I do this time?' Dapper shook his head.

Meanwhile, Jack was conversing with Myosurus.

'It would seem your mind is made up, Jack. Are you sure this is what you want?'

'Absolutely!'

'Very well, you must therefore accompany me to sacred ground, so I can enlighten the great spirits of your intentions. It will be necessary to ensure your safe keeping as an Islander.'

'Whatever, you wish, Myosurus. Where is it?'

'On top of a mountain, not far from here. I was going there anyway, tomorrow. Now, I have you to escort me. But *keep* it to yourself. Meet me here at first light. Now go.'

'I'll be 'ere and thank you. Goodnight.'

'Goodnight, Jack.'

As Jack left, Lance popped his head inside. 'Just came by to say goodnight.'

'Come in, Lance.'

'Is everything OK Myosurus?'

'Perfectly. You have travelled many paths in a short space of time. Although you are still a boy, I feel you are much wiser now.'

'Yes, I must agree, I do feel somewhat - different.'

'What you did for Miles was very mature of you. You should be proud of yourself. For being able to bring good out of evil is a rare quality.'

'I never stopped loving him as a brother.'

'I know Lance. Will you both stay on Echoco?'

'Oh yes!'

'Good. Now remember all that I have taught you.'

He gazed, dubiously at her. 'Myosurus, you talk as if ...'

'Go now Lance. Your path is truly set.'

Bidding her farewell, he paused and turned back saying; 'You *will* see them off with me. Won't you?'

'But of course I will. I promise!' she said, warmly smiling.

Everyone retired for the night and the camp fell into darkness.

Jill lay with her face squashed into her pillow, muffling her sobs as she cried herself to sleep.

Jack was worried he would not wake up in time and tried to stay awake. But, he eventually drifted off.

*

In the early morning hours, Jack woke abruptly. He looked around the teepee, where Matt, Podge and Dapper were fast asleep. Quietly, he crept out.

The black of night had turned a dark shade of grey and a sharp frost threatened to chill his bones. Blowing his fists, he looked towards Myosurus's teepee, where he spied her coming out, struggling with a cloth bundle. He hastened over to help her.

'Here, let *me* take that!'

'Thank you Jack.' She had a thick blanket, wrapped around her.

'Will yeh be warm enough?' he inquired.

'Oh, amply. Come, we must hurry, before the others awake.'

Jack lifted the bundle over his shoulder and followed closely. Myosurus hesitated outside Calyx's teepee and circling her arms, quietly muttered a few words before they continued on their way.

On reaching the outskirts of the camp, they began to climb a steep incline. Jack was surprised at how agile she seemed, almost as if she'd found her youth. Up and up, they continued.

*

It was half-light when they reached the top. Jack stared out and across a range of snow capped mountains.

'Wow!' he exclaimed.

'Breathtaking, isn't it.' He nodded as he breathed in the fresh, light air, and then, began to look about a little bemused.

He looked back down through wafting clouds, at the camp below and then round about the area where they stood, but could see no indications of sacred ground. 'I don't understand?' he queried. 'I thought we were goin' to the top of a *mountain*. Is this it?'

'No! *There's* the mountain, right there!' stated Myosurus, pointing to one, directly opposite.

Jack stared at the peak that seemed to strangely resemble the head of a unicorn. 'Forgive me for soundin' a bit thick, Myosurus. But shouldn't we 'ave gone down to the base of that one, before we came up?'

'Oh, Jack. You are amusing. Open your mind. It will reveal more if you open it fully. Look, there! Do you not *see* it?'

'See wot?' Jack was beginning to think she'd lost her marbles.

'*There*, the ridge! We merely walk straight across to the other side. Come, follow me,' she said cheerfully.

Jack looked on horrified, as Myosurus, stepped out. 'NOOO!' he screamed, dropping the bundle and trying to grab hold of her, but he was not quick enough. Jack couldn't believe what he was seeing, and gawped, goggle-eyed in disbelief as she stood in thin air. Blinking, he looked towards her feet, at what appeared to be a ghosting image of a rock bridge, which did indeed go across to the other side.

He picked up the bundle and sheepishly put a foot forward. On feeling the bridge take his weight, he breathed deeply and followed her across.

Once on the other side, they climbed to a clearing at the summit, near which a rock swivelled to a point in the clouds. Small totem poles littered an area of earth encased by jagged boulders that resembled a crown.

Myosurus walked over to one in particular, that lay flat on the soil near the edge and sat, crossed legged, beside it. 'Come, join me,' she beckoned.

Jack sat, placing the bundle beside her. Myosurus opened the cloth, which seemed to contain all her belongings. She removed a flask made of hide and offered Jack a drink. Accepting, he pulled a face as he drank the bitter tasting water. She then withdrew a beautiful, twined circle of twigs, which was adorned with beads and feathers.

'Here, this is my welcoming gift to you.'

'It's amazin'. Wot is it?' he inquired, taking it from her.

'It's a dream-catcher. Hang it above your head, wherever you sleep. It will ward off bad spirits and make all your dreams, happy ones.'

'Thank you, I shall treasure it always,' he said smiling, taking it from her.

'Now, prepare yourself, Jack. I must call upon Aquila.'

''Oo's Aquila?'

'Someone who has been expecting you. He will take you on a journey and show you of things to come. As you come back, you will travel down the forked tongue of a snake. You must choose a path, right or left.' Jack looked at her bemused. 'However,' she continued. Upon returning here you will remember nothing. Then you must return to the camp and depending on which path you chose, you will either leave Echoco or stay. One day in your future you will experience a *strong* dejavu, when you may recall this day.'

'But, aren't yeh comin' wiv me?'

'No, Jack. I need to stop here awhile, alone. Besides, Calyx will come, presently. Now, put your dream-catcher down, close your eyes and empty your mind. But on *no* account look behind you! When you feel your body lift from the ground, open your eyes and focus straight ahead.'

Jack did as she bid. For some reason, he wasn't afraid. Myosurus picked up a handful of dirt from the ground. Chanting, she rocked back and forth as she summoned Aquila.

Soon, Jack heard the sound of wings beating behind him. Closer and louder, till he could feel the rush of air on his back. Aquila landed, and then as if the great winged animal had entered his body, he felt his whole being lift into the atmosphere. He heard a snorting grunt, as with nostrils flared, Aquila's hooves pounded the air. His mane whipped Jack's face. Opening his eyes Jack saw the twisting horns in front of him. Together they soared, as one, high above the mountains and beyond, towards a great yellow light that shimmered with rays of gold splaying from all sides.

Travelling into the light, they entered a tunnel that seemed never ending. Suddenly, they burst out the other side and were flying over fields, where he spied a young girl grooming a pony. She glanced up at him with tears in her eyes, but Jack didn't recognise her.

The image of a man's angry face suddenly filled the air in front of them. As they surged through, it dispersed into hundreds of large white feathers that bombarded him, succeeded by black ones. Following which, one of each colour, quills forward targeted his eyes and penetrated his pupils. As excruciating pain seared through them, he squeezed his eyelids tightly shut.

When he opened them, Aquila was thundering down the long winding body of an enormous black and white snake. As they came over its head, Jack saw the tongue of which the forked paths lay ahead.

Aquila stilled his powerful wings, at which Jack's arms began to move up and down, causing Aquila's wings to do the same. He knew he was now in control. *Right, left - No, right!* he thought. He came to the fork and swung to the right. Aquila regained control and swooped back down to the mountaintop, where Jack could see a beautiful young girl, dressed in the same attire as Myosurus, dancing around where he sat.

As if waking with a start from a bad dream, Jack opened his eyes. 'I feel a bit strange Myosurus, but nothin' 'appened! Myosurus?' She didn't reply.

He turned to see her head bowed and eyes closed. She wore a contented expression on her face, which was ashen in colour. 'Oh, Myosurus!' he cried, realising she had passed away. A tear trickled down his cheek as he wrapped her blanket tightly round her.

Picking up his dream catcher, he uttered, 'Good-bye Myosurus and thanks for *everythin'*.' He then made his way back to the ridge.

Believe, believe, open my mind, he thought, as he stepped out onto it. Once safely across he began his descent to the sound of tom-toms that were beating in the camp below.

Presently, he met with Calyx, Lingua and some of the Elders, who looked at him knowingly as they continued past him.

'JACK! Where 'ave yeh bin? I've bin looking everywhere for yeh.' called Matt, running to meet him.

'Just for a walk.'

'Everyone's ready to leave. Are yeh stayin' Jack?' asked Matt as they reached the others.

Jack didn't hesitate in replying. 'Yes!'

'Then *so* am I!'

'Matt, I can't believe what you're saying!' cried Jill.

'It's what I want, Jill. Besides, there's nothin' for me to go back to!'

'Time to go,' interrupted Lance.

As the storm began to build in the distance, they began the journey back to the lake, where everyone had gathered to see them off.

*

'Jill, Jill!' called Peony, as they approached.

Jill went over to Peony, who studied her face. 'Why are you so sad?' Jill smiled, scared to speak, as tears filled her eyes'. 'I think I know. Why don't you tell him how you feel?'

'Not that easy - Oh here,' she said passing her the lipstick. 'I'm sure Scelaratus won't mind you having it now.' Peony smiled. 'Goodbye my friend.'

'Goodbye Jill,' she replied. Peony felt sad as she watched Jill walk over to join the others where the Orbs and Kindreds were preparing to leave.

'Are yeh sure, yeh know wot yer doin', Jack?'

'Sure I'm sure, Podge!'

'Wot about you Matt?'

'Yep! Take care of this bunch for me, Podge. I don't think The Rocks will give yeh too much grief from now on.'

'No sweat. Besides I'm gonna be a magician. M-a-tt, I was thinkin', them grains-'

'Don't even go there!' said Matt, cutting him short.

'Jill? What are we going to tell mum and dad! We'll probably be grounded for a year!'

'It's all right, Dapper,' said Eyebright. 'They are worried sick, but they know where you are. Your Auntie Margaret told them. I'm sure they'll just be pleased to have you back, safe!'

'Margaret!' muttered Jack, walking away.

'Look on the bright side, Dapper, It'll almost be the summer 'olidays again when we get back,' said Podge.

'Yeah, but we missed Christmas!' groaned Dapper.

'Yes, and *I* missed my birthday, *that* means I'm now twelve!'

'Ah, Yes Jill, but six months younger!' smiled Woodruff.

Lance walked over to Jill. 'I don't know what to say Jill. Eleanor would have been *so* proud of you.'

'And of you Lance.'

'Well, you were right about one thing, the moon certainly *was* on our side! I'll think of you all every time I look at it.'

'Me too,' she replied. Hugging Lance, she kissed him on the cheek before walking over to Jack.

'Are you all right, Jack?'

'Yeah. Would yeh pass a message on to Margaret for me?'

'Of course.'

'Tell 'er, I'll never forget 'er 'n give 'er a kiss from me.' Jill's eyes welled.

'You could tell her yourself if you came back with us. I feel like we've only just found you and now we won't *ever* see you again. Why *are* you staying, Jack?'

'Lance 'n Miles are my family too. I can't explain it Jill, but I feel like I'm - 'ome.'

Vicia called out to Jill, Dapper and Podge, to join Woodruff who was holding a plate on which Furse stood holding three grains.

'These grains will return you to normal size when you get back. They are also infused with our secrecy decree,' stated Furse, as he handed them one each.

Woodruff, instructed them to place them on their tongues, but *not* to swallow. 'I imagine there is much you would like to remember from your adventure. Do you swear to keep secret all you know?' queried Woodruff, raising his hand. They all nodded eagerly. 'Hum. Not that anyone would believe you,' he uttered.

Waving his hands above their heads, he proclaimed; *'These three swear, no pen shall write nor lips shall speak, these grains will block but the memory keep.'* He then bid them to swallow.

'MOUNT UP!' called Furse.

Jill stared at Matt, as they prepared to leave, but had to look away, as her heart pained so much, the tears began to fall.

'We'll *never* forget you!' cried Lance.

Suddenly, Blizzard began to howl from high up on the mount. Aquila ascended from behind him, soaring above Cumulus in the clouds, at which point Lance heard a voice in his head; *I never break a promise, Lance.* 'Myosurus!' he whispered.

As they all stared, gobsmacked, Cumulus proudly butted the air as another cloud moved majestically ahead of him. 'CRACKED ICE!' gasped Lance.

'HEAD OUT!' yelled Furse.

'WAIT!' shouted Matt. Jill's heart skipped a beat. 'I feel - I should be - wiv 'em - I -'

'That's OK Matt.' Jack reassured him. 'Yeh've gotta do wot feels right mate.' They hugged.

Furse quickly ushered Matt over.

'Hey Matt!' called Jack after him. 'Keep an eye out for those flashin' street lights, I may need yer 'elp someday!'

'Will do. If there's n' 'urricane anytime I'm passin', I'll toss in some new batteries for yeh!'

They smiled at each other.

Furse gave Matt a grain and Woodruff quickly swore him in. Everyone cheered after the vast entourage as they flew out to sea, towards the storm.

*

They all returned safely.

Podge and Matt discovered they were listed as runaways, as was Jack, who was then put on a missing file. Jill and Dapper were quite surprised at how understanding their parents were. To compensate for Christmas and Jill's birthday, a special day was planned at their grandparents in Cornwall to which Matt and Podge were also invited.

Margaret and Bob came up for the special day. Pamela had kept all their presents and had also bought some for Matt and Podge. One of which was a magician's set, which Dapper had suggested to his mum.

They had a brilliant day, with a scrumptious turkey dinner and all the trimmings. Jill made a wish as she blew out the candles on her belated birthday cake. Margaret guessed what she'd wished for, after picking up on her affection for Matt. Her main present was Eleanor's notebook, to which Margaret, as a precautionary measure had added a closing entry, which read; *A Fantasy, by Eleanor Pearce.*

After dinner, while everyone relaxed, Margaret drove Jill to the cemetery, to take some flowers she had bought. It was the first chance they'd had to talk since her return. Margaret listened intently to the whole story.

When they pulled into the parking area, she told Jill that Matt had mentioned he was thinking of taking her to the cinema with him when they returned to Southend, as there was a film he wanted to see.

As they walked towards the graves Jill asked her if she was sure, at least twenty times, also what tone of voice did he use and what expression did he wear. Margaret found it all highly amusing.

Margaret pulled up a few weeds, and then went to fetch some fresh water. She was deep in thought, as she tried to come to terms with the fact that she would probably never see Jack again.

Jill placed a bunch of wild flowers on Whitlow's grave that had amongst them, woodruff and furse. Kneeling by Eleanor's head stone, she filled a vase with lily of the valley. She then removed from her bag a small trinket box, containing a tiny silver key, which she wedged into the earth beneath the vase. 'Well, Great Nana, it was an adventure I'll *never* forget. Now your secret's safe with *you!*'

Margaret returned and filled the vases with water.

Jill kissed her on the cheek as she stood up. 'What was that for?' queried Margaret.

'It's from Jack. He said to tell you that he'll *never* forget you.' Margaret smiled, as a joyful tear, trickled down her cheek, and then they hugged.

(So! What *did* Jack see, when he journeyed with Aquila, which now hides in his subconscious? ... Well, that's *another* story.)

About the Author

Maria Boosey lives in Corringham in Essex. She studied music privately, dance and drama at college, and runs her own private school for singing and piano. Maria also spent a year teaching at the David Morris theatre school. Her hobbies include composing, painting, and writing, and she is presently working on the second book in The CUP of Destiny trilogy.

Printed in the United Kingdom
by Lightning Source UK Ltd.
119125UK00001B/221

9 781425 988098